COMPLICATED RELATIONSHIPS

HOT TREE
PUBLISHING

Complicated Relationships is a work of fiction. All names, characters, events and places found therein are either from the author's imagination or used fictitiously. Any similarity to persons alive or dead, actual events, locations, or organizations is entirely coincidental and not intended by the author.

For information, contact the publisher, Hot Tree Publishing.

WWW.HOTTREEPUBLISHING.COM

EDITING: HOT TREE EDITING

COVER DESIGNER: CLAIRE SMITH

FORMATTER: RMGraphX

ISBN-13: 978-1-925655-34-6

Second Edition

10 9 8 7 6 5 4 3 2 1

More From Amy

The Southern Devotion Series
For the Love of Gracie (#1)
Curves in the Road (#2)
Complicated Relationships (#3)

Standalones
Across the Way
A Little Spark

Trade Me Collection
Still You

Complicated : consisting of many interconnecting parts or elements; intricate

Relationships : the way in which two or more concepts, objects, or people are connected, or the state of being connected

The course of true love never did run smooth
~ William Shakespeare

Chapter One

INDECENT EXPOSURE

I wasn't prepared to find my roommate, Angel, in my bed, especially without clothes. I stopped midshift, my head throbbing with the movement and from the morning light shining through the curtains. Pulling my pillow over my face, I struggled to remember the previous evening.

Last night was the wedding of Mary Jane, my best friend. I remembered that much as well as the venue. I knew for sure the reception was at her husband, Derrick's, nightclub where I bartended. I groaned, remembering the game called Beat the Bartender I was dragged in to play. The goal was to outdrink me. As the memory replayed, it dawned on me I'd lost count after ten shots.

After that, everything was bleary, too murky to grasp. I sighed, pissed off with myself. I was lucky I'd slept with a beautiful woman instead of ending up with alcohol poisoning.

Angel was gorgeous; I'd noticed her from day one, but I never expected us to sleep together. Removing the pillow from my head, I looked over at her. Gazing on her caramel skin against the pillow, though, I had no feelings except remorse. I didn't want this to make things awkward between us.

She rolled over rubbing her eyes. "Turn the lights off," she whined.

I had multiple ways of handling the situation, yet the only one was to be honest and hope I wouldn't come across as a jerk. "Kind of difficult since it's the sun," I replied sardonically.

Her eyes shot open wide as she glanced at me, then pulled the covers up to look beneath them.

"Hey!" I called out, my tone aiming for lightness, as I jerked them back to cover myself. "You obviously remember as much as I do so eyes off the package."

My eyes widened when she stood up stark naked. "This—I didn't—Tristan, I like you, but—"

I raised my hands to stop her. "I like you too, as a good friend. We're on the same page." I grasped for the right words, wanting to make sure our friendship and living arrangements could survive this. "Sleeping together was a… mistake. Don't get me wrong, if I could remember, I'm sure it was great, but it definitely won't happen again." I paused, my eyes locked on her nakedness. "Can you put some clothes on, please?" At only twenty-four with a round, sexy-as-hell ass, and large, perky breasts, it was difficult to pull my eyes away from her. Her impressive assets along with her Hispanic heritage, which colored her skin in sexy tones, were doubly hypnotizing.

"Maybe we didn't have sex?" she suggested.

I pointed to the nightstand where there was an open condom wrapper.

"Damn. Well, at least we were safe." Without even as much as a glance and appearing completely unaffected, she turned, saying over her shoulder, "I'm going to shower," before she traipsed away to her room.

"Angel, my sister might see you!" I whispered loudly. Immediately her pace picked up as she took off in a sprint to avoid being caught in the hallway.

My sister, Macy, and I moved to Nashville with Angel and Mary Jane nine months back. Macy was fourteen, and I'd raised her since she was nine. Our mom was in a nursing home suffering from the effects of early-onset Alzheimer's disease. She had been there for four years by then. On my eighteenth birthday, my dad signed over guardianship of Macy to me. After obtaining a lawyer to get a special-circumstances divorce, he vanished from our lives. The only decent thing he'd done was to make sure I had legal guardianship of Macy so she didn't go into foster care. I strived to be a good role model for Macy. She barely remembered her mother, was abandoned by her father, so I had the responsibility to give her stability in life. For this reason, I didn't want her to see Angel and get the wrong impression.

The smell of eggs invaded my nose as I stepped out of my bedroom in my T-shirt and shorts. "Did you make breakfast, squirt?" I asked as I ruffled Macy's hair.

She smacked my hand away and grumbled, "If you can call it breakfast at two in the afternoon. You and Angel were pretty drunk last night so I thought you'd want some eggs for the hangover."

"How do you know we were drunk?" I asked, praying she didn't see us go to bed together.

"When Maria dropped me off, the two of you were still drinking and being loud." Maria, Derrick's mom, took care of the kids for most of the reception so the rest of the "adults" could party. We weren't exactly the best role models for adulthood last night.

"Oh, sorry, squirt. Move over, and I'll make some bacon and toast."

"Too late. The plate of bacon is in the oven staying warm, and the toast is"—the oven timer dinged in the middle of her sentence—"done, now."

Lightly pushing her aside, I grabbed oven mitts to pull the toasted bread off the oven rack where it had broiled. "You're the best sister, you know it?"

She grinned. "I know."

"I have to work tonight so I can drop you at Ashton and Gracie's if you want so you aren't home alone." Macy finished filling two plates of food and handed me my plate.

She shrugged. "What about MJ?"

Macy loved Mary Jane from the moment she met her. They spent a lot of time together when we all lived in

Florida, and since we moved, she missed her a lot. The fact she had a new family was hard for Macy to accept. "She leaves for her honeymoon tomorrow. I'm sure getting ready is keeping her busy."

Macy mumbled. "It's not technically a honeymoon, she's taking Katelyn."

Taking a seat at the table, she dug into her breakfast.

Mary Jane and Derrick were taking Katelyn on a four-day Disney cruise. Katelyn was Derrick's six-year-old daughter; born when he was only sixteen. Because they were a family and Katelyn's biological mother had never been in her life, they didn't want to exclude her from the trip.

"Look, I know you miss spending time with her, but she has a family now, and things are going to be a little different. You know she'll still come around and see you as much as possible."

"You miss her too, don't you?" she asked. "I know you're in love with her." *Damn.* Moments like these were the ones I wanted to avoid. Knowing how attached Macy was to Mary Jane, I tried to never let her know about my feelings. I thought if she believed we were only good friends, she wouldn't get hurt or feel abandoned by someone else. Apparently, my baby sister knew me better than I thought. As smart as she was, I sometimes wondered if she was the one raising me.

"Whatever feelings I had for MJ no longer matter. I'm happy for her, and you should be too. Don't you like Derrick and Katelyn?"

Macy sighed. "Yeah, I do."

"Well, so do I." The feelings for Mary Jane were still there, but I genuinely was happy for her. Hell, my night with Angel might have been my stupid way of attempting to move on.

The alarm on my phone buzzed. "I have to go. I need to run a few errands before work this evening. Go grab your things quickly." While Macy ran upstairs, I scarfed down the rest of my breakfast.

Ashton and Gracie were excited to have Macy stay over. They had an eighteen-month-old, Autumn, and loved having extra help. Gracie answered the door, and Ashton sat on the floor trying to reason with a screaming child.

"She doesn't sound happy" was the understatement I made at an inopportune moment in front of a tired mom.

Gracie, normally a very sweet and happy individual, cocked her head to the side and snapped, "Gee, I must be new at this because I thought it was the sound of joy." *Yikes.* Based on the anger heating her cheeks, I barely escaped an *Exorcist*-type moment where her head would spin around. *Note to self: Don't use sarcasm around new moms. Their sense of humor doesn't exist.*

Macy pushed passed me. "Forgive him, Gracie. He's a doof." Macy moved toward Ashton and began to sing a soft lullaby. Autumn's sobs lessened as she listened to my sister's melodic voice. The song was one mom used to sing to her as a baby. Her soothing voice cast a spell on me just as it did Autumn.

Ashton grinned, relief obvious on his face, and wrapped an arm around Macy's shoulder. "I love this kid. She's the toddler whisperer. Can she move in with us, just until Autumn starts kindergarten?"

I chuckled. "Sure, why not?"

Gracie closed the door and offered an apology. "I'm sorry I got smart with you, Tristan. It's been a long night. I'm exhausted, and it makes me extra bitchy."

"No apology necessary. I've never known you to be bitchy, and we're all entitled to our moments. Besides, Macy was right. I am a doof." I turned to Macy. "Give me a hug, squirt. I have to get to work."

On the drive to work, I tried to let myself go with the music, but I couldn't stop thinking about Angel. We'd barely spoken about what happened. I wasn't even sure if she remembered any more than I did. Would things be awkward between us? I couldn't afford to take on the house payment by myself. I was barely able to pay all the bills as it was. And Macy would be heartbroken if Angel moved out. When I arrived at work, I sent a quick text to Angel.

Me: Last night is weighing on me. Can we talk later?

Angel: We can, but Tristan as far as I'm concerned, everything's fine.

Me: Angel, we had sex.

Angel: Nothing's different

Me: I still want to talk.

Angel: OK. We'll talk about it at home. But stop freaking out!

Me: Yes, ma'am.

Chapter Two

COCKTAIL HOUR

A Shot in the Dark, the club I worked for, was packed when I started my shift. Every seat at the bar had a body filling it, but all the glasses were empty. Tag teaming with Marcus, the other bartender on duty, I started on one end with refills while he started on the other. By the time, we reached the middle it was time to start again.

Weekends were always this busy, which meant killer tips so I couldn't complain. Macy would be ready for college in a short time, so I had to start saving up more money. The pay I made as the supervising bartender was twice as good as any job I'd held before, not including tips. Tips were deposited into a savings account to buy things Macy needed. It was hard work and meant growing up faster than I wanted to, but Macy was worth it. Her intelligence would take her far in life, and I would do anything possible, including work my ass off, so she would succeed.

The crowd died down enough for me to begin cleaning for the night while Marcus tended bar. We still had some time until closing, but I liked to get ahead when I could. It would mean we could head home sooner rather than later. A woman with dark auburn hair stepped up to the bar on my end, drawing my attention to her. Her strapless top showed very little cleavage though it still looked sexy as hell. She ran her fingers through her hair, sucked in a deep breath, then exhaled, causing a piece of hair hanging down over her eyes to fly up momentarily. She appeared to be rather annoyed by something or someone. Throwing the dishrag over my shoulder, I sauntered over to check on her. "Hey there, sweetheart, would you like something to drink?"

"Something to take my mind off men," she replied morosely. She was definitely pissed off.

"Broken heart?" I asked. It pained me to see a beautiful woman looking downtrodden. Her beauty was natural with subtle makeup, a nice change from the normal club girls with raccoon eyes and blood-red lips. Her pouty lips shined with pink gloss, while her hair had been gathered together on one side leaving part of her neck exposed. I almost missed her answer distracted by the expanse of skin.

"Lonely one is more like it. Tonight marks another bad first date down the tubes. I'm beginning to think it's me. No scratch that, I know it's me."

Momentarily I moved away from her to grab a drink. "Here's a drink for you, 'a kick in the balls.' And I find it hard to believe there's anything wrong with you, darlin'." I was hoping to get a smile from her, but instead she cringed.

"You're not a native around here, are you?"

I gawked at her. "Is it obvious?"

She grinned. "Your southern accent is, well, atrocious." She took a sip of the sweet drink and closed her eyes. "Mmm, delicious. Thanks."

It wasn't the first time I'd been called out on my poor attempt at an accent, but hell, I'd never been shot down quite so fast before. "You're welcome." Her eyes met mine. "Even though you insulted me." Her eyes widened in realization, her mouth parting in a small O, and I was sure there was a slight blush crawling up her cheeks, though it was hard to tell in the dim lighting. I smiled, letting her off the hook and wanting to make it clear I was just joking with her. Extending my hand, I introduced myself. "I'm Tristan."

The small crease between her brows eased as she accepted with a strong grip. "Nice to meet you, Tristan. I'm Melanie."

"It's nice to meet you too. Sorry about the accent." I threw her a wink. "I'm trying to let the locals rub off on me." My comment earned me a small smile. "My best friend's from Kentucky, and her accent is incredibly thick. Maybe she'll change me." She threw me another small, tentative smile before looking away and then at her drink. The confidence from a few moments earlier disappeared. With a glance around the bar, I saw Marcus still appeared to be handling the few customers waiting for drinks. I could've just let her pay for her drink and carried on with cleaning, but my feet were rooted to the spot. I didn't know what I was going to say till I opened my mouth to speak. "So, tell me about the man troubles." I would've rolled my eyes at myself if her gaze hadn't jumped to mine.

She waved her hand as though dismissing me. "You don't want to hear such drivel."

"Ma'am, I'm a bartender. It's in my job description. Besides, if you don't talk, I may try out more of my southern accent." When I said "southern accent," I reached down low for the deepest twang possible to put in those words.

She puffed her cheeks out with a boisterous laugh. "Please no, anything but that. I'll talk! No more torture!" Her laughter calmed to a soft chuckle. "Hmm… where do I begin? I've had four dates in the past year, all doomed before they started. My first one was with a student's parent."

"Oh?" I questioned, thinking there was a scandal of sorts coming in her story.

"I'm an elementary school teacher, and I thought the guy was hot, so I asked him out. Little did I know he was madly in love with some other girl and on the rebound. I'm sure they're blissfully married by now. They seem the type of couple everyone strives to be. Maybe one day I'll know how it feels."

"Ouch." I took her glass and poured another drink.

"In his defense, he's a nice guy and his wife is incredibly sweet. I suppose my problem with him was a case of meeting at the wrong time. We only went on two dates and didn't have a lot in common either. I'm embarrassed to admit when I met his girlfriend, I acted quite catty toward her."

She covered her mouth and mumbled something I didn't catch.

Leaning down closer, I asked her to repeat herself.

She peered up at me, the hue of embarrassment on her cheeks, and admitted, "I hinted at her being unattractive. She should've slapped me. I'd have slapped me! The woman is gorgeous."

"It's understandable. And don't be too hard on yourself. I think we've all done *and said* crazy things in the name of finding love." I was impressed she admitted her fault in things not working out. When she first mentioned man troubles, I thought for sure she'd spend the evening bashing the entire male species. "What about Mr. Wrong number two?"

"The second guy, well our first date wasn't terrible. We had a lot in common."

"What went wrong?" Still engrossed in her story, I noticed the man next to me trying to get my attention by waving an empty bottle around. I grabbed a beer from the cooler, popped the top, and slid it over to him.

She chuckled as though I was missing an obvious joke. "He was a grade-A asshole. When he romantically asked me out for our second date by saying, 'We can go out again as long as there will be sex this time,' I knew he was Mr. Right-out-the-door."

Shrinking back, I bowed. "Let me apologize for the asshat and promise you all men are not so bad." She passed her empty glass back across the bar. "Do you want another?"

Shaking her head, she replied, "No, I better get going."

She stood and wobbled heavily.

Instinctively I reached out to grab her elbow and steadied her. "Can I call you a cab?"

She shook her head again. "No, I'll call my friend Sara to come get me. Will you be open a little longer? She'll be a few minutes."

Smiling, I replied, "Yep, there's time. You're welcome to camp out here."

She placed her hand on mine and gave a small squeeze. "Thanks, Tristan."

For the next hour, she sat at the bar waiting for her friend while I cleaned up. Occasionally I caught her watching me. Each time our eyes met, she glanced away with pink cheeks. It felt good to have her focus drifting to me. She was an attractive woman and seemed nice enough. Just as I headed toward her to take a break, she stood up and waved. "My ride's here. Thanks again."

I watched her go, throwing her a small wave and chin lift. Disappointment settled in my chest, causing me to frown. It wasn't like I'd planned to ask for her number or anything; she just seemed like someone I could have a decent conversation with. But still, it no longer mattered. She was gone.

Chapter Three

FRISKY FRIENDS

"Good Morning, ladies," I exclaimed, walking into the kitchen where Angel and Macy ate cereal. They both grunted a response. "You two are grouchy in the mornings."

"We can't all have gymnastic sex at all hours of the night." I spit coffee all over the back wall.

"What?" My voice hit a disturbingly high-pitch as I wiped my mouth of coffee spittle.

"You and bimbo?" Macy explained, "I'd gotten up to use the restroom and had the lovely experience of seeing her bouncing her way naked into the kitchen for a nighttime snack."

I sighed in defeat.

After Melanie had walked away, one of the club's regulars, Bailey, had appeared. She'd approached me a few times before, and I turned her down each time. Last night seemed as good a night as any to take her up on the offer of no-strings-attached sex.

Admittedly it was stupid since I'd just slept with Angel, but she assured me nothing changed between us. We were still just friends. And Bailey sweet-talked me into it, or rather her mouth around my dick while in the storeroom with a promise of more did. Yeah, she wasn't my best decision, but hell, I was single and had needs. The biggest mistake I made was bringing Bailey home with me where Macy could witness my shitty behavior.

"Her name is Bailey, and I'm sorry." Honestly, I never remembered her leaving the room either. I must have passed out after our second time.

"You got this one's name? Well, that's something I guess," Macy scolded. Hearing those words from my little sister crushed my spirit and opened my eyes to the reality of my downward spiral since making the move to Nashville. What kind of role model was I being for my sister?

"I'm sorry, Macy. It's been a hard time for me lately. I'm making a change though. There won't be any more one-night stands for gymnasts or anyone. I promise. In fact, I met a girl at the bar last night who seemed sweet. I'm hoping she comes back, and I get to know her better. And I'm going to take it slow with whomever I date now." I wasn't spouting bullshit to make her feel better either. The words I spoke were a promise to her, and the one thing I never did was break a promise to Macy. Seeing the disappointment on her face, hearing it in her tone, was a wake-up call for me.

Things were going to be different.

"You deserve a good girl, Tristan. You're a decent guy, and I know raising me hasn't been easy for you, so I realize you're sowing your wild oats."

"Whoa, sis. Where did you hear that phrase?"

"Doesn't matter." She shrugged nonchalantly.

The kid forever kept me on my damn toes. "Yes, it does. You're fourteen and too young to know anything about sowing oats."

Angel rolled her eyes and decided to put in her two cents. "Chill, T, she's a teenager. They know more about oats than we do most of the time. I know I knew more about it than my parents."

Placing my hands over my ears, I yelled out, "Augh. No, do not compare my sister to you, please."

Angel stood up, mouth agape, her eyes practically on fire with the anger behind them. "I didn't know you thought so low of me."

I could have punched myself. The last thing I wanted was to make a potentially awkward situation with Angel worse by insulting her. "Macy, can you give us a minute?" Macy left the room while Angel slammed drawers in the kitchen. I sighed, my voice low, apologetic, "I didn't mean it that way, Angel."

"How did you mean it?" She turned to face me, crossing her arms over her chest. "I'm not sure how you'll talk yourself out of this one."

"You're the first one to admit you sleep around, Angel. I want more for my sister. I didn't mean to hurt your feelings.

I'm sorry."

Angel kept her angry stance as she thought it over for a moment. "You're right. I've never denied sleeping around. You're forgiven. Be careful with your words next time, please." Her words changed from understanding to an undertone of hurt.

Stepping forward, I wrapped my arms around her in a friendly hug. "I promise, Angel." I cleared my throat, wanting to get any awkwardness over with. "And shit, about me bringing someone else back, after you know, the other—"

She stepped back and held her hand up to stop my rambling. "Please. No offense, but yeah, it was obvious we got it on since we were both naked, but hell, T, I don't remember the specifics, and like I already said, I have no desire to do that with you again."

I held back my amused smile, wondering if I should be offended by her dismissal or by the fact that my performance didn't rock her world. Instead I nodded in agreement. "Sounds like a plan."

"And you're not exactly Prince Charming either, not lately at least. Find yourself a decent girl, T. You deserve it, and Macy wants you to be happy." With a firm nod, seemingly happy that she'd fixed whatever this was, Angel kissed my cheek before walking away leaving me with my thoughts. The main one being, I really needed to make sure I didn't bring home any more one-night stands.

Chapter Four

BOYS WILL BE BOYS

The bar emptied by two in the morning. Being Derrick's first night back since the honeymoon, he was in the bar much later than usual helping us catch up. Normally he worked daytime hours, scheduling musical acts and placing orders with the distributors.

Derrick, Ashton, and I were taking inventory to place the next order for supplies. Ashton lifted a case of liquor to fill up the bar shelf, and it appeared to weigh nothing when he hoisted it over his shoulder. I tried to mimic the motion and only managed to lift the case to the height of my waist. "Damn, Ash. You're like the freaking Hulk or something. I can barely lift this thing."

Ashton gave a gruff chuckle. "Well, I guess you don't want to make me angry. Maybe you should come to the gym with Derrick and me some time. I've been helping him with weight training. I could do the same for you."

"Sounds like a plan. Maybe it will help me get a great girl like Gracie if I have guns the size of yours."

Derrick laughed. "Good luck getting arms like those trunks Ash carries around. I swear we have the same DNA, but somehow, he's a beast. I've been working out for years and still can't get the size he is unless I want to take some drugs that shrink my boys, and I refuse to do that."

"How'd you get to be so big, Ash?"

"When I lost the woman I loved, I began working out nonstop to take my mind off the grief."

"Wait, what? I thought Gracie was the love of your life?" My brows dipped in confusion.

"She is, but I didn't know back then. I was in love with a girl named Addison, Gavin's sister. She died during a convenience store robbery while there buying cigarettes."

"Wow, I'm sorry, man. I had no idea." Some of the stories I'd heard now made more sense, such as why Cameron and Gavin named their daughter Addison. For a moment, the air was thick in the room. I needed to lighten things up again.

"You get a massive set of muscles, good looks, money, and two great loves. Do you hoard four-leaf clovers or what? Where does all the luck come from?" The one time I'd been in love the woman loved someone else.

"I wouldn't call it luck. My first love was murdered, and my wife and I got together after she was brutally attacked by her ex-boyfriend. That kind of luck can make a guy question if he brings bad luck upon those he's around,"

Ashton replied sadly.

"Sorry, man. I can see what you mean. Still, you two have fantastic women. Tell me your secrets. I've been sleeping around since I moved to Nashville, and it's getting old. I'm a terrible influence for Macy too. Since you're both white knights, maybe you can tell me the secret?" I'd take any advice they had to offer. Making a change was a serious goal for me. It was what I wanted, to be a better role model for Macy.

Ashton grabbed three beers out of the cooler and motioned to a circular table in the bar. "Let's have a beer and talk." We popped the tops on our beers, and each took a swig before Ashton began. "Gracie and I were best friends. Cameron introduced us while she was dating Hudson." His voice grew angry as he spouted the name of Gracie's ex. "I fell in love with her pretty quickly, but she fought her feelings for me. He'd broken her, made her feel like she wasn't worth being loved, and it convinced her to stay and ignore the signs of his inevitable abuse. She finally allowed herself to give in to her feelings for me, and when she broke up with him, he flipped out. You know the rest of the story. My point is there is no secret. Patience, understanding, and friendship are some of the ways to a happy life. They worked for me at least."

"You know my story," Derrick began. "Hell, you were part of it. I'm not sure I was patient enough at times. Letting her go to take the internship in Florida was the hardest thing I've ever done. I knew she was the one for me, and I didn't know if I'd ever see her again. Two years and several hundred miles apart, we still managed to find our way back to each other. Of course, she walked back into my life pregnant and with you on her arm, something I never expected. But finding out she was a surrogate for my brother made me fall in love with her all over again. None of it was easy, but in the end, it all worked out. I think the moral of these stories is everyone's different. There's no consistent formula to falling in love. There's no true happily ever after or anything else fairy tales teach us. Love is work, and in the end, the payout is greater than anything else in life. You'll get there, T."

If they believed it, I should. Connecting with someone had been difficult for me. Attraction wasn't the hard part. There were plenty of beautiful women in all shapes and sizes around, but none I thought twice about, until Melanie. Something about her stuck with me. Perhaps if I follow Derrick and Ashton's advice, I could find my happy ending too.

"Another beer?" I offered. Both gave a nod, so I ran to the cooler and pulled out three more bottles. "I suppose you two don't know the meaning of life either?"

They both laughed, and I threw them a grin as I handed each another beer. I hadn't had many bosses I could call friends. Most of the jobs I had before came with supervisors who felt the need to boast their superiority over their employees. Derrick and Ashton Collins were content letting their employees run things most days. They treated us as equals. Our friendship had grown stronger since I began to work for them. When I first accepted the job, I thought it would be the opposite; I was glad they'd proved me wrong.

"Have you considered Angel?" Derrick inquired.

"Considered Angel for what?" I asked perplexed.

"Girlfriend material. You two live together and seem to be good friends. Any chance for romantic feelings there?" Derrick's eyebrows rose with curiosity as he took a long sip of beer and waited for my answer.

"Angel is a knockout. She has a firecracker attitude, a big heart, a sexy Latina accent, and her body is amazing. As much as I adore her, I feel like we'd never work as a couple. We've been living together for a while now, and we fight worse than siblings."

"Do you love her?" Ashton brought out the heavy question.

"I'm not *in* love with her. I care about what happens to her though. Where'd this come from, did she say something?" His question made me wonder whether the night we shared meant more to Angel than it did to me.

"Nah. You know how girls want everyone to be in love the way they are. MJ and Gracie both have been itching to find love for Angel, and they were considering the possibility of you and Angel together," Derrick replied casually.

"If I thought it would work, I'd try it. I don't think Angel's the one for me though, as cheesy as it sounds."

"It doesn't sound cheesy. People know when they've found the right person, which also means people know when they haven't." Ashton offered his words of wisdom.

Derrick's phone rang, cutting through our conversation. "Hey, baby, are you having trouble sleeping?" He laughed quietly at her response. "I'll be leaving here in about twenty minutes. I'll stop and get you a frosty and fries on my way home. I love you too."

"Pregnancy cravings already?" I asked.

"MJ cravings. Her weakness is to have fries with a chocolate milkshake. She doesn't eat it often, but she really wants some now." He glanced at his beer and shrugged. "At least I only drank a little of it. I'm going to get on the road and get home to my girls. You two ready to head out?"

Ashton stretched and yawned. "Yep, I have a couple of girls waiting for me at home as well." They both looked over at me and guffawed at the same time. Ashton explained the joke I missed. "Technically you have two girls at home too. You aren't as different from us as you think."

"You have a point. Unfortunately, one is only a friend, and the other is my sister. Not quite the same. I'm heading out though too. I'm exhausted, and I hear the bed calling my name from here."

The house was eerily quiet when I got home. As usual, I leaned my head against Macy's door to listen for sounds. Her snores were loud and clear so I moved to the next door down the hall. Angel had a habit of not coming home at night, so I was shocked to see her wrapped up in her own bed. Every night I checked on her and usually found nothing more than an empty unkempt bed. We were a lot alike. She couldn't seem to settle down either. I wanted her to find someone too, but hoped Mary Jane and Gracie hadn't convinced her to pursue me. Friendship was all I wanted from her, but I didn't want to hurt her either. Grabbing the doorknob, I eased the door closed and released the latch slowly to keep from waking her.

Even though my body was tired my mind raced with thoughts, I knew I'd never get to sleep. I went downstairs and sprawled out on the couch to watch a movie.

The curtains in the living room had been left open so shortly after falling asleep, the bright sun awakened me through the white blinds. With a grunt, I rolled over and covered my face with my arm. With the light problem solved, I was drifting back to sleep when the scream of a blender began. Grumbling once more, I pulled a throw pillow over my face to drown out the noise. Next came the unpleasant smell of burnt eggs.

Trying to sleep had become impossible. I stood up, stretched my back until it cracked, and lifted my shirt to my nose to cover the foul smell from the kitchen. The shirt smelled like a mixture of beer and cleaning fluids, so it wasn't much better. I pulled it over my head as I walked into the kitchen barefoot and dressed only in jeans.

Macy stood at the sink scraping the obliterated eggs down the garbage disposal. I inched up behind her to help and noticed she had her earbuds in. She poured a fresh cup of coffee and when she turned around, she screamed, and her hands shook enough to spill the hot liquid on my chest. "Shit!" I screamed out and grabbed a hand towel from the stove bar to wipe the hot liquid off my skin.

"I'm sorry, T!" Macy cried out. She wet a washcloth and pressed cold water against my skin to keep me from burning. I grabbed it from her hand and finished getting the spots she missed. She pulled her earbuds out and said, "Don't sneak up on me, T."

"Next time, don't use earbuds, a garbage disposal, and a blender all at once and you might hear me. What are you doing in here?"

"Trying to cook breakfast. I was trying a new recipe, and it didn't work out. I thought you'd still be in bed."

"I fell asleep on the couch."

"Oh. Sorry," Macy apologized.

"No worries, squirt. I'm going to head upstairs to catch some real shut-eye though. Don't worry about breakfast for me. Make something simple. There are frozen waffles, strawberries, and syrup. Go a little nuts today."

"Okay, want me to wake you up in a few hours? We could have a movie day?" Back in Florida, when it was the two of us, we'd have a day together once a month. No phones, no friends, no computers, just Macy, me, and a stack of movies.

"Give me at least five hours of sleep, and I'm all yours, kid."

When Macy woke me, at the time I requested, I felt refreshed and ready to sit up for a bit. Just as we settled down to watch a movie Derrick called to ask if I could work. Macy was disappointed but understood I had to go.

CHAPTER FIVE

CHIVALRY ISN'T DEAD

"Hey there, pretty lady," I called out as I spotted Melanie at the end of the bar again.

"Hi, I spoke to you last week." She informed me as though she was only another face in the crowd. She had no idea her face had starred in a few very vivid dreams of mine.

"I know. I'm glad to see you back, *Melanie*. You only got through the two jerks this year and had two more stories to tell me." Judging by the shocked look on her face, she didn't expect me to remember her name or story. "Did you think I'd forget?" She stumbled over her response, so I saved her by leaning down close to her ear and saying, "I told you, not all of us are jerks."

Someone yelled out "Bartender," so I excused myself to go tend to the individual whose speech was thoroughly slurred at this point. "Did you know if you have a certain type of car key, you win a free drink?"

The guy took the bait, reached into his pocket, and slammed his keys on the bar. "Sheck 'ems out, besha I gots one" was how it came out in a breath full of whiskey.

Grabbing his keys, I clicked my tongue. "You don't have the magic key. However, you did win a free sober ride home!" Sometimes they argued with me or got angry. This guy looked excited; he cheered before dropping his head to the bar to take a nap. I motioned for Bobby, our bouncer, to come get him.

We had a special room to the side of the door for our sober-rides pickup. We called it the drunk tank. The room had three plush couches for customers to pass out on comfortably. Each sofa had a wastebasket next to it ready to assist in sobering them up. Whenever a customer was too sloshed, we convinced them to give up their keys. Then we'd figure out which car was theirs, so we didn't tow it, and we'd send them off to take a sober ride. Most of the time they were coherent enough to give the driver their addresses. Their keys were returned before they got out of the car, and they always came back the next day to retrieve their vehicles. It was a lot of work but worth it to save them from getting on the road. Occasionally we ended up with an overnight guest who had to be babysat by security until they awoke feeling crappy the next day. We would send them off the next morning with a bottle of water and a dose of ibuprofen.

"What would you like to drink?" I asked Melanie when

I returned to her end of the bar.

"Beer, please, whatever your favorite is. I'm trying new things."

I reached into the cooler and picked out my favorite brand, popped the cap off, then slid it down the bar to her. She brought the cool bottle up to her plump pink lips and took a long taste.

"How was it?"

She pulled the bottle away, placed her hand against her mouth to catch a drop slipping down her chin. My teeth bit down on my bottom lip hard as I imagined I caught the drop with my tongue as it dipped into her mouth. "It's good."

"Did you have another bad date? Is this your bad date getaway now?" It took every bit of focus I had to concentrate on her words instead of her body. Her fingers fumbled with a necklace above her cleavage. Occasionally my eyes dipped down to her plump breasts.

She grinned. "No. I like this bar. I love how you do so much to make sure people get home safely."

"My bosses' father was killed not long ago by a drunk driver. And I mean bosses, plural. The owners are brothers. After his death, they spent extra money investing in a sober ride business. They wanted to make sure they weren't responsible for anyone else losing a loved one. We do our best to keep an eye on people who are leaving here to make sure they aren't driving. We've even had to call the cops on a few of our customers who got behind the wheel wasted."

"Wow, that's very responsible." Her brows lifted, seemingly impressed, and my chest warmed. Rarely did I worry about what people thought, but with her, I wanted to make a good impression.

Out of the corner of my eye, I spotted a guy rough handling a woman. "Excuse me a moment," I requested before turning and yelling, "Hey, Marcus! Keep an eye on the bar!" Pushing my way through the crowd, I tapped the guy on the shoulder.

He turned around angrily. "What?"

"You need to keep your hands off the lady or get out of the club."

With a step toward me, he put his nose against mine. "Who's going to make me?"

A hand slammed down on his shoulder, and a gruff voice stated, "That would be me." When the man turned around, he looked up at Ashton. I was no scrawny guy, but Ashton was over six foot five and solid muscle. I knew he was complete mush inside, but he was intimidating to look at nonetheless. "This is my club. Ma'am, are you with this guy?" She shook her head. "Good. So, you're bothering my customer, which means you're bothering me. You can leave her alone, or you can just leave. Make a choice. If I see you manhandle anyone else in here, I'll call the police. You got it?" The only response received was a grunt before the idiot stalked away.

"Thanks." The woman batted her eyes at Ashton. She ran her hand along his bicep and asked, "Can I repay you?"

Politely, he moved her hand from his arm and replied, "I'm flattered, but I'm a very happily married man. My friend Tristan here is single though."

Hurt from Ashton's rejection soon changed over to checking me out. Before she answered, I pointed toward the bar. "I have to get back to my station. I'll be behind the bar if you need me."

The woman was cute, but she seemed to want any guy she could get, and I wanted something more substantial. Plus, I wanted to get back to the auburn beauty at the bar who had captured my attention. Melanie wasn't sitting where I left her. After a glance around the room, I spotted her dancing with a guy. It stirred something inside me. Jealousy. The same thing I felt when I first saw Mary Jane and Derrick together.

My eyes focused on her. The way her hips swayed back and forth hypnotized me. Her dance partner moved his hand down her sides and began to lift her dress up her thighs. Anger boiled inside me; I was ready to pounce. For anyone else, I'd be flagging down our bouncer to get rid of the guy, but I wanted to rescue her myself. I strapped on my metaphorical superhero cape, and as I approached—to save the day—I noticed she had not only pushed his hands away but punched him in the nose as well. She turned red when she spotted me, and I raised my hand up. "High-five." She smacked my hand. "It's hard to believe you complain about jerks. Looks like you can take care of yourself pretty well."

"I have three older brothers who taught me how." She pushed passed me, reclaiming her seat at the bar. "Can I get another of those beers?"

"Sure. And if you tell me about the other two guys, it's on me."

"Deal," she agreed. After I had popped the top on the beer, she took a long pull and then began her story. "Guy number three thought he was all that and a bag of chips. He was nothing but crumbs if you ask me. He took me to a strip club. I'm open-minded and all, but a first date… at a strip club?"

"Ouch. I agree. There should be a warning and intimacy already present. What kind of perverted weirdo was he?"

"See, told you I know how to pick them. Last, but not least, the date from the night I met you. We had a great time. He's charming, sophisticated, well-mannered, all around great guy."

"I'm not getting a problem with him," I said, thoroughly confused.

"There was no problem. Until he reached out to touch my hand on the table, and a wedding ring circled his finger."

"Whoa."

"That was my reaction!" she exclaimed with annoyance. "He told me his wife cared more about the kids than him these days, and it was practically a dead marriage."

"What was your response?"

"I told him to call me when he found a woman to believe that line." She took another swig from her beer bottle. "I'm done dating for a while. I'll find something else to occupy my time." And my bubble burst with those words. Maybe I could change her mind about dating?

"How'd you end up here the other night? Is this where you met?"

"No. A friend of mine told me about this club, and I'd

wanted to check it out. Ending the date abruptly offered the perfect opportunity." Peering up at me, she added, "The night definitely ended better than it began."

"Tristan!" Marcus yelled from behind me. When I turned, he waved his hands to show the fullness of the crowd in front of the bar.

"Shit! I'll be back." I sprinted across the bar to take orders. Normally someone can shout something at me, and I can get it easily. With Melanie clouding my thoughts, I wrote everything down with descriptions of who ordered it. Gorbachev: Bud Light beer. Barney: a shot of whiskey. Ginger: Jägerbomb. Fake boobs: cosmo. Mullet: MGD. With five orders written down, I stopped to get them ready before taking five more and repeated this until the bar was clear. Turning to Marcus, I said, "Sorry, man. I was distracted."

"I noticed. She's hot, by the way. I'd be distracted too. Sorry you missed out on talking to her."

"Oh no, she's…." I started to say as I turned toward her. Her seat held a large, hairy, redneck-looking man. I cursed at missing a chance to ask her out. My relief bartender for the night, Xander, walked toward me from where I'd left her.

"The hottie at the bar paid her tab, then gave me this for you." He handed me a twenty-dollar tip wrapped around a business card. "She suggested you give her a call and she'd finish telling you a story."

The business card was one of ours from the bar. She'd written her number on it with her name below and a heart dotting the letter I. Staring at the heart, I grinned widely. She was into me too. Having her number meant I didn't have to wait and hope to see her again. As soon as I had a free moment, I planned to call her and could hardly wait to hear her voice again. I programmed it into my phone and then pulled my wallet out of my back pocket and slipped the card in behind a school photo of Macy.

CHAPTER SIX

LIFE'S COMPLICATIONS

My plan to call Melanie the following day didn't pan out the way I wanted. The morning instead began with a mopey Macy lying on the couch in the living room. "Hey, squirt, what's up?"

She grumbled a low, "Nothing."

"What's wrong?"

Another low rumble. "Nothing."

Her mood required drastic measures; I grabbed the remote off the table and switched off the television. "As convincing as that sounds, sit up please and persuade me a little more."

She rolled her eyes and sat up reluctantly. "Why do boys not do what they say they'll do?"

"Is this about…" I squeezed my eyes shut trying to

remember the name of the boy who Macy went on her first date with a few months back.

"Carter… his name was Carter. And yes, it's about him. Our first date was a lot of fun, and I thought we hit it off, but he hasn't called me this summer like he promised."

My big-brother instinct made me want to beat the kid up for making my sister sad. The teenage boy of my past understood why he might be acting this way. Choosing my words carefully, I said, "He's a putz." Okay, so that didn't come out as I'd intended. Sure, I didn't curse or make threats, but I meant to be a little more comforting. "What I mean is he's a teenage boy. When I was a teenager, do you remember how many girls I dated?" Macy's expression told me those words were no more comforting than my first.

Angel spoke up as she entered the room. "I think what Tristan is trying to say is Carter's young and naïve. When a teenage boy says he'll call, it may not mean right away. It doesn't mean he didn't have fun with you or doesn't like you."

"Thanks, Angel. Maybe he's waiting until school starts again? He may have a busy summer." Macy began making assumptions to comfort herself.

"That's the spirit. I'll see you two later, I'm off to work." Angel gave us each a kiss on the cheek and sauntered out the door.

Back in Florida, Macy and I used to spend a lot of time together. When Mary Jane came in the picture, the three of us began to hang out together. Since moving to Nashville, everything had changed. Mary Jane married and had a stepdaughter, and I spent many hours at work. We hadn't spent a single day together in over a year at least.

"Remember our tourist days in Florida?" Macy nodded, so I continued, "We haven't had one of those in Nashville. Let's have one today, just the two of us." Her face lit up with excitement I hadn't witnessed in a while, which made me happy and sad at the same time. I had neglected my sister, the most important person in my life. My life needed to be prioritized, and Macy belonged at the top. As anxious as I was to talk to Melanie again, I'd have to put my potential love life on hold for a little longer. Putting a smile on Macy's face made my whole day brighter. "Go upstairs and get dressed in your best tourist clothing."

Macy bolted up the stairs, and I followed her. During our tourist days in Florida, we would wear attire only non-Floridians would wear such as shirts with catchy phrases about the state or extreme Disney attire including a pair of Mickey Mouse ears. In Nashville, the tourist population wore cowboy hats, boots, and fringe or rhinestones. The stereotypical country attire, something most native Nashvillians never wore.

Macy stepped from her room in a plaid button-down shirt, tucked into a pair of dark jeans, and a pair of cowboy boots Mary Jane bought her when they first moved here. "I need a cowboy hat for full effect," she said spinning around.

For my attire, I donned a pair of jeans I'd never wear normally. They were a size too small and so tight I was afraid my voice would be higher than Macy's for the entire day. I also chose a plaid button down and paired it with an

"I ♥ Nashville" belt buckle also bought by Mary Jane as a joke. I had a set of cowboy boots from when I lived in Florida.

"We'll buy hats first thing when we get downtown today. After, we'll grab breakfast at the Pancake Pantry and then figure out from there what tourist thing to do next."

Macy clapped happily."I'm excited, T! I've missed these days!"

Second Avenue and Broadway Street downtown were the best places to shop for a cowboy hat because you could find every style imaginable. They weren't cheap, but I had worked a lot of overtime lately, so I made the choice to splurge a bit. The smile on Macy's face made it worth every penny. She chose a beige hat with an Aztec design on the band. For me, she picked out a black cowboy hat with a brown leather band.

"Where do you want to go?"

Macy's eyes bulged as they landed on the green and gold sign of a bookstore across the street. Grabbing her hand, we ran across the road together and ventured inside. A musty smell greeted us the moment we opened the door. With aisles barely wide enough for two people to pass, I followed behind Macy. The books were all old, and some were even first editions. It felt like we'd stepped back in time. Ever since she was five, Macy loved to read. She ran her hands along the shelves in complete awe of the contents. Each book she pulled down, she viewed with the intensity of someone seeing one of the seventh wonders of the world. One book made her eyes mist with tears. Seeing her excitement over reading made me proud. Girls her age were getting excited over social media, makeup, and boys. I'd raised a girl genius with a massive love for reading. I only wished I could afford to buy her a few of these first editions she swooned over.

"It's *The Lion, the Witch, and the Wardrobe*. The first book Mom read to me; it was her favorite." Macy held the book against her chest with her eyes closed in thought. "When I tried to read it to her at the hospital one day, she told me the story was stupid."

Our mother's Alzheimer's had hit Macy the hardest, and I don't know why I thought ignoring the situation instead of talking about it would make her forget. "It was the disease talking, Macy, not our mom."

"Doesn't make it hurt any less."

She had a point. Of all the people in the world, the expectation is that your parents should always remember things about your life since they were the ones there for almost every moment.

"She shoved me too."

"What?" I asked in shock. Our mother never laid a hand on us in anger or frustration. She never believed in spanking. "You never told me."

"I didn't want you to worry or get angry. As you've explained, it's the disease. I'd left the room for a moment, and I came back in to hug her goodbye. She gasped with horror and shoved me away telling me to get out of her room. The shove was hard enough to knock me down. She started screaming she didn't know me and to keep my hands off her. The nurses came in to restrain her, and I ran out crying. I accepted she wouldn't come back to us." Although she fought to hold back the emotion, Macy's tears flowed as she relayed the painful story.

I pulled Macy against my chest hugging her tightly. Smoothing her hair, I let a few tears fall from the hurt she had to endure. A similar experience with Mom caused my hope to die as well. Mine came when I walked into her room, and she flirted with me. The moment was sad and creepy for me, but still better than Macy's.

"Will you buy this book for me, T? I'd like something to remember her by, and I left my copy there."

The price was a bit high for the hardcover edition. Crunching a few numbers in my head to be sure I could pay bills, I bought it for her, deciding I'd live off the free snacks at work for meals until next payday.

Once the door closed behind us, she turned and asked, "Can we skip breakfast. I'm not hungry anymore." One thing Macy always had was a hearty appetite. Her abrupt change of plans concerned me. She never talked about stories of Mom with me, and I feared I hadn't handled the moment properly.

"Sure, squirt. Where do you want to go?" All I wanted was to put the smile back on her face. Whatever she chose to do, I'd make happen.

"Can we go home and watch a movie? Maybe when Angel comes home tonight, the three of us could play something." We kept a closet full of board games at the house. On the rare nights I got Angel to stay home, the three of us had game night. We gambled with household chores; the two of them ganged up on me a lot.

"Sounds like fun." I placed my arm around her, pulled her close to me, and kissed the side of her head. "I love you, kid." She peered up at me with a smile that melted my heart.

Our evening ended with an enjoyable round of Monopoly with Angel. My stacks of money were low, and I owned some of the cheapest properties on the board. "I'm calling it a night. You ladies have practically bankrupted me."

"Poor, Tristan. You're such a bad sport when you don't get Park Place or Boardwalk," Macy teased good-naturedly.

"I still think you cheat." I grinned and mussed her hair. We packed up all the pieces and went to our separate rooms. I grabbed a towel and a pair of shorts, then headed to get a shower before bed. Blocked by Macy at the sink, she turned and grinned at me with a mouthful of toothpaste. I closed the toilet seat lid and set my fresh clothes on it while she finished up.

After spitting and wiping her mouth, she wrapped her arms around my neck and kissed my cheek. "Thanks for today, T. I had fun."

"Me too, kid. We'll have to do it again soon. I promise we'll get back to our traditions." Life needed to be the way it was before Mary Jane. I loved having new friends in my life, but Macy should always come first. She couldn't handle any more letdowns in life from parental figures.

CHAPTER SEVEN

SAVED BY THE BALD

My day out with Macy meant extra shifts to cover the bills this month. If I wanted to spend more time with Macy, I had to find cheaper activities for us. During the week, the crowd was minimal, which made the evening drag on. I preferred a crowded Saturday night, running back and forth across the bar, over staring out at a few lonely people.

Only one bartender worked during these nights unless there was a special occasion or holiday. Even then, the bartender barely had anything to do so we'd spend the evening staring at the television screens or chatting one-on-one with the customers who were there simply to drown their sorrows.

It would have been the perfect time for Melanie to show up. I'd have all the time in the world to listen to her sweet voice. The two times we'd spoken were on weekend nights. I knew she was a schoolteacher, and it was the end of May, so I decided to give it a shot. I sent her a quick text.

Me: Hi, it's Tristan. It's slow at the club tonight. Thought maybe you'd want to stop by and finish telling me the story?

Melanie: Sure. I'll be there in an hour?

Me: Sounds perfect.

"You look happy. What are you up to?" Ashton asked approaching the bar.

"I asked a girl to come see me tonight. Hope that's okay, boss."

Ashton chuckled. "You know it's fine. Sounds promising. Who is she?"

"I met her here not long ago. She left me her number, thought I'd give her a call." Butterflies attacked my stomach as I grew nervous about seeing her again. I wanted to make an even better impression on her this time.

"Good luck! Since it's slow, I'm going to head home and spend time with my beautiful wife. Gracie texted stating Autumn is finally asleep. We haven't had alone time in a while." He bumped his elbow against my arm and grinned.

"I get it."

"I know you do. Macy may not be a toddler, but she does take up a lot of your time," Ashton commented.

"It's worth it though. And I'm going to start spending more time with her again. We hung out the other day, and she admitted something to me about our mom. She's still having trouble coping, even now."

"You know Gracie is a psychologist. If Macy needs to talk to someone, she'd love to be there for her. I'm not suggesting she needs professional help. But as a friend, Gracie may be better suited to help her since she's not as close to the situation as you." As shy as Macy was, I could never get her to talk to a stranger about what our parents put her through. She loved Gracie though, and it would be a great opportunity for her to work through her history.

"Sure, that would be great. I'll talk to Macy. In exchange, maybe she could babysit so you guys could have a few date nights out."

Ashton gave me a strong hug. "Brother, you read my mind." He patted my back and then waved as he left.

"Am I too late?" A soft female voice called out from behind me. Melanie lifted herself up onto the bar stool and leaned forward with a smile. I grabbed two beers from the cooler and popped the tops as I strolled over to her.

"Nope. Just in time to share a beer with me." Her fingers grazed my skin as she took the bottle. An electric spark passed through my body with the contact.

"Can you drink on the job?"

"Yeah, as long as I don't get drunk. I'm on the clock for about"—I checked my watch—"five more hours, so it's my one drink for the night, and I want to share it with you."

"I'm honored. I honestly didn't think you were going to call." She took a long sip of beer waiting for my answer.

"I wanted to call sooner; it's just I needed to spend some time with Macy, my little sister. She's having a hard time— boy troubles."

She pointed the bottle at me. "Those are the worst troubles. I feel for her. How old is she?"

"Fourteen, she's about to be a senior in high school." I forgot how it sounds to people when I say it out loud.

Melanie choked a bit on her beer. "What? Wow! She's like a Doogie Howser?"

"Like a who?" I asked perplexed.

"Doogie Howser… teen doctor… Neil Patrick Harris? Ring a bell?"

"Neil Patrick Harris… he's on *How I Met Your Mother*, right?"

Melanie shook her head back and forth. "Um… yeah. He started acting at a much younger age though. It was a show in the late eighties, early nineties, called *Doogie Howser, M.D.* He played a sixteen-year-old genius who became a doctor. You never watched it?"

"I was born in the early nineties, what do you expect?" The moment the words were out, I wanted to suck them back in.

Melanie held her hand up feigning offense. "And you think I am older than you?"

"No, of course not." Stumbling over my words, I tried to backtrack to save face.

She laughed. "It's fine, Tristan. I'm joking. I watched it when it came out on DVD. I love anything and everything from the eighties and nineties. Now if you told me you never watched *Saved by the Bell*, I'd be offended."

I glanced at my beer bottle, cleared my throat, and asked, "Need another?"

She gasped. "Seriously? Zack? Slater? Kelly Kapowski? Screech?"

I cleared my throat again and repeated, "So… that beer?"

Melanie set her bottle down, stood up, extended her hand to me, which I took hold of, and said, "Thank you for the beer. It was nice meeting you. Good night."

She began to walk away, leaving me dumbfounded. I waited for her to turn back. When she didn't, I called out to her. "You're leaving?"

"Yes." She raised her hand and waved without turning around. I ran after her, reached out, and spun her around gently. Lips sucked between her teeth she tried her best to hold back the laughter.

"That was downright mean. I thought I offended you."

"You did. I can recite each episode, down to the songs 'Zack Attack' performed."

"Zack Attack?" I asked still completely lost.

Melanie smacked her forehead. "You make me sad. Let's change the subject."

"Deal. Come sit back down?"

She followed me back to the bar where I grabbed a cold beer to replace her last one. A bald man sat a few seats down from hers, and he tossed back his third shot of the night. He glanced up and held his glass up to her. "How you doin'?"

"Good, Joey Tribiani, and you?" She chortled and gave an entertainment reference I completely understood for a change.

"*Friends* is one I know," I stated, relieved at the smile on her face.

"Thank goodness, now we can talk and it might go somewhere." The innuendo in her tone filled my heart with hope.

I leaned down close, tucked her hair behind her ear, and trailed my finger down her cheek as I asked, "Where might this be going?" She shivered at my touch, and warmth spread through my body. If baldy hadn't been in the room, the bar might have gotten a bit X-rated. She bit her bottom lip and drew in a sharp breath.

"Can I get a refill?" Baldy called out from behind me. As I pulled away, I noticed a blush filling her cheeks. I needed to call this guy a cab soon. After I had filled up his shot of whiskey once more, I scurried back to Melanie's side.

"So, where were we?"

"Probably someplace we weren't ready to be. Tell me a story from your high school days. Were you a player, a geek, a jock?" she asked, changing the subject. We were making great progress, and it's like she leaped back three feet. We'd never reach the next step if she kept pulling back. Patience was one of the virtues both Ashton and Derrick had mentioned in finding the right person. I had a feeling Melanie was worth the wait, so I let her redirect without question.

"Um… okay. I wasn't a typical high school kid. I wanted to play sports, but it didn't work out with my mom's illness. I spent a lot of time with my sister instead." Our conversation took a more serious turn than I wanted, but it was too late to retract my comment.

"What illness?"

"Alzheimer's. The doctors diagnosed her before my first year of high school. Macy was only four. As soon as I turned eighteen my dad signed custody over to me and left."

Her mouth dropped open in surprise. "Not at all what I expected to hear. You know we got off subject earlier but tell me again how Macy is a senior at fourteen?"

"Well by the time school starts she'll be fifteen. Her birthday is at the end of July. But she's incredibly intelligent. She started school a year early and skipped two grades. She's always loved school, gotten top grades, even exceeded top grades because she did all the extra credit projects too. She wants to go to medical school and become a doctor. I think her dream is to find a cure for Alzheimer's so no one else goes through this pain." I choked up a bit as I related that bit of information. I hated to appear vulnerable in front of this stunning woman.

Walking behind the bar, Melanie wrapped me in an embrace. Her arms pressed against my back pulling me tightly against her. My hands landed on her lower back, and my nose pressed against her neck taking in the scent of her skin as she consoled me. I lifted my head to face her and moved in for a kiss when Baldy interrupted us again. "I need another drink."

I sighed and let go of her. Instead of pouring another shot of whiskey, I cut him off and informed him a cab was on the way. When I turned to make the call for the cab, I saw Melanie gathering her things. "Are you leaving?"

"It's late. I enjoyed talking with you though. I'll come back this weekend if you'd like. Or you could give me a call," Melanie suggested. Feeling dejected, I watched her walk away. Just before going out the door she pressed her palm to her lips and pulled it away again, blowing me a kiss. I couldn't wait to find out where the intense attraction would lead us.

Next time I saw her I planned to continue what Baldy interrupted.

CHAPTER EIGHT

FRIENDS FIRST

"All right, guys, I'm heading to the grocery store since it's my turn to shop. Any requests before I go?" I asked Angel and Macy.

Macy replied first. "Mouthwash."

"What? We had a whole bottle the other day?" I asked, confused.

"If we did, we're out now."

"Okay, mouthwash," I mumbled as I added it to a list I'd made on my phone for reference. "Anything else? Angel, do you have any special requests?"

"Feminine hygiene products," she replied with a smirk.

"Um, it's better if you get those yourself. I'll screw it up." Thankfully I'd avoided the dreaded feminine products aisle in the store for most of my life.

"Get some for me while you're at it," Macy requested.

Covering my ears, I chanted, "La la la, I don't want to know that my sister has hit puberty."

"Two years ago, T," she said nonchalantly.

"How have you been getting the stuff before?" She never asked me to pick anything up at the store for her, and I'd never seen them in the bathroom.

"Allowance money is how I bought them. It's not exactly something I wanted to mention to my big brother. Then when you met Mary Jane she bought them for me."

"I'm sorry, kid. You should've come to me."

She shrugged. "It's fine. I made do with what I could."

Macy amazed me more and more each day at how independent she could be. For a fourteen-year-old who had been through as much as she had, I expected her to act out much more. I was lucky she let it mature her instead of allowing it to break her down.

With a deep resounding sigh, I caved to their demands. Handing them the paper, I instructed, "Write down specifically what you want. I mean brand name, with or without those wing things, length, color, whatever it requires, so I don't screw it up. In fact, it would be best if you can take a picture of the packaging and text it to me."

Together they stepped up and kissed my face. "Thanks, Dad," they chimed in as though they'd planned it.

"Weirdo's," I muttered, before winking and walking out the door.

The grocery store was dead on a Thursday morning, which was why it was my favorite time to shop. My first stop was the feminine aisle so I could grab up what they needed and bury them below the rest of the groceries. "Tristan?" I heard as I pulled a giant package of tampons off the shelf. Embarrassment spread rapidly across my face once I saw the owner of the voice.

"Oh," she said, noticing the package in my hand. "Girlfriend send you shopping?"

"Little sister and roommate did, actually. Is this your way of asking me if I have a girlfriend, Melanie?"

She blushed at being caught. It's clear to me why she stood out more than anyone else I'd met at the club. No matter what she wore, she looked irresistible and had a way of making me smile in an instant.

She avoided the question completely. "It's nice you're willing to pick those up for her. Even most dads won't do the feminine hygiene products."

"To be honest, they laid the guilt on pretty heavily." And the box still clung to my hand, screaming out to everyone who passed. Tossing it into the basket, I shrugged towards Melanie.

"It only proves you're an even more amazing guy than I thought. And I already thought you were pretty amazing." She gave a sexy wink turning the temperature in the store up several degrees.

"Would you like to go on a date with me?" *Please say yes. Please say yes.*

Her lips spread into a wide grin, she bowed her head as if embarrassed and then responded. "I thought you'd never ask."

***

Since the moment Melanie accepted, I hadn't stopped thinking about her. We were supposed to meet at the restaurant at seven. Having a Friday off was a rare occurrence for me. When she accepted the date, I wasted no time in making it for the next day. She chose to meet there instead of letting me pick her up. If I thought about it, the reason could possibly be due to the bad dates she experienced recently. It was always good to be cautious about who knows where you live, especially as a single woman. Although, I was positive Melanie could take care of herself in any situation.

When I arrived at the restaurant, the hostess took me to a booth to wait for my date. My phone rang, and it displayed Marcus's name. "Hey man, what's up?"

Marcus's voice on the other end sounded scratchy and horrible. "I'm not going to make it in tonight, boss. I ate something terrible and have been upchucking all day."

"No problem, man. Feel better. I'll call and see if Grayson can cover you." I tried Grayson's number with no luck. My stomach tightened knowing I'd have to go in myself if I couldn't find someone to cover. The only other bartender on duty was Xander, and he'd never handled the weekend crowd on his own. Attempting Grayson's number two more times, I resigned myself to looking for Melanie's number next.

"Sorry, I'm late," she expressed as she slid in across from me. She lifted her phone as I hung up. "Were you calling to see where I was?" she asked smiling.

"No. Unfortunately, I was calling to cancel. I have to go to work and cover for one of my bartenders. He called me a few minutes ago and has food poisoning. I can't get my other guy to answer his phone, so I have to cover. I'm sorry, Melanie." If my face displayed even half the disappointment I felt, she'd understand I didn't want to leave. As soon as she said yes, I'd been planning the night, hoping to make it special for her. The last thing I wanted was to be her next bad date story. More importantly, I wanted to know more about her, but work kept getting in the way.

And I'd never been sorrier than at the moment I laid eyes on her. Her black dress cut low in the front and hugged her waist, before flaring out into a skirt that fell a few inches above her knees. "I'm sorry. Would you like to come to the bar with me? Drinks on me?" We stood up to leave; I handed the waitress a tip in apology for bailing on her table.

"Maybe we can do this some other time." Her words were despondent, and I worried that she'd given up on me already.

Reaching out, I grabbed her elbow gently and pulled her to the side when we were out the door. "You're terribly mad at me, aren't you?"

She shook her head. "No, not at all. I understand. I'll admit I'm disappointed, but not mad. When is your next night off?"

"Tuesday."

She thought for a moment and replied, "With school being out, I have a part-time job during the summer, and I have to work Tuesday night. Maybe this isn't meant to be."

No! I couldn't let her back out of this before we even had a chance. I raised my hand to graze her cheek. She closed her eyes, and shivered at my touch. "You want this to happen as much as I do."

She chewed her lip and dipped her eyes to the ground. "I do."

Not wanting our first kiss to be rushed, I brushed my lips against her cheek. With my mouth close to her ear, I murmured, "I'll switch shifts with Marcus for tomorrow if you can make it." She nodded, then moved away quickly to her car. Her body shivered with each word I spoke. I affected her, and I liked it. When I called, Marcus was more than willing to cover my shift so he wouldn't lose any hours.

The next night I sprinted downstairs to find my shoes when I found Angel lying on the couch. Normally this wouldn't have been concerning if she weren't face down. Kneeling beside her, I moved her hair from her face and coughed as I inhaled the fumes of whiskey trailing from her mouth and clothes. Her breath was shallow, but it was there.

Shaking her and repeating her name over and over didn't help. Panic rose in my chest as I stared at my unconscious friend. I struggled to lift her body off the couch; the dead weight was too much for me to handle alone. "What did you do, Angel?" I rolled her over to her side, scooting her back against the couch for support. The movement didn't faze her in the least. Tugging at my hair, I searched the room trying to figure out what to do. The sense of dread subsided long enough for an idea to form. In the kitchen, I filled a cup with ice and water, gave it a few seconds for the ice to disperse its coldness before draining the water into another cup with no ice. *She'll thank me for this later*, I tried to convince myself as I threw the cold water on her face.

She jumped up screaming with fists flailing for a target. When she steadied, I said, "I thought you might be dead. How much did you drink?" I tried to control the anger in my voice, but all the fear had turned into adrenaline and I couldn't come down from it.

She flailed her arms in anger. "I don't know. What's it to you?"

Next to the couch, I noticed two bottles of whiskey. "Tell me you didn't drink both of those by yourself." Living with Angel, I should've seen something was wrong. I'd been so preoccupied with work and sleeping around I'd missed what had been going on at home.

She stepped up, standing nose to nose with me. "Of course not, I'd be dead. Now, get off my back, asshole. You're not my dad, my boyfriend, or my husband. You're my fucking roommate. Learn your place, T." Angel had never been this drunk or this hostile in the time I'd known her.

"I'm not going to take what you say to heart because I know you don't mean it, Angel."

She scoffed, "What if I do? Why don't you move the hell out and take your brat of a sister with you?" *Ouch.* Luckily, Macy had stayed with a friend tonight, or her feelings would've been hurt. Angel moved forward to leave the room and stumbled toward the ground.

"Shit," I blurted, before helping her back onto the couch.

With Angel on the verge of passing out, I helped her upstairs to my room since it was the closest proximity to a bathroom. After running to the bathroom to throw up, she collapsed to the ground crying. I scooped her up in my arms once more and carried her to bed. With her head on my lap, she cried herself to sleep. I sighed and turned the television on, not wanting to disturb her by moving her head.

Pulling my phone out of my pocket, I called to cancel on Melanie, again. Once more, she sounded disappointed. She claimed she'd call me later when she had her schedule in front of her so we could pick another day, but it sounded like a blow off. I apologized profusely until she finally said she had another call coming in and had to go. As much as I hated having to cancel on her, I knew I had to be here for Angel.

Thankfully *The Walking Dead* marathon was on or I'd have been bored out of my mind sitting there. For the next few hours, I watched the gore- and drama-filled show until my legs started to fall asleep. Carefully I pushed Angel aside, and she woke up startled. "Tristan? Where am I?"

"In my bedroom."

She grabbed her head. "What hit me?"

"You almost passed out from drinking possibly two bottles of whiskey. Care to explain why you're drinking so much alone?" With the amount of time passed, my words came out much calmer, filled more with concern than anger.

Angel stood up, her stance wobbly at best. "I'm going to

take some ibuprofen."

Steadying her arm, I reached behind me. "Beat you to it. Here take these and drink this entire glass of water."

She glanced at the clock on the nightstand. "Didn't you have a date?"

"I did. I was worried you might have alcohol poisoning. I wanted to make sure you didn't need to go to the hospital. I couldn't leave you here alone." I couldn't tell if she was embarrassed, angry, or grateful by the look on her face. "Tell me why you're drinking, Angel." Silently she trudged out of the room. Following close behind her, I vowed, "I'm not letting this go."

As I grabbed her arm, swinging her around to face me, I noticed the stream of tears on her face. "I don't know, Tristan. I can't answer you," she conceded in a whisper of shame. Once I wrapped her in my embrace, she released the sobs she'd been holding inside. "Don't tell anyone, please. I don't want them to know." Methodically smoothing her hair with my hand, I swore to keep it our secret. "Did I do anything crazy?"

"You told me to get out and take my brat sister with me." After seeing how appalled she was at her words, I thought I shouldn't have said anything, or told her she was belligerent without adding anything further.

"I'm sorry, T! You know I love Macy."

Covering her mouth gently with my hand, I said, "I know. Now to show us how much you care, I want you to stop drinking." She opened her mouth to argue when I interrupted. "I mean it. There's a difference between getting drunk with friends and getting drunk all alone. If I'm going to keep your secret, you have to be willing to change."

Defeated, she sighed and promised to put her best effort into it. We started with the fridge and liquor cabinet, ridding both of every alcoholic beverage known to man. We spent most of the night talking about her options, looking up groups on the internet. Angel wanted to try it on her own first. She asked if I would help her, I agreed as long as I noticed an improvement. I had my reservations about whether I'd made the right decision to keep Angel's secret. Time would tell whether the two of us had the strength to get her better.

CHAPTER NINE

KNIGHT IN SHINING ARMOR

At work, I checked out the room hoping to spot Melanie. She hadn't been back in since the second time I canceled our date last week. She probably found a new hangout where she'd tell the bartender about her bad experience with guys this year, including me.

A hand pressed against my arm causing me to turn around. "Looking for someone?" Mary Jane asked with a smile.

"Hey, beautiful," I beamed before giving her a friendly kiss on the cheek.

"I need some T and Macy time. Can we schedule a day together? The three of us like old times?"

"Yeah. I know Macy has missed you like crazy! How're you feeling?" I asked as I noticed her rub her slightly extended belly.

"Not bad. The morning sickness is better this time than it was with Addison." Mary Jane was a surrogate who carried our friends Cameron and Gavin's daughter, Addison. They were having trouble adopting due to the fact they're a same-sex couple. Mary Jane stepped up and offered herself as a surrogate. It's one of the reasons I fell for her.

This pregnancy was her first child with Derrick, her new husband. "When do you find out what you're having?"

She grinned. "At our next appointment in July. I can't wait, but I think Katelyn is more excited than anyone. Now enough about me, who were you looking for?"

"A girl I met in here a few weeks ago. We've tried to go out a couple of times, and I had to cancel both times. I think she's given up on me."

Mary Jane frowned. "I can tell you're disappointed. Why did you cancel?"

"I had to fill in for Marcus when he had food poisoning the first time. The second time, Macy was sick." I couldn't tell her about Angel, or I'd be breaking my promise. Lying to Mary Jane made me feel like I swallowed a bowling ball. Deep in the pit of my stomach was a weight of guilt eating at me for not telling her about Angel's sickness.

"You could've called me to take care of Macy."

With one eyebrow raised I emphasized, "You're pregnant, MJ. I couldn't take a chance of you getting sick too." The ease of the lie left a bitter taste in my mouth.

"Got it. So, tell me all about her," she urged, leaning into the bar for support.

"I will but right now I have to work, my bosses are real hard asses." I gave her a wink because my bosses consisted of her husband and three brothers-in-law, and they were some of the nicest guys you'd ever know.

"Okay. But you owe me the scoop. See you later. Love you, T." Palm pressed to her face she lowered her hand and blew a kiss my way.

"Me too, MJ." We always closed our conversation with "I love you," but I'd stopped saying the actual words when my feelings grew stronger for her. Instead I responded with "me too," or "ditto."

As soon as Mary Jane sauntered away, I spotted Melanie on the dance floor with a guy. My stomach clenched with jealousy. I had to remind myself she could see anyone she wanted whether I liked it or not. Her eyes met mine, and she smiled before turning back to the guy and patting her throat to demonstrate thirst. He stayed on the dance floor, moving on to the next girl he found.

"Hey, Tristan, can I get a bottle of beer?"

Grabbing her favorite cold beer out of the cooler, I popped the top and handed it to her. "Can we try this date thing one more time?"

She sighed after swallowing her first sip. "Maybe we should give up on the idea."

"You're not interested anymore?" Her rejection stung more than any other before. I wanted to know more about this woman.

"I am, but it doesn't seem to work in our favor." Her eyes wouldn't meet mine.

"One second, let me take these orders and I'll be back."

I filled a few orders and then strolled back to Melanie when I was stopped midway by Bailey, the gymnast. "Hey, sexy!" she yelled across the bar at me as she leaned down to place her full cleavage on the bar top.

"What's up, Bailey?"

"I was wondering if I could show you more of my moves again at your place? The other night you only saw a third of them." *Fuck*. I glanced over at Melanie hoping she hadn't heard and misunderstood.

Her head whipped around, and her mouth fell open just before tears filled her eyes. She threw a ten-dollar bill on the bar and mumbled, "Keep the change, asshole."

Yelling after her was pointless. "Bailey, it was fun, but I'm interested in someone else right now." Marcus stood behind me, so I grabbed the neck of his shirt and pulled him around. "Watch the bar, I'll be back. Keep Bailey entertained. She's a gymnast." Marcus's ears perked up and the flirting began. At the door, I pulled the bouncer aside. "Bobby, did you see a pretty auburn-haired girl come out here?" Bobby pointed over to the parking lot where I saw Melanie walking to her car.

A male figure stepped out from behind the car next to her, grabbed her purse, and began to struggle with her. He shoved her to the ground and took off running. She seemed fine but shaken up. "Bobby, get her inside!" Adrenaline kicked in, and I took off after the thief. From behind me, I heard Melanie screaming my name.

I was chasing a teenager who weighed probably one

hundred pounds soaking wet. He ran fast, but I caught up with him thanks to my long legs. We struggled before he pulled a knife on me. I had him cornered, and he fought back slicing open my palm. "Shit!" I cried out. Lunging one more time, I pinned him against the wall and grabbed the purse from him before he slipped out of my grip running back down the alley. Back in the parking lot, Bobby comforted a worried Melanie. When I approached her, she ran toward me.

"You're bleeding!" She grabbed for my hand, and I yelped in pain. "Sorry," she gasped, letting go again. "Need me to call 911?"

I shook my head. "No. I'm going to head out for the night though and get this checked out. Here's your purse." With my noninjured hand, I returned it to her. I always kept a bar towel hanging from my back pocket for easy access. I pulled it out and wrapped it around my hand.

"I don't care about the purse, Tristan."

"Well, that sucks since I put myself in danger to retrieve it." In all honesty, I hadn't cared about the purse either. I saw Melanie in danger and needed to protect her whatever the cost. For someone I barely knew, it was an odd feeling.

"I'm grateful, but you could've been seriously hurt! I'm driving you to the hospital. Bobby, can you tell his boss?"

Bobby nodded. "Sure thing, ma'am."

The ride to the hospital was filled with awkward silence. I hated knowing she was angry with me. "When Bailey talked about the other night, it wasn't literal." Melanie stared ahead without blinking. "We had a one-night stand weeks ago. It was the first night I met you." Her hands clenched the wheel tighter. "Damn. What I meant is, it was before you, and I hadn't even talked about going out."

"You have nothing to explain to me, Tristan." Putting the car into park, she hid her purse under the front seat. "I have no delusional fantasies of a fairy tale relationship. It's not as though I thought you'd see me and swear off all other women."

"What if I want to be that guy?" Placing my good hand over hers, I noticed she didn't pull away from my touch, which was a good sign.

She rolled her eyes and released an audible sigh. "Cut the cheesy lines, Tristan. Let's stay in reality." She acted angry and aloof when I knew she was hurt and putting up her defensive walls. I intended to prove to her I wasn't like those other jerks, no matter how long it took.

"I'm sorry. Look, Melanie, I promise this is nothing." I held my hand up, which had stopped bleeding. "You can go home. I'll call someone to pick me up," I told her.

Melanie looked appalled at the mere suggestion of leaving. "You risked your life to save my purse. The least I can do is wait to make sure there's no permanent damage to your hand."

Swallowing my pride, I admitted the real reason for stalling. "I can't afford unnecessary medical bills, especially from the ER. If I go in there, it's going to be an outrageous bill to pay. It's too late at night for a quick-care place. I promise I'll have it checked out by my regular doctor one day this week."

Starting the car back up, she pulled back onto the road. "My home isn't far from here. I need to make sure your hand is bandaged up. You're coming to my house, and I'll take care of it and then take you home."

As she drove, she stared ahead in silence. I knew I didn't owe her an explanation for sleeping with Bailey, but I wanted her to know I hadn't lied to her or stood her up so I could have sex with someone else. "I told her I'm interested in someone else. Before I came after you, I introduced her to my friend Marcus."

Ignoring me still, she remained focused on the road. "Give me a chance, Melanie. I'll prove to you I'm not like the others. I promise."

The anger in her expression softened when I hit the nail on the head about what was wrong. She'd confided in me that she'd been hurt by men. Based on her stories, it was clear she didn't trust easily. My goal was to be sure she trusted me.

"You can't make that promise yet, Tristan. Let's start over." We pulled into a driveway, and she put the car in park. After a moment, she mocked surprise and exclaimed, "Oh no, how'd you hurt your hand?" For a brief second, I thought she was schizophrenic until she winked and held out her hand. "I'm Melanie, you are?"

I grinned. "Tristan. I helped a damsel in distress, and this is what happened."

She hissed slightly. "The knight in shining armor gig isn't all it's cracked up to be, is it? I'm sure she was grateful."

"I hope so. I'd do it again if I had to." Without even

sharing a kiss, I already knew I'd do anything for her. She had me wrapped around her finger without even trying.

Her tone grew very serious as she said, "Thank you, Tristan."

She led me into her house and sat me down at the kitchen table while she dashed to get her first aid kit. When she returned again, she set everything on the table. "Come over to the sink. Let's look at your hand." She unwrapped the bar towel I used to staunch the blood. Running hot water, I stuck my hand beneath the flow so she could see the cut better. "This will sting a bit," Melanie warned before using alcohol-soaked gauze to clean the blood away. I hissed in pain and ground my teeth trying to maintain my manhood when all I wanted was to curl up into a ball and cry like a small child. I might have been a wuss on the inside, but no one would ever see me show it.

"You're lucky it looks pretty superficial. I'm going to put some ointment on it and wrap it. You'll have to clean it every day and make sure it doesn't become infected." With a cotton swab, she dabbed ointment over the cut, placed a cotton square over the wound, and wrapped gauze around my hand securing it with tape.

For a brief second, I stood and took in her appearance. She was easily one of the most beautiful women I'd seen in a long time. Reaching for my hand, she brought it to her mouth and kissed it gently. "My students say when they get a booboo and their mom kisses it, it's the best medicine." Her face contorted, nose scrunched up, she cringed. "That seemed sexier in my head, but after saying it, it's rather creepy."

Together we laughed at the awkward comment. "Yeah, it was a little weird, but sweet."

"I suppose you need to go back to work?" Eyebrow cocked curiously.

"Nope. I texted my boss. They've covered me for the night. We could go out and grab a bite to eat? Try again for a date."

"Let's order a pizza instead? We could talk a bit?" My text alert sounded as soon as she finished her question. Melanie appeared apprehensive I was about to bail again.

"It's my sister, Macy. My boss called home to fill them in on what happened, so she's just checking on me. I'm staying, don't worry."

Her shoulders slumped as the worry left her face. Instead of ordering pizza, we made sandwiches in the kitchen and plopped down at the table to talk. Being alone in a house with Melanie, I was amazed at how well I'd done in not touching her so far. All I wanted to do was kiss her. Once the conversation got going, we lost all track of time. We weren't aware we'd talked the night away until she gasped and said, "The sun's coming up."

I grabbed Melanie's hand and led her outside to the front porch where I'd spotted a swing when we came in. Being smooth, I stretched before dropping an arm around her shoulders. "Nice move," she quipped.

I didn't want the night to end. I'd grown comfortable sitting there with my arm around her, waiting for the right moment to kiss her. Her eyelids grew heavy, and she could barely keep them open as her head rested against my shoulder. "I should let you get to bed."

I kissed her forehead before helping her to her feet. "Do I need to take you to your car at the club?"

"No" was the only word I spoke before I placed my hands on either side of her face, leaned in, and captured her lips with mine. Her lips, soft as silk, moved cautiously against mine. I wanted more. She closed her eyes and released a soft whimper as I deepened the kiss. As my tongue slipped passed her lips, I groaned at the instant reaction my body had. The kiss was electric, unlike anything I'd experienced before. Her hands moved around my waist, sliding up my back. I moved my hand from her face and dropped it to her waist. Playing at the hem of her shirt, I let my fingers dance against her smooth skin as I moved the shirt up.

She pulled away first. "I'm not a prude, but I don't want to be a one-night stand to anyone, Tristan." I wasn't ready for the kiss to stop, but I respected her wish. Lately, by the time I'd kissed a woman, we were naked within minutes. As much as I wanted Melanie, things between us had to be different from with other women.

Caressing her face with my palm, I agreed, "I don't want you to be either. As much as I want you, I want to take things slow."

"I should get you home before we change our minds." Melanie smiled and stood up first. "Are you sure you want me to take you home instead of the club?"

As I rose, I said, "Yep. Home is closer, and you're tired enough. I'll get a ride to the club later to get my car." She went inside to grab her keys, and after locking her door, I grabbed the keys from her. "Do you mind if I drive?" She shook her head.

The drive home was better than the ride there. Things between us were progressing nicely. We hadn't officially had a first date, but I'd gotten the kiss I'd been imagining since I met her. Once I backed out of her driveway, I rested my arm on the console and Melanie reached for my hand. Holding my free hand, her thumb lightly caressed the spot I'd injured. Listening to music, she was so quiet I assumed she'd fallen asleep at one point.

"We're here." She startled slightly, then exited the car. She came around to the driver side and leaned forward to give me a goodbye kiss. I made sure she got back in the car and then said, "I had a great night. Text me when you get home so I know you made it without falling asleep."

"I will. See you soon, Tristan."

Chapter Ten

A HELPING HAND

After the success of our spontaneous date, we began talking for a few hours every night. During the day, we'd send text messages back and forth with little quips about our day.

Melanie: How's your hand?

Me: Almost completely healed. Some hero I am, right?

Melanie: Superheroes heal superfast you know.

Me: You're good at building a guy's ego. :) I'm surprised you aren't telling someone else about our crazy date.

Melanie: You know I've had crazier ones.

Me: Talked to a guy today who told a girl he built a time machine. Did you date a bald guy named Terry in your search for Mr. Right?

Melanie: Lol, no, but he sounds perfect for me. You should give me his number. I was puked on by a student today. I could use a time machine.

Me: Or you could make the best of a bad situation.

Melanie: How would I do that?

Me: I could come give you a bath. ;-)

Melanie: Sounds nice. We can talk more about it on our second date.

Our second date was the following Saturday. It had been a long time since I'd had a night off on a weekend.

During the middle of the week I received a text from Melanie.

Melanie: This may sound desperate of me, but I want to see you before Saturday

Me: I'm working tonight if you want to come by.

Melanie: I'm off tomorrow so that sounds great .

Things were slow so I dialed Melanie up instead of texting more. "Hey, I was wondering if you wanted to go bowling tonight?"

"Bowling?" Melanie asked, sounding perplexed.

"There's not much open at 2:00 a.m. and that's the time I get off tonight. I thought we could have a couple of beers and hang out."

"What time does the club close?"

"One. I need about an hour to clean up though. I'm closing." Closing up meant wiping down tables, sweeping, closing out the till. The till alone usually took more than an hour on a good night, but it was a weekday. We barely had any customers.

"What if I come by just before closing and help you? Would you get in trouble?" The thought of being alone with Melanie, no interruptions, gave me goose bumps. "No, I have the coolest bosses ever. Be here around twelve thirty tonight, sound good?"

"I'll be there."

As if on a timer, she arrived precisely at twelve thirty. Wearing a light-blue tank with tight-fitting jeans, she sat under a lamp and I groaned when I saw her nipples begging to be freed from her bra.

With a smile on her face, she waved at me with four fingers fanning so femininely as though she were drying her nails. Giving her a nod, I turned to my customers at the bar and gave them the thirty-minute warning for closing time.

Trying to get all the customers out of the bar in a hurry was like herding cats. A few of them had to take a last minute pee break, a couple were finishing up a last game of pool, and one or two just wanted more alcohol.

"Drinks are cutoff. You're a regular. We go through this every time you come. You're always the last customer of the night, and I have to send you packing." Wendell groaned ready to argue more so I leaned down and lowered my voice, "Look, man, I need a favor. Leave now and the next time you come in, the first drink is on me."

The promise of free alcohol had him hustling toward the door. After checking the premises to make sure everyone was out of the public areas, I locked and bolted the door and turned off the neon sign. The music still played overhead, so I went to the control box and lowered the volume to a decent level where we still heard the music but could talk too.

"Where do you want me to start?" Pointing toward the back, she asked, "I've seen you go in there before. Is that where the broom is?" I nodded.

"You don't have to clean. They pay me for that. You can sit and talk to me."

"I don't mind helping." I pulled the tills out and began to count the money for the evening, matching it with receipts. I had to count one cash register three times because I was distracted by her movements.

When she swept past the jukebox, she stopped to select a couple songs before picking up the broom again. Her musical taste varied, much like mine. The first song was "School's Out for Summer" by Alice Cooper. I lifted my brow in amusement. "Nice choice." I grinned when she held the broom up to her stomach and pretended it was a guitar. I wasn't sure about the choice of song until I remembered she was a schoolteacher.

Once the drawers were balanced, I locked them away in the safe and returned to Melanie, who was bent over scooping up the trash from the floor. Her ass was perfect.

I ventured out on the dance floor just in time for a slow song to come on. "Care to dance?"

Resting the broom against a booth, she took my hand. We danced with so much space between us it took me back to my teenage years when I was afraid to get too close to a girl. Her arms were extended straight out, resting her hands just over my shoulders. I chuckled to myself as I thought about asking her to go steady.

"What's funny?" Melanie asked.

Mimicking a nervous, apparently Italian teenager I said, "Yo, who you got for biology this year?"

Her brows furrowed, and she glanced down at our bodies. We both laughed and I took a step closer. "You were Stallone as a teenager?"

I shrugged. "Honestly, I have no idea where that accent came from. Was it better or worse than my attempt at a Southern one?" Her head bobbed side to side as her shoulders shrugged. "I get it, both atrocious."

"Just be you." She smiled and laid her head on my shoulder. I dropped my hands to her lower back and held her close.

"Where'd you grow up? What's your family like?" The barrage of questions began as a way of keeping my mind off her body. Her breasts pressed against my chest were hard to ignore. I needed a distraction if I wanted to keep my promise of taking things slow.

"Nashville. Lived in or around the city my entire life." Her fingers ran through the back of my hair as she spoke. I tried to focus on her voice instead of the tingling sensation coursing through my body. "My parents were less than ideal. I don't talk about them much."

Our feet stopped moving at the end of the song. "Let's sit. I'll grab us some beers."

We sat in the corner booth with two bottles of beer and chatted about life. "I can't imagine having a mother with Alzheimer's. My mom didn't care who or where I was most of the time, but it was by her choice. It's not fair the way life is sometimes. You know?"

"Believe me, I know. I question things often. As much as I've missed my mom, Macy and I have a bond I wouldn't trade for anything." At times I wondered what might have happened had my mom never gotten sick. Would Macy and I have been close or would the difference in our ages have kept us from bonding? Telling this to Melanie seemed a bit too deep for the moment.

"What do you think you'd do if you saw your dad again one day?" Melanie pulled out the big thinker. The question I'd asked myself many sleepless nights since he'd left.

"I haven't decided if I'd punch him or thank him for giving me the best gift ever." Her delicate fingers danced across my skin as she reached for my hand and grasped it.

"Macy's lucky to have you. I have three big brothers, and they always had my back, but we don't see each other much anymore."

"How was your mom with them?"

"Her downward spiral began after they moved out. Each one left home just after high school and got a job. I think being stuck raising me was too much for her to handle. My memories of her revolve around the bad times. I don't remember the good ones." Her past was important to me, but I hated to see her so sad. We needed a subject change.

Moving closer to her, I leaned in to kiss her when I heard, "Shit! You scared the hell out of me, T!"

Papers scattered the floor around Cameron who stood with his hand on his chest. Melanie jumped up to help him gather them. She locked eyes with Cameron and his head tilted curiously. "Have we met?"

"Not that I recall. I'm Melanie." They shook hands and returned to picking up the papers.

"Cameron is one of the owners," I stated. Melanie's eyes widened.

"I didn't know you had a date tonight, T." Cameron threw me a wink.

"It's not a date. I was waiting on my sober ride." Fidgeting nervously, Melanie handed the papers to Cameron. We both laughed at her adorable attempt to cover for me.

"Cameron's cool, Melanie. I told you my bosses all are." I wrapped my arm around her shoulder. "We're on a date. She's helping me clean, and I'm paying her with my good looks, charm, and a few free beers."

"How romantic?" His eyebrow cocked. "I didn't mean to interrupt. I was working on some inventory statements." He rolled his eyes backward and mimicked a snore. "I'm headed home to my family. You two be safe when you leave."

"Want me to walk you out?"

"Just watch from the door to make sure I get out okay?" Things got a little iffy downtown late at night. Employees parked around back, but part of Bobby's job was to move the closer's car to the front lot before he left. The owners shared two spots out front since they were rarely all there at once.

"No problem." I removed my arm from Melanie's side and walked Cameron to the door.

"She's cute. Did you get set up by one of the girls?"

"No. She's been coming into the bar. She was the one I chased the mugger for. Why?"

"Oh, no reason. I just thought maybe the girls were matchmaking. You two look good together." I glanced back to see Melanie checking out the jukebox again.

"Thanks. She's pretty great."

"Tell MJ about her. She'll be happy to know you're dating." I cocked my head to the side in confusion. Cameron patted my shoulder. "Macy's been telling her about your conquests. MJ worries."

"Got it. I'll talk to her." He nodded and proceeded to sprint to his car with a wave back at me once he was inside. I watched him pull out of the drive just to be sure and then locked the door.

"I thought that was something guys only did for girls, watching them get to their car."

"Criminals often carry guns. Even guys aren't as tough as guns. After what happened to you the other night, we're all being a little more cautious." Ashton and Derrick both reamed me for chasing the mugger on my own, but I knew they'd have done the same thing. We all agreed to be more careful though.

"I didn't mean anything by it. I just thought it was sweet of you. I like that you look out for your friends." She grinned.

"Where were we?"

"Right about here I think." Fisting my shirt, she yanked me forward until our lips met. I expected to taste beer, but peppermint exploded in my mouth instead. Her feet moved backward as I pushed us toward the booth we'd been in before. Tumbling forward, I fell on top of her breaking the kiss as we both chuckled. "Ouch," she mumbled against my lips. I pushed up off the booth to give her a chance to straighten up.

"At least that will be a memorable kiss for you."

"Every kiss with you has been memorable, Tristan." Pink filled her cheeks. I kissed each one feeling the warmth against my lips. Stopping to look in her eyes, I saw her heated gaze looking back at me. I moved my mouth down to her neck and peppered her skin with kisses. My hand slid down the front of her shirt, and when it grazed her pert nipple, she gasped in my ear. Cupping her breast, I continued my trail of kisses along her collarbone, up the opposite side of her neck, then back to her lips. Our tongues danced while my thumb and index finger played with her nipple through the thin material.

With both palms against my chest, she pushed back biting her lip. "Slow."

"Sorry." I started to say, but she pressed her finger against my lips to silence me.

"Don't be. I was reminding myself, not you." She glanced around the room a moment. I watched as she walked over to the bar and looked around. "Is there any food in here?"

"Just peanuts, cherries, olives, stuff needed for drinks. If you're hungry, I can go check the back offices for something."

"Do you mind?" I left Melanie while I went to the back on a search for food. I knew Cameron kept snacks in his drawer, so I raided it and would replenish later. Returning to the main room, I dropped the variety of snacks on the table in front of her.

"Granola bars, chips, and gummy snacks is all I could find. I could run out and grab us something." She grabbed my hand quickly as I started to stand. Her fingers trembled and her eyes were wide. "What is it?"

"Flashbacks of the last time you left the club for me, I guess." She grabbed the gummy snacks. "These will be fine. And in a few hours we can go grab breakfast. What do you think?"

"Sounds great." I ripped open the first packet of gummies and fed one to her.

"Oh, what about Macy?" she asked, covering her mouth as she chewed.

"I texted Angel a while ago to make sure she'd be home with her tonight. So we're good."

After popping a few more gummies in my mouth, I pushed the bag away. "This isn't cutting it. Let's get out of here and grab something to eat." We gathered up the trash, dropped the snacks back in the office, and I led her to the door. Turning out the light, I locked the door and walked her to the car.

"We'll take yours, and I'll ride in with someone tomorrow."

"You leave your car here a lot," she commented.

"Our employee lot is fenced in. It's pretty safe there. I never had Bobby move it out for me once I found out you were coming by." The sky had begun to lighten. I glanced at my watch and saw it was after six in the morning. "We've been talking for over five hours."

"Time flies when you're having fun," she said with a grin. After grabbing breakfast, we ended the morning with Melanie dropping me back at my house around nine. "Are we still on for Saturday? Or have you had enough of me?"

She wrapped her arms around my neck, pulling me into a hug. "Nah, I think I could handle seeing you again in a few days." She winked. "Text me details later. Go get some sleep." A quick kiss on the cheek and she drove away.

The house was quiet when I got home. I stripped down to my boxer briefs, curled up under the covers, and was asleep the moment my head hit the pillow.

Chapter Eleven

MAKING PLANS

I scheduled time with Mary Jane and Macy for the day. The two of them arranged our afternoon activities while I was at work the night before. Lucky for me the plan was to meet around three, so I still got a decent amount of sleep.

We began our day at our favorite local diner to chow down on greasy burgers and salty fries. Junk food was a weakness and a very rare occurrence between the three of us. While in Florida, we began a junk food challenge. We'd eat healthy at every meal and then agreed once a month we'd pig out on whatever sinful treat we wanted. Somehow it never failed, we decided on burgers and fries.

"Derrick and I are going up to Fall Creek Falls this weekend, and we wanted you and Macy to come along," Mary Jane stated as soon as we sat down.

Macy's excitement couldn't be denied as she bounced in her seat. "Yes, please, Tristan, can we go?"

"Well, being I'm off for a change, I have a date this weekend with Melanie. I really don't want to cancel on her given my track record so far." Nothing short of the apocalypse would keep me from seeing her this weekend. Especially after mentioning a bath.

"This is the girl you told me about? You two are dating now?" Mary Jane asked. Her shoulders lifted and an optimistic smile filled her face.

"Yes. We finally worked things out to spend time together, and I don't want to mess it up again."

Mary Jane didn't hesitate to respond. "Bring her along! We'd love to meet her."

"I'm not sure we're serious enough for an overnight trip. We've only been on a couple of dates." Two dates and two amazing kisses, but things were still new. Asking her to go away for the weekend with me alone was a stretch, but asking her to meet my family at the same time had potential to scare her off for good.

Mary Jane placed her hand on top of mine. "You two have been talking for a while though, right? Ask her, you never know what she'll say. And if it makes Melanie feel better she can share a room with Macy and Katelyn, and you can sleep on the pullout sofa." The prospect of an entire weekend with Melanie was enticing.

Macy sat with her hands together in a praying fashion, and her bottom lip jutted out in a pout. Once Mary Jane noticed the pose, she mimicked it. "Fine, I'll ask her." They both cheered victoriously.

Both nervous and excited about the idea, I had to come up with a way to present it to Melanie so she wouldn't get freaked out. The more I thought about it, the excitement began to outweigh the nerves.

***

The next evening I took Melanie out, so we'd have had three official dates before the weekend trip idea was brought up.

There's a great theater on the outskirts of town with the outward appearance of a barn. The tickets were a little pricey, but included an all you can eat buffet dinner.

Once shown to our table, I held the chair out for Melanie before taking a seat across from her. Small talk between us flowed with rarely any awkward silence. During the meal, I brought up Fall Creek Falls.

"So, this weekend I know we were supposed to go on a date, but something has come up. Some friends of mine are going to Fall Creek Falls overnight, and they asked Macy and me to go with them."

"We can always reschedule our date. You should go with them and enjoy yourself. It's a beautiful park." She seemed eager to get out of going. My pride took a nosedive momentarily. Her response made me second-guess the idea. She jumped so quickly to assuming I'd go, maybe it wasn't the best idea to invite her along. Macy could go with them, and I'd get a raincheck for another time. To allow myself time to think, I took a large bite and took my time chewing.

After considering it, I decided to stick with my original plan instead. If she said no, it would speak volumes about where we stood. "I turned them down because of our date. And they asked me to bring you along." The pleased grin on her face improved my self-esteem.

"Oh, wow. Um, yeah I'd love to."

"You would?" I exclaimed, sounding more surprised than I intended to.

She read me wrong because she said, "Were you hoping I'd say no?"

Our signals seemed to get tangled around each other often. "No. Of course not. I didn't know if we were serious enough for an overnight."

Melanie shrugged. "Who decides when we can do stuff in a relationship?" As soon as she uttered the word "relationship," she began to backpedal. "Um, I mean a friendship relationship. Err… dating. I…"

I covered her hand with mine. "I know what you mean, and it doesn't scare me for you to call it a relationship." *Well, it scared me a little.* She breathed a sigh of relief before taking a bite of her salad. "Your friends, are they a new couple as well?"

"Um, no. They're newlyweds. Macy would also go with us because they have a young daughter who will be there. My friend suggested it would be fine for you to share a room with the girls, and I could take the pullout couch. It can be a strictly platonic weekend. I'll be a perfect gentleman."

"Sounds like fun. We can determine the sleeping

arrangement later." Her flirtatious comment ended with her biting her bottom lip.

"You keep biting your lip like that, and I know where you'll be sleeping."

She grinned. "A weak threat."

"More like a strong promise," I countered.

She picked around her plate, moving food from one spot to the next. Eventually, she placed her fork on the side. "Do you think they'll like me?" she asked, changing the subject.

Putting my hand over hers on the table, I rubbed my thumb across her skin. "I don't know why they wouldn't." The broad smile lighting up her face made all the nerves I had fade away. The getaway couldn't come fast enough.

***

The following weekend we made plans to meet at the Nature Center at Fall Creek Falls. Macy spent the night with Mary Jane and Derrick because she wanted to ride up with Katelyn. There's a huge age difference in the two of them, but they get along like best friends. Melanie and I headed up a little earlier so we stopped and picked up supplies along the way.

When we arrived at the Nature Center, I texted Mary Jane, and she let me know they'd be there in a few minutes. Melanie had been to Fall Creek Falls Park before, so she started to show me around a little. We strolled first to the overlook for Cane Creek Falls. She stood against the banister, and I leaned up against her back. "Waterfalls are very romantic," she sighed.

"They are," I agreed as I bent to plant a tender kiss on her exposed neck. She turned in my arms, placed her palm against the back of my neck, and pulled my face down to hers to kiss me.

Wrapping my arms around her, I lost myself momentarily until I heard the words, "Get a room man, this is a family park."

Melanie turned back toward the falls embarrassed, though I recognized the voice. "Hey, man, it's about time you guys got here."

Derrick and Mary Jane stood on the steps looking down at us when I noticed their mouths dropped open. I turned to introduce Melanie and noticed she wore the same expression.

"Lanie," Mary Jane stated.

Confused, I asked, "Lanie?"

"It's the nickname I go by," Melanie explained.

"You know each other?" I glanced back at Mary Jane.

Katelyn jumped down the stairs and hugged Melanie tightly. "Hi, Ms. Harris."

Melanie returned the hug and commented awkwardly, "Hey, Katie, I hope you're enjoying your summer."

And then everything clicked into place. Mary Jane sensed I needed some private time and suggested, "Katelyn, why don't we go on down to the Cascades so you and Macy can swim. Lanie and Tristan will meet us in a few minutes."

As soon as they were out of sight, I faced Melanie. "Katelyn is the student whose father you went out with?"

She nodded and then asked, "Which means the best friend you're in love with is Mary Jane?"

"*Was* Mary Jane, past tense."

"Are you sure, Tristan?" she asked without a hint of jealousy, only curiosity in her tone. Part of me wished there had been a little jealousy. As hard as she was to read sometimes I wasn't sure we felt the same attraction. Although we'd only been on three dates, we'd flirted with each other over a span of two months.

"Positive. Why didn't you tell me you go by Lanie?"

She shrugged. "When I met you it was a low point in my life. You know I'd had one terrible date after the next. All I wanted was a fresh start. So I used my full name for a change. And after you became my personal knight in shining armor, I thought maybe the name change helped. You can call me Lanie though."

"Okay then. *Lanie*, are you going to be uncomfortable spending the weekend with them?" She entwined her fingers in mine pulling me in for another kiss.

"I'm here to spend the weekend with you, and I'm excited about it." I believed her when I stared into her eyes and saw no regret or unease. We began our trek down to the Cascades swimming hole.

At the bottom, Mary Jane had a towel laid out on the rocks, and she wore a tank top and shorts. Her shirt rode up a little over her baby bump. "She's pregnant?" Melanie asked.

"Yep. She's due the end of November." I couldn't contain my smile as I stared at Mary Jane's barely swollen belly remembering the last time she was pregnant and everything we experienced.

I spoke the truth to her before; my feelings for Mary Jane were in the past. It didn't mean I couldn't be happy for her as my closest friend.

Glancing around I noticed Katelyn and Macy were already using the natural-rock slides to go into a swimming hole. They seemed to be taking care of each other. Derrick sat on a rock not far from away taking photos of them with the falls and surrounding area.

"May we sit with you?" I asked Mary Jane.

She patted the ground next to her. "Of course, please. Lanie, I apologize for the shock today. Tristan had told us your name was Melanie, but I didn't put the two together."

"No worries," Melanie answered sincerely. She stood up, removed her shirt and shorts, and revealed a tasteful, yet sexy as hell, bikini. Her breasts were perky, and her nipples noticeable beneath the light blue bikini top. I couldn't think straight as I stared at them. Pornographic images flooded my mind. Her long smooth legs wrapped around my waist. Our bodies connected, writhing together.

Melanie turned around and bent over to get into her bag where she pulled out a bottle of lotion. The position she stood in made things quite painful for me in a certain area. Mary Jane reached over to smack my leg getting my attention and letting me know she noticed my ogling. I adjusted my shorts and cleared my throat.

"Can you put some lotion on me before I go in to swim?" she asked handing me the bottle of suntan lotion. Stammering out a yes, I squirted a large drop in my hands and rubbed it onto her back. While I lathered her up, she pulled her hair from the ponytail it was in, ran her fingers through it, and tied it up in a bun on top of her head. My fingers massaged her shoulders, and I zoned out into a fantasy again.

"Thanks, Tristan. I'm going to swim with the girls for a few minutes if you don't mind?" Melanie brought me out of my X-rated fantasy, and I shook my head to clear myself of any more inappropriately timed thoughts.

"No problem." She leaned forward to give me a quick peck before taking her turn down the rock slide. She swam over to join Macy and Katelyn as they played.

"You two are cute together," Mary Jane commented as she watched me observe Melanie.

"I like her a lot. Is it weird for you?"

Mary Jane sat up. "We made peace a long time ago, Tristan. She's a sweet woman. She and Derrick had a couple of dates while we were broken up, so there was no cheating involved and she has apologized for the way she spoke to me when we met. We had a rocky beginning, but she's Katelyn's favorite teacher, and it looks like Macy likes her too." She pointed to the water where Melanie and Macy laughed and played together. Katelyn must have done the introductions for me. I wished they could've met before the trip, but it didn't seem to matter.

"Is it weird for Derrick?"

Derrick stepped up behind us. "Is what weird for Derrick?"

"Lanie and me?"

He shook his head. "Not in the least. It doesn't seem weird to you either based on the hot lip-lock we interrupted. Do me a favor though, Katelyn doesn't know Lanie and I went out, so don't tell her, please." I could easily keep the promise. I didn't want Macy to know either because it seemed a bit weird to even think about.

Melanie swam over and stepped out of the water; I observed Derrick to see if he noticed her, but he didn't. He only had eyes for Mary Jane as he bent to kiss her belly and spoke to their unborn child. I wrapped up Melanie in her Minion-covered beach towel. Her lips quivered with the cool breeze hitting her wet body. She took a seat between my legs, and I draped my arms around her to warm her up. She leaned her head back. "Thank you for inviting me this weekend. Macy's great."

"How long have you two been dating?" Derrick asked.

"Not long, we met at a club downtown; it's new…." Her voice trailed off as recognition hit. She covered her mouth and said, "Oh my gosh! You own A Shot in the Dark?"

Derrick laughed. "Yep. My brothers, Ashton and Gavin, and my brother-in-law, Cameron all run it together."

"What about your sister?"

He seemed confused. "I don't have a sister."

Melanie was equally confused after his comment. "Oh sorry, I guess he's your brother-in-law because he's MJ's brother?" We all tensed up worried she had an issue with same-sex marriage.

"He's married to my brother Gavin."

Light dawned in her eyes, but there was no disgust or

even surprise. "Duh, sorry that was stupid of me to ask."

"They had a dual marriage ceremony in New York with Ashton and Gracie," I added trying to ease the awkward moment. "MJ had told me all about the ceremony after we met. She hadn't been able to attend because of her internship, but they sent her a video and several pictures of the event. I felt as though I had attended myself."

Melanie smiled. "How sweet. I was thrilled when they finally legalized same-sex marriage."

Macy shouted, "Tristan!" causing me to tense up until my eyes landed on her at the top of a rock slide. She held up her hands, mimicked taking a picture, and then pointed to the water. Derrick handed me his phone, so I snapped a few pictures of her as she slid down into the creek below.

She began her swim over to me, and I yelled out, "Bring Katelyn in too!" Macy grabbed Katelyn and together they swam over to us.

Mary Jane opened her backpack and pulled out bottled waters for the girls. They downed them as though they hadn't drank in days. "Are you girls hungry?"

They both nodded without letting go of the bottles. "Why don't we go check into the cabin and get some lunch? We can also swim at the pool or maybe fish if you'd like. Your dad brought his fishing equipment," Mary Jane said to Katelyn, before turning her attention to me. "Tristan, do you fish?"

"I've never tried fishing, but I've always wanted to."

We hauled ourselves up the two flights of stairs back to the parking lot. The walk down wasn't too bad; the walk up was a lot more difficult. Melanie seemed to be making a great effort to act normal, but I wasn't sure whether it was simply an act, or if she was as happy as she seemed. I wanted to give her a way out if she needed it. At the top, I pulled Melanie aside. "If this weekend becomes uncomfortable to you, at any point, we'll leave. Okay?"

"I'm fine, Tristan. Derrick and I had two dates; it's not like we had this long-term relationship or even feelings for each other."

"All right. I wanted to make sure."

"And that's one of the things I like about you, you're very considerate." She kissed my lips softly, then took my hand and pulled me toward the car to catch up with the others.

CHAPTER TWELVE

SOUTHERN COMFORT

The girls swam at the pool with Mary Jane watching, while Derrick, Melanie, and I fished from the deck of the cabin. The three of us couldn't have had a more awkward past together, but if you walked up, you'd never have known we weren't the best of friends. Any discomfort had passed not long after we left the Cascades area.

The inside of the cabin was very simple but had all the amenities of home; two bedrooms, two baths, a full-size kitchen, and a pullout couch in the living room. Derrick and I carried all the luggage to the different rooms to get everyone settled for the night.

"Can we roast marshmallows before we go to sleep?" Katelyn asked, pulling on Derrick's arm.

"Kid, we didn't bring marshmallows."

Timidly, Melanie spoke up. "Um, I did." We all looked at her to elaborate, so she shrugged her shoulders and said, "I love roasted marshmallows. When Tristan told me we were coming this weekend, it was the first thing I bought. If you don't mind, Derrick, I'd be glad to roast them with the girls."

"Sure. I can start a fire in the pit outside," Derrick offered.

"No need. We can use the stove." She led the girls over to the stove and flipped on one of the eyes. "We'll turn it up to high and you roast it the same. Oh, is there a hanger or something we can use?"

I searched through the drawers of the cabin and found a large cooking fork. "How about this?"

"Perfect." She speared two large marshmallows on the fork, held them above the glowing orange eye of the stove, and we watched as they began to brown. One caught fire, and she turned it slowly letting the flame spread along the fluffy treat to coat it evenly. Once it was sufficiently toasted, she extinguished the flame with a quick breath and handed the first two treats to Katelyn and Macy.

"Tristan, we have to keep marshmallows at the house now so I can do this more often." Macy had a mouthful of the toasted sticky treat as she mumbled these words.

"Sure, why not." I laughed at the sticky mess on her face.

Macy had taken to Melanie quicker than I expected. I loved watching the two of them laugh together. One of the key things I wanted in a relationship was for the woman to get along with Macy. Connecting with my friends was a plus, but relating with Macy was a must. I raised her. She was more my daughter than my sister in some ways, even though she wasn't far from being an adult. She was a huge part of my life.

"I need one or four of those marshmallows please, for the baby, of course," Mary Jane requested with a wink.

"Yes, ma'am, let's get the pregnant lady what she wants." I grabbed the fork from Melanie and toasted two more.

An hour later, we were filled up with the sugary goodness of burnt gooey marshmallows. It seemed like bad parenting to send the kids to bed all hopped up on sugar, but at least they had a TV to keep them occupied.

Around midnight we vacated to our separate rooms to sleep. Melanie and I took the bedroom with two double beds after Macy and Katelyn begged to be able to sleep on the couch so they could watch television. I certainly didn't argue. Melanie seemed perfectly content sharing a room and immediately claimed the bed closest to the window. I wanted to be closer to the door in case Macy needed me. She was nearly fifteen going on thirty, but I'd always see her as a little girl.

"Good night, Lanie."

"Good night, Tristan."

I turned off the light and lay down on the too-soft bed. My tossing and turning drove me to the brink of insanity. At one point, I glanced over at Melanie's bed, and the moonlight illuminated her body. Her back was to me, and she wore nothing but a tank top and short shorts, which allowed me to see the line of her dark lace panties.

The dull murmur of the television from the living

room was the only sound I could hear. I needed to think of something besides Melanie's body. My mind wandered through different scenarios; each one grew dirtier than the next. The bedsprings creaked from Melanie shifting in her bed. The tank top inched up exposing her lower back. The top of a tattoo dipped down beneath her shorts, and I wanted to know what it was. I groaned out loud unintentionally. She rolled over. "Are you having trouble sleeping?"

I sighed. "Yeah, what about you?" Instead of answering my question, she stood up and moved next to the bed I occupied. She pulled the covers up and slid underneath, then wrapped her arm around my stomach with her head against my chest. "Is this too forward?" she asked.

"No. I promise to keep my hands to myself." I grunted through clenched teeth as my body began to respond to her closeness. All the fantasies I had came flying back into my mind making it hard to concentrate. Making a lot of things hard actually.

Her bottom lip poked out, then she whispered, "I was hoping you wouldn't."

Was I dreaming? "Are you sure? It's like our fourth date." I stuttered, overwhelmed at the thought I could do things to this woman I'd envisioned since I laid eyes on her.

"Tristan, when a woman is of sound mind and body, completely sober, and asking you to touch her, don't ask questions." She cupped her hand behind my neck and pulled me forward into a fiercely passionate kiss, slipping her tongue between my lips. There would be no more arguments from me. Only she could stop us, my engine was on go and full speed ahead. Pushing her shirt up, I ran my fingers over her silky skin. My mouth against her neck, I tasted the coconut and pineapple flavor on her skin.

She lifted up onto the bed and pushed me down on my back. Straddling my waist, she raised her shirt exposing a little skin at a time, all the while teasing me with her hips gyrating against my shaft. My hands followed hers as I helped push her shirt further up. Tracing the underside of her breasts with my thumbs, I hardened even more beneath her. Getting hard had never been a problem, but with Melanie, just a look from her made me crazy. Feeling me between her legs, she gasped and rolled her hips. Pushing her shirt over her breasts, I rubbed my palms over her taut nipples, rolling them between my fingers. Sex usually meant getting off and having fun doing it. What we were about to have was more than just sex. I wanted to get off, but I wanted to please Melanie more than anything. Admiring her body by moonlight, I relished watching the lust fill her eyes, the sexy way she sucked her bottom lip in on one side, and listening to her soft gasps of pleasure. She tossed her head back and bucked her hips against me until I couldn't take it anymore. I yanked the shirt over her head and lifted her off. Together we jerked our shorts and underwear off in a rush. I reached over and grabbed my pants off the floor to retrieve a condom in the back pocket.

"I came prepared just in case. This wasn't planned."

"You aren't the only one. Now stop talking and put it on already." I tore open the package and slipped it on. As I thrust inside her, she bit her bottom lip.

She pushed me over onto my back to straddle me again. As she rocked above me, I tossed my head back against the pillow in pure ecstasy, enjoying the feel of being inside this amazingly beautiful woman. I cupped her breasts, rubbing my fingers across her nipples as she bounced. Sitting up, I rolled her to the side, slipped my arm under her leg, and entered her from behind. When we came together, I also came to my senses. "I'm sorry. This wasn't very romantic."

"Tristan, stop acting like I'm a virginal school girl who needs her first time to be perfect and romantic. We're both adults; we've both had sex before, and we were both hot for each other tonight. Am I right?"

"Yes, but I don't want you to be a one-night stand. I want us to be more." I pulled her face to mine, kissing her softly. "If you're up for it, I can show you the romantic side now."

"Oh, I'm up for it." Something changed between us after the first time. Our connection felt stronger; we were more in sync.

Starting at her jawline, I traced affectionate kisses down her neck, over her collarbone, and at the top swell of her breasts. When I took her nipple in my mouth, she arched her back with a moan of pleasure. A glass of water was beside the bed so I reached over and grabbed an ice cube from it. She drew in a breath as I touched it to her breast and then relaxed as my mouth trailed the ice to gather up the moisture. Moving down her body, I allowed the frozen cube to melt against her abdomen, dripping trails of water in different directions over her skin. My tongue darted out to catch the drop running towards her core before dipping down to taste her. She rounded her back again and let out a deep moan before covering her mouth to stay quiet. I wanted to hear her moans, but I knew we had to keep from waking the others. Her legs rested against my back. Each time I hit the right spot her toes curled against my spine.

She flailed around, and I knew she was close. Slipping on a new condom, I climbed above her and moved between her legs, teasing her until she begged me to be inside.

Afterward, she pressed up against me with her head against my chest, legs thrown over mine. "Definitely more romantic," she sighed.

Kissing her forehead, I said, "I hope this doesn't sound cheesy or weird, but I really like you, Lanie." The word like seemed not only cheesy, but also weak in comparison to how I felt about her. But it was too soon to use stronger words.

She smiled up at me. "I really like you too."

The next morning, the night before felt like a dream until I noticed the beautiful, naked woman lying in my arms. Her hair fell over her eyes, and her lips were pursed in a pout as she slept. It would be easy for me to fall in love with this beauty. In fact, I think I'd already begun my descent.

Chapter Thirteen

GIVING IN TO TRUST

Once she fell asleep, it appeared Melanie could sleep through anything. I'd spent the last hour staring at her. I planted kisses along her skin, and even sucked on her neck trying to wake her. She moaned but never stirred awake. "Lanie," I whispered against her ear, flicking my tongue against the lobe.

The door opened, and Macy exclaimed, "Good Morning, Tristan." I tossed the blanket over Melanie quickly and sat up keeping myself covered. "Oh. Sorry!"

Macy closed the door quickly with a giggle. Embarrassment crept up my face with what she would relay to Mary Jane and Derrick. I sighed and slid on my boxer briefs and a pair of jeans before going to greet them. I kissed Melanie's head and tried to wake her once more with no luck.

Closing the door behind me, I stepped into the living room area where Mary Jane and Derrick glanced up at me with the same knowing smile on their faces. "Sleep well?" Mary Jane asked.

"Locks on these doors would've made it better," I said ruffling Macy's hair.

"Where's Lanie? Derrick's got breakfast ready, which is why we sent Macy to wake you up." Mary Jane peered around me at the closed door.

"She's a heavy sleeper. I've tried everything to wake her."

"She must have been exhausted," Derrick said with a smirk before Mary Jane smacked him playfully.

"Mature, Derrick. Can we act like adults now?"

"What fun would that be?" Derrick asked. He tipped his head toward the kitchen. "Go grab you some breakfast. We'll save her a plate."

Melanie stepped from the bedroom looking as beautiful as ever. Her long hair was pulled up into a ponytail, and the sweet aroma of her perfume drifted into my nose as she approached. "Good morning," she said, before giving me a kiss on the cheek.

"I tried to wake you up."

"I'm practically dead to the world when I sleep." She turned her attention to Mary Jane and Derrick. "Good morning. Did you sleep well?"

Mary Jane grinned. "Yep. Tristan said you two had no troubles either."

It had taken a moment before Melanie peered up at me

with shock. I held my hands up in surrender. "I don't kiss and tell. Macy barged in this morning and saw us in bed together." Melanie sighed with relief. For a moment, I saw some of her insecurities surface, but it was gone as soon as it appeared. It would take some time for those uncertainties to go away completely, but I was up for the challenge. I'd do whatever it took to keep her happy.

Mary Jane gathered up a tote bag with some snacks and cold waters from the fridge. She turned to me and suggested, "Why don't Derrick and I take the girls to hike down to the falls and give you two some alone time?" She must have noticed Melanie's demeanor as well. A little time alone was just what we needed.

"Sounds good to me." Melanie smiled and nodded in agreement with me. A few minutes later, we had the cabin all to ourselves.

"What should we do while they're gone?"

"Get to know each other a little more? Let's sit outside and talk." Not the response I hoped for, but I did want to know more about Melanie.

Taking a seat on the wooden bench outside the door, she patted the spot next to her. Once I sat down, I wrapped my arm around her. "Tell me about yourself then. I want to know it all."

"I've never had much to be happy about in life, Tristan. My parents were never around for me. My dad has never been in my life because my parents never married. I told you about my issues with my mother. The only people who ever cared about me were my older brothers, but they all have their own families now, and I rarely see them." Every family had their black sheep and crazy history. My chest hurt to hear of Melanie's loneliness over the years.

"When I turned eighteen, I qualified for a full scholarship to college, and I worked my butt off to graduate with honors in childhood education. Teaching children had been my dream because I had a teacher who had been better to me than my parents ever were, and I wanted to pay it forward to another child. Falling in love had never been in the plans."

Falling in love? I moved my arm away from her and put a little space between us. With the mention of her teaching career, my fear came back to light. *Was it possible she had feelings for Derrick, which still lingered?*

"After college, I found a job with a local elementary school. I was the youngest teacher they had at only twenty-two. They started me out with another teacher, Bradley, whom I shadowed for my first year. During the year, we grew closer and then one day…."

Her words trailed off, and I tried to make sense of everything in my head. "Wait, so Bradley is the one you fell in love with, not Derrick?"

Melanie's head whipped around. "What? Tristan, I told you, Derrick and I had two dates. Not even so much as a kiss happened. There are no feelings there."

"I'm confused. I don't understand why you're telling me this?" *Was she still in love with this man?*

"I'm getting to the point," she promised sincerely. "I fell in love with Bradley, head over heels. He seduced me, then trashed me to the principal afterward. He told them I came to him and offered my body in exchange for help during the year. They fired me for fraternizing with a colleague and perceived I needed more time to mature. The next year I took a job at Katelyn's school. You'd think I'd learned my lesson about mixing business and pleasure, but I still asked Derrick out. The reason I'm upset is I like you."

"Women are confusing," I mumbled, shaking my head. "I'm so lost."

"The one time I've been in love, he demolished me, Tristan. He trashed my dreams and broke my heart at the same time."

Tracing my thumb across her cheek, I vowed, "I'd never intentionally hurt you. It's not who I am." Pausing, I thought about everything she said and something dawned on me. "You're falling in love with me?"

"I could be." She bit her lip as a smile spread across her face.

I thought the prospect of commitment would terrify me, but instead, I wanted to jump up and down, whooping and hollering. We were on the same road, still completely in sync.

With my hand behind her neck, I pulled her close capturing those sweet cherry lips with mine. I pushed my fingers through her hair as she moaned against my mouth. She lifted herself up and straddled my lap on the bench.

"Do you want to go back inside?" I asked.

"Yes."

We stood with our hands clasped as she pulled me into the cabin and straight to our bedroom.

CHAPTER FOURTEEN

GETTING TO KNOW YOU

"Was Mary Jane the first girl you fell in love with?" Melanie asked as her finger traced lines across my chest. I tensed up at the question. "I'm sorry."

"No, don't be. My feelings for Mary Jane were different than I ever had for anyone. I'm not sure now if it's because our friendship is so strong and I confused it with love or what. The truth is, what I'm feeling for you now doesn't feel anything like what I felt for her, which makes me think I'm falling in love for the first time now… with you." Since we'd met, I knew Melanie was who I wanted. My one night with Bailey stemmed from my attraction to Melanie, and the next morning I woke up with a desire for more in life than just sex because of her.

"Tristan, I—so, is it too early to define what we are?"

To me it seemed obvious what we were, but I knew Melanie needed to hear me say it.

"If it's okay, I'd like to call you my girlfriend." If she'd hesitated, I might have freaked out a bit. The smile on her face at hearing the ten-letter word put my fears at ease.

"It's more than okay."

Melanie took a shower while I started fixing us a snack from some of the fresh fruit Mary Jane had packed. Picking up my cell phone, I sent her a text to let her know they could come back whenever.

Me: Thanks for the time alone.

MJ: Is everything good between you two?

Me: Better than good. We're officially exclusive now.

MJ: Great! I think you two are cute together.

Me: She may be the one, MJ.

MJ: Aww, T, I'm happy for you.

Me: Thanks. I'll see you guys soon.

MJ: K. We're about to start our hike back up so we'll be at the cabin in another hour or so. Love you.

Me: Love you too.

Once the message was sent, I realized it didn't hurt to say I loved her anymore. On this day the sky seemed bluer, the lake clearer, the trees a deeper shade of green.

As Melanie strolled out of the bedroom, even she seemed clearer to me. The deep auburn of her hair against her ivory skin, the shape of her breasts, her hips, her toned calves, there wasn't a flaw I could find on this girl. I appreciated everything about her down to the spattering of freckles under her eyes.

"You're staring," she said with a smile that met her eyes. Putting a genuine smile on her face and knowing she trusted me gave me a sense of pride.

"You're beautiful," I replied stepping up to her.

"Good response. Do you still want to go for a hike or stay here and get to know each other better? And by better, I mean talking," she elaborated with a knowing grin for where my mind floated.

"Let's stay here. I do want to know one thing about you first."

"What?" she asked.

"I noticed your tattoo last night when you were sleeping, and I wanted to see the full picture."

She grinned and swiveled around to raise her shirt and display the intricate wing design, which spanned across her lower back.

I traced my fingers over the design causing her body to tremble. "How long have you had this?"

"Since my eighteenth birthday; it was a spring break girl's bonding thing. My best friend and I each got one. She got the name of her boyfriend, whom she broke up with a year later, and I picked these wings."

"Why'd you choose a tramp stamp?"

Melanie cringed and lowered her shirt. "I hate when people call it a tramp stamp. I wanted it somewhere unnoticeable by most people. A place of intimacy for my lover I suppose you could say."

"You can see it when you're wearing a suit though?"

"Did you notice it when I was in my bathing suit yesterday?" she asked with a raised eyebrow. When I stopped to think about it, I hadn't noticed. Her small bikini shorts sat a bit high on her hips covering it from view.

"It's very sexy," I purred against her ear.

We curled up on the couch, and she sat with her back against my chest. Her fingers entangled with mine as she compared our hands.

"Tell me about your roommate. You never mention her."

"Angel?" Not the topic I wanted to explore because there were too many secrets I'd promised to keep for her. "She's MJ's best friend. They lived together down in Florida, and originally we planned to all rent a place when we moved here. For years, they lived together in Nashville and only moved for MJ's internship at Disney. Derrick proposed after MJ came home, and it left the two of us to figure out our housing. Angel and I decided to go ahead and live together so we could afford a nicer place. She's now one of my best friends, practically a sister." Saying she's like a sister had a bit of a creep factor to it since we slept together, but it's not something I wanted to get into with my new girlfriend.

"So, nothing romantic has ever happened between you two?"

The last thing I ever wanted to be was a liar, especially when it came to my relationship with Melanie. The tough part was I promised Angel I wouldn't tell anyone about our drunken roll in the hay, and I didn't break promises.

"Nope, nothing romantic." Technically I didn't lie. What happened to Angel and I wasn't romantic in the least. In fact, if we hadn't woken up naked in the same bed, with a used condom wrapper on the nightstand, I'd never have known we slept together. The night was still a blur to both of us.

"Does Macy get along with Angel?"

"They love each other. Angel helps her with her honors Spanish classes, and they do all the girly stuff like painting their nails and crap."

Melanie laughed at my creative phrasing. "You're poetic, Tristan. You should be a writer." She shifted her weight slightly and brushed up against my shorts. "Oh." She blushed, obviously noticing my body's response to her.

As she turned and leaned forward to kiss me, the door opened, and Derrick called out, "We're back, put your clothes on!"

He came around the corner with a smirk. "No worries, the girls are outside, so they didn't hear me."

"Thanks, Derrick. Did you guys have fun?"

"Yep. Don't freak out, Macy has a knot on her head." Before I zipped into panic mode, I took a few deep breaths to give Derrick time to elaborate. "As we hiked back up from the falls she fell forward and smacked her forehead on some rocks. She didn't lose consciousness or anything, but she has a nasty bump. There was a nurse behind us on the trail, and she checked her over and advised we put ice on it."

"Where did you get ice?"

"I carry a first aid kit with me pretty much everywhere I go," Mary Jane advised as she came in the door with Macy, who seemed embarrassed more than anything. "It has a cold pack in it. You snap it in half, and it cools down."

The bump was noticeable. "How's your head feeling, kiddo?" Since the day Macy was born, I'd played the big-brother-protector role. After taking over the responsibilities of a parent for her, I freaked when she had a papercut. Over the years, I'd gotten better about flying straight to panic mode, especially due to her clumsy moments being frequent enough to give me permanent high blood pressure. So, inside I was coming apart a little with worry, but I kept it off my face for her sake.

Macy shrugged indifferently. "It hurts a bit, but I'm fine. Can I take a nap?"

"No." Mary Jane and I echo.

"Why not?" Macy asked, looking exhausted.

"I'd rather make sure you don't have any symptoms pop up to require seeing a doctor. For now, I need you to stay up so you can tell me if you start to feel nauseated or your vision gets wonky." Mary Jane was right. If she demonstrated any symptoms, we might have to take her to the hospital to check for a concussion.

"Wonky?" Macy asked.

"It's a fun word," Mary Jane said with a shrug.

"I brought one of our favorite card games. Let's sit around the table and play. Maybe later Lanie can roast more marshmallows for us?" Derrick suggested, looking to Melanie for approval. She nodded, and we all took a seat. I claimed the chair across from Macy so I could keep an eye on her just in case.

CHAPTER FIFTEEN

TWO'S COMPANY, THREE'S COMPLICATED

When we returned from Fall Creek Falls, Macy and I took Melanie to our house so she could pick up her car. Macy helped Melanie load her trunk while I took our luggage inside.

I dropped the bags by the door and turned to go back when I found Angel passed out on the couch. The scene before me was very familiar. Macy came in behind me and ran up the stairs, shouting she'd be right back down in a minute, completely missing the sight in the living room.

As soon as I approached Angel, I smelled the alcohol wafting from her body. I grabbed a water bottle from the fridge and poured it over her face. She jumped up screaming. "What the fuck?" I heard Macy's footsteps running back down the stairs, but it was too late to cover this up.

"You were passed out again, Angel. Have you been like this all weekend?"

Angel stormed passed me. "It's none of your fucking business."

I grabbed her arm. "It is my business when I share a house with you and my sister." I lowered my voice to a gruff whisper, and added, "And watch your mouth."

Angel stepped up inches from my face and shouted, "Don't tell me what to do. Just because we *fucked* one night doesn't give you the power over me."

I heard a gasp and turned to see Macy and Melanie standing at the door. Macy's mouth hung open in shock, while Melanie's face fell into a look of despair. "Lanie, it's not..." Before I spouted the terrible cliché, Melanie flew out the door and jumped in her car. "Damn it, Angel! You're ruining my life. I wish I'd never met you!"

She stumbled back at the tone in my voice. Through everything, I'd raised my voice, but I'd never gotten truly angry with her. I couldn't take back what I'd said by blaming a drunken tirade. Also, you can't take back the truth. At this point, I truly wished I'd never met Angel Simmons.

I couldn't leave Macy alone with Angel, but I needed to go after Melanie and explain things. After running up the stairs, I found Macy sitting in her room. "What's wrong with her?" she asked with a shaky voice.

"She's sick, Macy. I thought I could help her deal with this alone, but I was wrong. That's all I can tell you right now. Angel is not herself, but I'm going to get her the help she needs. For now, can you please let me drop you off at Gracie's so I can go explain things to Lanie?" Melanie wasn't more important than Macy, but I needed to explain the sex thing first. I did not intend to break my promise to Angel, even though she deserved it after the way she might have ruined things for me. Deep down, as angry as I was, I knew it was the alcohol speaking, not my friend.

"Sure. But first, explain them to me. What did she mean by you two f—" Before she uttered the f-bomb I never wanted to hear out of her mouth, I stopped her.

"Don't say the word. I'm not going to lie to you. Angel and I got really drunk at MJ and Derrick's wedding, and we had sex. Neither of us remembers it, but she felt the need to use it against me tonight." I tried to keep the anger from my voice, but the more I relived what Angel had done, the angrier I became.

"I'll go to Gracie's if you promise to tell me everything when the time is right. I live in this house too and deserve to know what's going on. If I'd come home and found her by myself, I wouldn't have understood why she was acting so mean." Macy was right. I don't know what would have happened if she'd found Angel that way first. She deserved the truth.

"I promise to tell you everything, kiddo."

Macy agreed to be dropped off at Gracie and Ashton's for a bit. Gracie said she'd use the opportunity to talk with Macy about her feelings over our mom's situation. I didn't go into any details, and Gracie was kind enough not to ask.

Melanie's car sat in the driveway when I arrived at her house. Part of me thought she'd go somewhere to avoid any chance of me finding her. My fist had hit the door with one knock before it swung open with ferocity. "What?" she asked, annoyed. Her eyes were red; she'd been crying, and it shattered my pride to know I caused her pain.

"Can I come in so I can explain things?"

Her hand swung past her body in a sweeping motion to silently allow me entrance. She sat on the couch, as far from me as possible, with her arms crossed and her eyes looking at the floor. "I didn't lie to you."

Her head whipped up in shock. "You told me you'd never slept with Angel."

I sighed. "You asked me if anything romantic happened between us, and I said no. We got drunk one night and ended up in bed together. Neither of us even remembers having sex. We were both naked, and there was a used condom, deductive reasoning says we did."

Figurative smoke poured out of her ears from the heat enveloping her face. "Excuse me for not being more specific in my question. I should've asked, 'Have you ever screwed your roommate,' but I wanted to show more tact. Next time I'll remember you need specifically worded questions."

Her voice cracked, and she began to cry again. I wanted to punch anyone who caused her pain, and being the reason for her hurt sucked for lack of a more poetic word. "This all happened the night of MJ and Derrick's wedding three months ago. It was at least a month before I met you."

Melanie stood up. "It's not about when it happened. I

don't care who you slept with before we started dating. You lied to me, Tristan. I asked you for honesty, and you lied. I hate liars. I've dealt with them enough in my life." I stood up reaching for her. She eased away from my touch. "Please leave. I need a little time and space."

Dropping my head in defeat, I began my slow retreat from her house. "I care about you, Lanie, more than you know." Her eyes dipped to the floor as I saw the emotion roll over her face again. Before I could cause her any more pain, I turned and walked out.

Feeling dejected, I sat behind the wheel of my car staring at her house, not wanting to leave. With my fingers wrapped around the door handle, I considered getting back out, walking up there, and making a grand romantic gesture by telling her I loved her. But I wasn't sure this was how I wanted to say it… or if I was even there just yet. I couldn't imagine anything feeling worse than the moment she asked me to leave, and I didn't want to risk finding out.

***

At home, Angel waited in the living room for my return. The moment I entered through the door she called out to me. "What do you want?" I asked with contempt.

Angel had sobered up some, looking guilty. "I'm sorry, Tristan."

"Save it," I answered, outraged. "Save it for someone who cares. I'm going to my room. I'd appreciate you leaving me alone until I am ready to speak to you." She dipped her eyes to the floor before I added caustically, "And stay away from Macy." Her eyes filled with pain at my words. Seeing Melanie hurt broke me, and I wanted Angel to suffer for what she'd put me through lately. Maturity and sophistication had left me the moment I saw the look of pain on Melanie's face.

My room resembled a bachelor's pad, something I felt like I'd be forever at this point. Clothes were strewn over the chair in the corner and thrown near the hamper, not in it, but near it. In the bathroom, a towel was on the floor from when I took a shower before I left. I had forgotten to hang it up.

As I stared in the mirror, my fingers scraped down my face, then raked my hair back. Macy's hair was all grown back, and mine had grown quite thick again. Thinking about the story made me miss my old friendship with Mary Jane. I needed one of those days, curled up on the couch with her griping about my problems while we ate pretzel M&M's and buttered popcorn.

Running my fingers through my hair once more, I remembered the night we spent on the beach after we first met at work. She asked me about my bald head. I had to tell her about my sister being bullied at school and how the nasty girls cut her hair in so many different lengths we had to shave it off. I shaved mine to make her feel less insecure.

As much as I loved my friendship with Mary Jane, I almost wished I'd never moved here to stay close to her. Macy was happier, which was important to me though. Living with Angel started out being fun, and Macy loved her, yet somehow all of us missed her downward spiral. I thought back and realized I'd never seen her spend an entire night without an alcoholic beverage in her hand. Gracie and Mary Jane had known her for years and never spotted it from what I could tell. *Why did I promise to keep her secret? Why am I trying to do this on my own?* My cell phone buzzed in my pocket.

Mary Jane: Macy called me and said something is wrong with Angel. She also claimed you and Lanie had a fight?

Me: I'm taking care of it.

Mary Jane: I want to help. I love both of you.

Me: I'll let you know if I need help with it.

Mary Jane: Promise?

Me: I'm done making promises.

Mary Jane: Tristan, what's wrong??

Me: I'll call you later. Love you.

Mary Jane: Love you too. You better call me later, or I'm coming over there.

Me: Don't threaten me :)

Trying to help Angel deal with this alone had been a mistake. She needed support, and we had the best group of friends for that support. I didn't have the strength needed to get her through this and take care of Macy at the same time, not alone at least.

Sliding down to the floor, I placed my head in my hands as I released a groan of frustration. My fingers dangled over the screen of my phone contemplating what to do. Finally, I opened the screen and began to research alcohol rehab facilities nearby. It was time to break a promise.

CHAPTER SIXTEEN

BABY STEPS

I tracked down the top rehab in Nashville. They informed me, since Angel was over eighteen and not married, she'd have to commit herself if she hadn't done anything illegal, like gettting a DUI. Seemed stupid to think she had to commit a crime before she got help. Drinking to the point of blackouts, meant you're a danger to yourself in my opinion.

Angel's bedroom had been quiet; the door closed her off from having to face me. I knocked three times before entering. Awaking when I sat on the bed, she rubbed her eyes. "I'm not drunk. I needed a nap."

I pushed her hair away from her eyes. "I can tell. You smell better than usual."

The saddest smile I'd ever seen appeared on her face. "If that's a compliment, you should work on your verbiage."

"You need help, Angel."

Angel sat up pulling the blanket with her to stay covered. "I know. Are you willing to help me?"

I shook my head. "You need professional help. You need to check yourself into rehab. There's a great place not far from here. I've done research on them. I'll help you pay for it."

She panicked. "Please, no. I can't be locked up, T. I promise, I'll do anything else. If you tell me no more alcohol, then fine. We'll get rid of everything in the house again." She grabbed my hand. "Please give me a chance to do this on my own first. If I can't do it, then I'll check myself in. I'm asking for a month. Please." My eyebrows creased as I thought about her offer. When I hadn't responded a moment later, she added, "I'll talk to Lanie for you. I'll explain everything. I'm sorry I'm ruining your life. You and Macy are my family."

Pulling her into my arms, I kissed her forehead softly. "You haven't ruined my life. I was wrong to say such a hurtful thing. You have to do this though, or I will have you committed," I threatened her, knowing I couldn't really do that unless she proved a danger to herself or others. "This is your second chance, you have to use it wisely because there won't be any after this one." Angel sobbed, and I pulled her closer. "What started this, Angel?"

She held tight as she confessed, "I'm always alone now. I'm tired of being alone."

"What do you mean by alone? You have a ton of friends who care about you, and you are out partying with people every night."

Angel moved away from me fidgeting nervously. "My friends have all moved on and gotten married. I go out every night and get so drunk I end up sleeping with someone whose name I can't remember in the morning. Waking up to you was refreshing because I wasn't terrified out of my mind. The only thing I do right is carry condoms with me. I've made it a regular monthly trip to go to the health center to get tested for STDs. My life is spiraling out of control, and I'm tired of feeling this way. I drink to numb the loneliness, T." She broke down in gasping sobs with her confession. "I'm utterly alone."

"Jesus, Angel. You can't go on like this. I wish you'd spoken up. You, me, and Macy, we can do things together. Hell, I'm not married and doubt it's in my future anytime soon."

She sat up, wiping her eyes. "I'll make Lanie understand."

"I didn't mean anything about Lanie. We're still new. Even if she forgives me, there won't be any aisle walking for a while except at the grocery store."

Angel snickered and smacked my chest. "You're so corny."

"It made you laugh though. Come on. Let's go downstairs and get something to eat. I'll grab Macy, and we'll have a family dinner."

"Sounds great, T." Wrapping her arms around my neck, she squeezed me close and then kissed my cheek, her lips lingering against my skin as she whispered, "Thank you."

Macy anxiously awaited our arrival at the bottom of the stairs. She bounced back and forth on the balls of her feet. "Need to pee?" I asked her with a teasing grin.

"Can we talk?"

"Sure, over dinner. Or did Ashton and Gracie feed you?"

"I had a snack there, but I could eat some dinner."

We didn't have much along the lines of real groceries, so we pulled together a few deli meat sandwiches with chips and apple slices. We hadn't sat down at a table together in a while; I'd missed it. "Now can we talk?" Macy asked anxiously.

"Yeah, sure. If you'll cut back on the hyper a bit."

Macy rolled her eyes dismissing me by swirling her hand around. "I have this brochure for a summer camp I *really* want to attend. It only lasts for a week, and it's at the end of summer. It's for kids like me who have excelled in school so much they've skipped grades. My friend Sammy is going, and it's not terribly expensive." Every word after brochure she sped through so quickly I barely kept up.

"Slow down, Macy. Take a breath. Does the brochure have the pricing in it?" Macy gave an affirming nod. "And is Sammy a boy or girl?" Macy's eyes rolled to the side as her lips puckered. "I'm assuming boy due to the look on your face."

Her shoulders pushed upward as she leaned her head to the side with an innocent-looking smile. "He's only a friend. They have boys and girl cabins though, of course. Tristan, please."

I placed my palm out and rolled my fingers back and forth in the international sign of "gimme." The pamphlet contained all the information about activities, lodging, food, and the price. "Wow. We need to work on your idea of what's inexpensive. It will cost a week's worth of pay and then some. You know what I'd have to do to make tips cover this? Don't answer that."

"MJ and Derrick offered to pay for it." Her face scrunched up as she nervously relayed this piece of information.

"What? When did you talk to MJ about it?"

"In Fall Creek Falls on the hike. MJ suggested I talk to you first and said if you couldn't swing it, she'd be glad to help."

Nothing stabbed a man's pride more than people assuming he was too broke to support his family. "Give me some time to think about it."

"It starts in two weeks, and there are only a few spots left." Macy rarely became so excited at the prospect of spending time with kids she didn't know. When I brought up the move, it terrified her to have to start a new school where she could be bullied again.

"Okay, give me two days to do the numbers. We're not asking MJ and Derrick to pay for it."

After dinner, Macy excused herself to play on her computer for the night while Angel and I detoxed the house again. "I didn't realize we had this many bottles of alcohol left in the house." Three bottles of Vodka under the sink, two bottles of Jack Daniels in the cabinet above the refrigerator, and four bottles of Bacardi 151 in the back of the pantry.

Angel shamefully confessed, "I've been buying it and hiding it so you wouldn't notice how much." Her problem was more advanced than I knew, and I felt like the worst friend in the world for not noticing the severity sooner.

Allowing her to deal with this on her own didn't work the first time, I'm not sure why I thought this time would be different. What also angered me was that she had so much strong alcohol in the house easily accessible to my teenage sister.

"Do you have it hidden anywhere else?

Angel hung her head down once more. "There are a few bottles in my car and my bedroom closet."

"In your car?" I shrieked out like a high-pitched female. "Tell me you didn't drink and drive, Angel, especially after the drunk driver killed the father of three of our close friends."

"No, I never drove after I drank. I kept it in there for safekeeping. Sometimes I'd go out there at night and drink."

"Jesus, Angel. I don't even know what to say." Part of me felt responsible for how far her addiction progressed. I should've paid more attention to what had been going on under my own roof. I knew it wasn't my fault, but I needed to focus on my family better. Any opened bottles were poured down the sink; the sealed bottles were put in boxes. We loaded up four cardboard boxes with liquor to take to A Shot in the Dark. The back of my SUV was loaded down with the boxes, and I promised I wouldn't tell them where they came from.

"I'm scared, T. What if I fail again?" She stumbled back a bit in fear. I caught her arm before she fell and wrapped her in my embrace. Running my fingers through her hair, I tried to calm the fear, her body shivered.

"I'll be here for you. Last time we tried this, I let you do it all alone, but I'm not making that mistake again. If it's too much to deal with, then we'll go to the professionals. In fact, I'm going to find you a weekly meeting, and I'll go with you."

"Thank you. I do better when someone else is with me. For years I refused to face my rape until Gracie had to face hers, and then we entered counseling together. Bad example. I haven't dealt with it so well either."

My mind still reeled from hearing someone had raped her. "Rape? When were you raped?"

"Sorry, I forgot you didn't know. My first sexual experience was in high school and he forced himself on me. I never told anyone until a couple of years ago when Gracie confessed about Hudson. We entered group therapy together, and I thought it was helping. Apparently once the therapy stopped, I dove into liquid therapy instead."

"How long have you been drinking like this?"

Her shoulders rose and fell as she kicked at imaginary objects in the grass beneath her feet. "Maybe a year now."

"Jesus, Angel."

She laughed, and I offered a look of confusion. "You've been saying those words a lot. If I were a dog, I'd start answering to Jesus Angel." She laughed teasingly, then became serious as she said. "You're a great friend, T."

"If I'm such a great friend why did it take me a year to notice you had a problem?"

Wrapping my arms around her, I hugged her closely and made a silent vow I would do everything possible to make her better.

Chapter Seventeen

MIXING IT UP

Melanie hadn't called, texted, or even emailed me since the day we came home from the falls. Every time I picked up the phone to text her, I had to stop myself so I could give her the time she needed. It had been almost two weeks, and it was time to take action. Sitting around doing nothing was not the way I rolled. Melanie had told me once she thought the best romantic moments were in movies from the eighties era, and she missed those small gestures nowadays. She wasn't one who enjoyed the cliché of giving flowers or jewelry, but she would rather have something from the heart. I called up my eighties movies expert to get some ideas for romantic gestures.

The doorbell rang, and I slipped downstairs to answer it before anyone else could. "You're looking studly as ever."

Cameron complimented me as I opened the door and waved him in. "What fabulousness do you need from me?" When I told him my idea of the eighties movies, I thought he'd pass out from the excitement. "Oh, my gosh! I have a million ideas for this, things I dreamed of myself. Like when the princess gave the criminal her diamond stud earring in *The Breakfast Club* or John Cusack held the boom box up to Ione Skye to win her back."

I stopped him. "From *Say Anything*, right?" Cameron nodded with excitement when I knew a movie he referenced because I was behind on those. "An awesome scene. Now we need a song for me to play for her."

Cameron tapped his finger against his cheek in thought. "Wait. No. The thing every girl loved during that era, something they found most romantic was mixtapes." My eyebrow arched with questions springing to mind. Before I could ask them, Cameron said, "We'll find some of the most romantic songs from back then, ones that remind you of her. Then we'll put them on a cassette tape, and I'll deliver it to her with a Walkman."

Bobbing my head, I asked, "Okay, so when are we going to rev up the DeLorean and go back in time to get a Walkman and a cassette tape?"

Cameron's face lit up at yet another movie reference I nailed, and he grabbed my face. "You are getting so much better, Tri-Stud! And haven't you ever been to a pawnshop or antique store? They have these things. Even if we can't buy an actual cassette to record on, we can buy a cassette of some crappy music, put tape over the square hole at the bottom and tape over it."

The explanation still confused me until he cried out in frustration. "You poor boy! Were you so privileged as a child you never had a cassette tape growing up? I mean, I know CDs have been around since before your birth, but come on now! My family was rich, but Gracie and I used cassettes all day long! In fact, we used to host our own radio show." He used his fingers to make quotation marks regarding their broadcasted show.

"This seems like a lot of trouble to go through."

Cameron smacked my forehead. "Exactly the point. She'll know you exerted yourself. Sure, you can download a mix flash drive to give her, but where's the creativity or the effort? Come on, we have some antiquing to do."

Surprisingly enough, we found a box of recordable cassette tapes at the second antique store we hit. We grabbed up a couple of them and found a small cassette player with the ability to record and play. Coming up with ten songs was easier than I expected.

> My list of "take me back" songs:
> "Time After Time" by Cyndi Lauper
> "Can't Fight This Feeling" by REO Speedwagon
> "When I See You Smile" by Bad English
> "I Wanna Know What Love Is" by Foreigner
> "I'll Be There For You" by Bon Jovi
> "Is This Love" by Whitesnake

"I've Had the Time of my Life" by Bill Medley and Jennifer Warnes—Cameron insisted on this one.

"Heaven" by Bryan Adams

"Alone" by Heart

And, of course, the list wouldn't be complete without "In Your Eyes" by Peter Gabriel, the song John Cusack played on a boom box for Ione Skye in *Say Anything*.

Cameron helped me record the songs onto a mixtape for Melanie and agreed to deliver them along with a short note I wrote to her which simply read:

> Lanie,
>
> I miss you. I'm respecting your request for time to think by not calling. Please, accept this mixtape so I can let you know how I feel through the words of these songs. I had my friend Cameron deliver it so I wouldn't put you on the spot.
> Tristan.

Cheesy wasn't my style, but have you watched an eighties movie? They're all cheesy, and the girls love them. So, I took a page out of John Bender's book and sacrificed a bit of myself to get the girl. It wasn't always necessary to keep up the tough guy exterior; it was acceptable to show a soft side from time to time. If the mixtape didn't work, I'd show up on her front porch in parachute pants and dance hammer style all over her front yard. Technically "Can't Touch This" came out in 1990 but I was willing to embarrass myself in any decade to win her back. Even though I was unsure if what I felt for her was love, I knew I liked *how* I felt about her, and I disliked being away from her.

Cameron left and promised to call after he dropped the package off at her house. The next few hours were excruciating as I stared at my phone waiting for one of them to contact me.

The doorbell rang saving me momentarily from my misery. Melanie stood on my front porch in a pair of jean shorts and a light pink T-shirt looking more beautiful than the last time I'd seen her. She lifted her arm and unclenched her fisted hand to reveal a small diamond stud.

"I don't have any piercings."

She grinned. "I bought a magnetic earring. In keeping with the eighties romantic movie gestures, I'm not a princess by any means, nor are you a criminal, but still."

I took the stud from her and placed it on my earlobe with the magnet in back holding it in place. "How does it look?"

She shrugged. "Well you're no John Bender, but it'll do." Neither of us could stop grinning.

"I love my mixtape. It's the most romantic gift a man has given me."

I smirked and decided to say my thoughts out loud. "Also in keeping with the eighties theme, you look pretty in pink."

She let out a burst of laughter, which echoed through the foyer. I always wanted to see her this way, laughing and happy. "Come in." I sat on the couch first so she could determine how close we sat to each other; I was exhilarated when she sat right next to me with our legs pressed against each other.

"Cameron is a sweetheart. I wish you'd delivered it, but I appreciate the reason you didn't. I've missed you a lot. The truth is since you hadn't called, I was terrified to make the first move." Before I could defend my actions, she stopped me. "I know I told you to give me time, but I'm a woman, and we rarely mean what we say." She winked at me. "Seriously, you hurt me pretty badly, Tristan. I need you to promise if we start this again we have to keep the honesty in our relationship."

"I promise." With a deep intake of breath, I closed my eyes and decided to break my promise to someone else. "Angel is an alcoholic. I spent the last few days helping her rid the house and her car of all liquor. I made a promise to her I'd help her get through this and regain her sobriety. I also promised I wouldn't tell anyone unless she didn't follow through on her part. I don't want to keep anything from you, so I need you to keep this secret for me."

"My lips are sealed. Tristan, you're taking on a lot of responsibility. Are you sure you can help her? Shouldn't she go into a program with professionals?" I knew she was right. I didn't have much faith I'd be able to help Angel, but I wanted to give it my best shot.

"She doesn't want to be locked up. I gave her a month to make significant changes. If she can't do it on her own, she promised to go into rehab. For now, I'm going to attend meetings with her."

"Oh, like the ones for loved ones of alcoholics?" Her voice didn't display jealousy as much as the uncertainty of my feelings.

"Angel and I are friends, Lanie. We slept together one night, vowed we'd never tell anyone, and it wouldn't happen again. If I had been sober, I'd never have slept with her. There has never been more than feelings of friendship between us."

"I believe you."

Three simple words never sounded more convincing. Past girlfriends had issues with me having female friends. Cheating was something I've never even come close to doing. My theory was if I was unhappy enough to cheat, then I didn't need to be in the relationship in the first place. When I had feelings for Mary Jane, I didn't even contemplate pursuing her while she still had feelings for Derrick; I am not that kind of guy. I've done one-night stands. My bad boy side was alive, but it had its limits.

"So, should we plan the next date?"

Melanie smiled. "Yep, I'd like to, and I have an idea for one if you're up for it." The grin on her face made me a bit nervous about what she had in mind for us.

Chapter Eighteen

BOOGIE FEVER

Melanie kept me in suspense about our date even to the point of driving us herself. When we arrived, I wished she'd spoken up beforehand. "We're at a skating rink."

She bobbed her head, grinning from ear to ear. "I've always wanted to go skating with a guy like in the older movies. You up for it?"

"I've never even put on a pair of roller skates."

"Shut up! Are you kidding?"

"At this moment, I wish I was." Dread washed over me as my manly pride slinked away into the back seat while the petrified scaredy-cat took over. I was glad she liked me, and hopefully she wouldn't hold my clumsiness against me.

"If you want to go somewhere else, we can." Her attempt to offer a way out brimmed with her disappointment. Inside I screamed for her to take me anywhere but there. Being a guy who wanted to impress a girl, I caved.

"How hard can it be, right?" Dumber words couldn't have been spoken. Any trace of confidence I might have had flitted out the window as soon as I tied the skates and stood up. "Whoa!" I shouted as my feet tried to roll out from under me.

"Go slow. You'll pick it up once you figure out how to maintain your balance. Watch." Melanie rolled out to the concrete rink as though she was a pro at this. My eyes left her body momentarily to search for the nearest exit. She skated a full circle around the rink, at one point doing a spin, then squatting down to make a curve, and standing back up again to swivel her hips as she danced back to me. Focusing on the way her body moved took my mind off the terror of falling on my ass. As I stood against the wall, she placed a hand on either side of me. The closeness of her body to mine made it difficult to concentrate, and my breaths came out faster. When I tried to shift my feet, they started to slip from under me, but I straightened quickly and clung to the wall again.

"Do you skate all the time?" My voice screeched more than I intended as fear took over.

"Nope. I haven't done this since I was a teenager. I think I was fifteen last time I tried skating." She held her hand out to me. "Take my hand, and we'll go slow."

One hand clasped hers while my other held onto the wall as I skated like an old man. Baby steps, stomping the skate down with each step, I'd never felt less sexy. Melanie let go of my hand and skated backward as she stepped in front of me. When we rounded the corner, her back was to everyone but me. She unfastened one button of her blouse giving me a view of her cleavage and taunted, "If you can skate to me, I'll unbutton more."

And suddenly I was inspired to try as my body remembered how it felt to be naked against her. Her pink satin bra mocked me as it held her perfect breasts the way I wanted to. I thought I'd found my stability to make my way to her, and then part of my body threw me off course. My feet slid forward without my body following, throwing me off balance, and the concrete floor grabbed my ass before hitting me in the head. "Ouch."

Melanie gasped, and then she skated over and bent down. "Are you hurt?" Her shirt hung open with her breasts fully visible, and if there hadn't been others in the skating rink, I might have pulled her down on top of me right this second.

"Just my pride." I tried to sit up and stopped myself. "Shit. I take it back, my head is pounding."

Melanie grabbed my elbow and helped me sit up. "Let's get these skates off before you stand up." She unlaced my skates the same as a parent would for a child, making my manhood shrink more.

Gently, I grabbed her hand. "Let me do it. I already feel childish enough."

Melanie pulled away from me, appearing dejected. She rolled over to the bench and closed the three buttons on her blouse. For a moment, she sat there deep in thought. The terrible rolling contraptions were off, and my socked feet were almost as slippery on the slick concrete as the skates were. The date had been a disaster. I needed to figure out some way to save it.

"I'm sorry about making you feel childish or embarrassed today. I only wanted us to have fun," Melanie said as she untied her skates.

Kneeling before her, I lifted her chin. "You didn't embarrass me. I embarrassed myself. I felt silly for not even being able to stand up on the damn things. I'd like a chance to make it up to you though." Melanie smiled and gave a nod.

Trying to figure out a way to accommodate another of her romantic fantasies was difficult for a guy who never lived in the eighties or knew very few movies from that era. While Melanie excused herself to the bathroom, I texted Cameron for help.

Me: Lanie took me skating, and I fell on my ass. I need another romantic sentiment from eighties movies.

Cameron: Skating? Ouch. Ooh, I have the perfect idea. Let's forego romantic for the moment and make her laugh instead. Give me a call, and I can explain.

Cameron's idea was not the one I expected at all, but it would make Melanie smile and probably get me a lot of points in the creativity department. I'd admit to her afterward how Cameron helped.

"Can we stop by my house for a few minutes?" I asked when Melanie returned. She agreed, so we headed home. Angel was at work, and Macy was spending the night with her friend from school. "Stay down here I'll be back." Melanie sat on the couch reaching out to grab a magazine off the coffee table to thumb through as she waited.

I changed into a button down white shirt and left my socks on, grabbed a pair of sunglasses and snuck back downstairs into the kitchen without her noticing my return. The song I needed was already pulled up on YouTube because I had to watch the video and learn the dance moves the best I could in the short time.

As the entry music played, I slid in my socked feet down the hallway until I stood in front of the living room entrance. I used my phone as a microphone, so the music stayed loud. Melanie looked up astounded as I reenacted Tom Cruise's entire dance scene in *Risky Business*. At the end of the scene, he flopped down dancing on the couch, but I couldn't do that with Melanie sitting there. I compromised and lowered myself above her as the smile on her face met with the desire in her eyes.

Our mouths crashed together as we frantically pulled at the others' clothes. The pink satin bra I'd been thinking about for the last few hours came into view, and I bowed my head to kiss the top of her breasts. She squirmed beneath me, and when I sat up slightly, she reached up and ripped my shirt open the rest of the way, popping buttons off in the process. Her eyes drifted down my body to my black boxer briefs. There was no way I was going to wear white briefs even to stay true to the movie. She bit her lip before pushing me onto the floor. With a leg on either side of my hips, she lowered herself onto my lap grinding against me.

The evidence of my desire for her pushed at the material of my boxer briefs. She removed her shirt from her shoulders, then reached behind herself and unlatched the bra, letting her breasts spill free.

Moving my hands along her soft alabaster skin, I grazed my thumbs below her breasts before cupping them. My hopes were high we'd make it to this moment so when I changed, I slipped a condom under the band of my boxers, just in case. Melanie leaned forward, giving my hands a chance to slip my boxer briefs down and slide on a condom, before she sat back and drifted into a state of ecstasy with me. Our make-out session started off frantic, but once the sex began, it became slow and different than anything I'd experienced.

After reaching our peaks, Melanie lay beside me on the floor with her leg across mine. She ran her fingers over my chest, drawing what felt like hearts with her finger. My lips pressed against her forehead and lingered for a moment. She sighed with contentment before drifting off to sleep. Lying with her in my arms, I watched her sleep for a few minutes. I could get used to her face being the last thing I saw at night and my first sight each morning. Thoughts of a future with someone were new. Everything with Melanie was new, and yet it was as comfortable as though we'd been together for years.

I leaned forward and pulled the blanket off the couch to cover us. No one was expected home for hours, but I didn't need to cause her any embarrassment if someone came home and found us naked on the living room floor.

Two hours later, we'd both had a decent nap. Melanie woke me up by planting kisses on my face. "Hey, handsome," she remarked when I opened my eyes. When my hand moved to cup her face, she turned her mouth to kiss my palm lovingly.

"I didn't get a chance to ask what you thought of my surprise."

Melanie giggled softly. "I thought I made my approval pretty obvious. It was great, Tristan."

"I have to confess I got the idea from Cameron. I haven't seen many of the eighties movies and he has. I hope you're not mad."

"No, I think it's amazingly sweet you wanted to do something so much you got help to make it special. I love… it." The 'it' sounded a bit choked as though she began to say something else. It made me nervous and excited at the same time to think she almost confessed her love for me. I still didn't know if I was in love with her, but I assumed when I was I'd be able to say it with no problem.

"I'm glad you loved it." I pretended not to notice her difficulty in changing the phrase. Knowing her feelings was one thing, but I wasn't ready to talk about them yet. I wouldn't tell her I loved her until I was sure. I'd never lie about love, especially to a girl like Melanie. She was much too important to me.

Melanie sat up and grabbed my nemesis the pink satin bra. Her arms were around her back trying to clasp it. Tracing my fingers over hers, I took the straps from her and clasped it before pressing my lips against her back. She turned her head to smile at me. "Don't make me get dressed only to get naked again."

Smirking, I replied, "Why not? It's more fun getting undressed."

Chapter Nineteen

MINTY FRESH

"Hey, kiddo, you ready for school?" I asked Macy. After things became copacetic with Melanie, and Angel seemed to be doing better, I'd decided I would ask Derrick and Mary Jane to help me pay for camp as a loan. They offered to loan me the money to cover it all, but I only needed half so I could pay them back quicker. Macy was ecstatic to hear she'd be able to go. It only lasted a week and seemed the best way to end her summer break. The week she had been gone was torture for me. When I wasn't with Melanie, I worked to earn extra money.

When Macy returned, she seemed happier and more excited than ever to begin her final year of high school. Several students from her school had attended, and it allowed her to make new friends.

The next few months zipped by without much drama for a change. Business at the bar was steady, and tips were filling my bank account nicely.

Macy was in her third month of senior year, and things seemed to be on track for everyone. Melanie and I had been going strong. We saw each other at least two nights a week when our schedules allowed it. Her school hours and my bartending hours didn't match up, of course, so it was a struggle to find free time. We made it work though.

"I have my backpack ready. There are a few toiletries I need though if you're going to the store today. Can you pick me up some mouthwash, shampoo, and conditioner?"

"There's plenty of mouthwash upstairs. Go grab the bottle out of my bathroom."

"I checked there this morning; you're out too."

My head spun around to face her. "What? Didn't I buy it a week ago? Are you freaking drinking it?" And then it dawned on me. "Never mind. I'll run to the store and leave it for you tonight before I go to work."

I left Macy in the kitchen and took the stairs two at a time. It occurred to me the mouthwash had alcohol in it and could be the drink of choice for someone who was being monitored for alcohol abuse as I'd been doing to Angel the past few months.

Her room was a mess; Angel had always been a slob according to Mary Jane. Her trash cans were full but nothing alcohol-related in any of them. The trash had built up so much I tied bags and trudged them downstairs with me. She had clothes strewn everywhere. The laundry basket sat empty by the window, so I started tossing things inside it. When I jerked up on a shirt sticking out from under the bed, two empty bottles of mouthwash tumbled from it along with several small airplane size bottles of alcohol. Angel was an alcoholic on a downward spiral beyond the realm of sobering on her own. I needed help in making sure she got sober and stayed that way.

Even further under her bed were empty bottles of whiskey, vodka, and moonshine. "Damn it, Angel."

"Tristan!" I heard Macy call from downstairs, "Mary Jane's here!"

Promise or no promise, Angel needed help. "Send her up to Angel's room, please!"

Mary Jane appeared a few minutes later. She placed her hand on her hip and peered around the room. "You should make Angel clean her room instead of doing it for her." She must have noticed the stress on my face because she sat down on the bed next to where I sat on the floor. "What's wrong?"

Holding up the bag of trash, I said, "Look at all of this."

Mary Jane's brow creased with confusion. "Maybe those have been over a long period?" When I reached in and pulled out the mouthwash bottles, her expression became distressed.

"I bought both of these less than a month ago. This one I bought last week. I think she's drinking it for the alcohol effect and covering up anything like whiskey on her breath. I found her passed out a few months ago, and when I tried to help her, she became belligerent. She stumbled and eventually passed out on my lap. I promised her I wouldn't tell anyone if she got help, and then I find these." I held up the mouthwash bottles again.

"You can't keep a secret so huge, T. This is too big for you to take on alone."

"I know. Every time I turn around it's affecting my relationship with Lanie too. I've been through a lot in my life, MJ, and I face things head-on and always get through them. Angel is beyond my help. I don't know what to do for her." Sympathy rolled over her features, for me, for Angel, for all of us. Alcoholism had a way of breaking relationships, of ruining a person's life. If we confronted her and she refused to get help, then she'd turn away from us diving deeper into despair.

"You care about her, don't you?" Mary Jane's question played on repeat in my ears. How *much* I cared was the question I couldn't answer.

"She's my friend, MJ," I answered in the only way I knew was true.

"Let me talk to Gracie and Cameron and see what they think about doing an intervention. Angel's stubborn, it won't be easy to get her help, but I'll be damned if I'm not going to try." Mary Jane moved to the closet, then returned a few minutes later with another handful of small bottles.

"Dammit. I emptied this entire house with her this summer. We cleaned out four or five boxes of hard liquor from the house and her car. I thought she was doing better."

Mary Jane took inventory of everything we had gathered. "She's probably drinking less than before but enough to keep from getting the shakes. I'm betting she rinses with the mouthwash several times a day to kill the liquor smell. She may be drinking it too as you think, but there are enough liquor bottles here it doesn't seem like she'd need to."

"What the hell? Can't a girl get any damn privacy?" Angel stormed into the room grabbing the bag of trash from my hands before pushing her palm against my chest knocking me backward. "I've warned you about my privacy, Tristan!"

"And I warned you about what would happen if you keep drinking!" Getting up in her face my voice grew louder. Mary Jane put a hand on each of us trying to calm us down. Angel released a guttural scream and shoved against Mary Jane's hand causing her to stumble backward and hit the floor. It happened in slow motion as Mary Jane tumbled backward landing hard on her hips.

Angel stood there dumbfounded while I bent to help Mary Jane. "Go get the car ready now! And don't think about driving. I'm getting her checked out."

Mary Jane pressed her hand to my shoulder. "I'm fine, sweetie."

"You're pregnant. We need to make sure the baby is fine."

Angel panicked. "MJ, I never meant to push you. I'm sorry."

I shoved against Angel pushing her away. "Get out of here! Stay the hell away from her." At this point, Angel was crying but I didn't give a damn. I wrapped Mary Jane's arm around my shoulder to support her as I lifted her up off the floor. Once she was standing up, she bent forward slightly letting out a groan of pain. "Is it the baby?" She grabbed my shirtsleeve while nodding her head.

"Call Derrick for me, please. I want to go to the hospital, after all."

If anything happened to Mary Jane's baby, none of us would ever forgive Angel. Derrick arrived in record time, panic rising from him as expected. He was already very overprotective of his first child; the new one on the way was no exception.

"Call me and tell me what the doctor says."

Mary Jane agreed and then requested, "Don't be hard on her, Tristan. It's a disease. She needs help to overcome it, and she needs her friends now more than ever. What happened was an accident. Angel would never hurt me on purpose. Promise me you'll help her?"

I hesitated, unable to make such a promise as I wondered if my best friends were going to be mourning the loss of a child shortly. Mary Jane didn't let me get away without answering though. "Promise me, T. Please."

"I promise," I replied through clenched teeth, hating the taste of the words in my mouth. "Be careful and don't worry about anyone but yourself and your little one."

Angel hadn't shown her face since everything happened. I took some time to myself to calm down from the events before going to see her. I searched the house for her finally noticing the closed bathroom door. Knocking seemed futile since she wouldn't answer when I called out her name. "I'm sorry I screamed at you. We need to talk. Can I come in?" No answer. "Angel, answer me or I'll come in on my own." Still no response, so I turned the knob. She sat fully dressed in the bathtub with tears streaming down her face as her body trembled.

Before I knelt beside her, I grabbed the box of tissues sitting beside the sink. Angel didn't acknowledge my presence as though she was completely unaware of her surroundings. Her eyes were puffy; her hair disheveled from where she pulled at it. "Angel," I whispered her name as I reached out to blot her tears. She still didn't move or speak or even shift her eyes. Grabbing a hand towel, I wet one end with cool water to clean her face. The moment I touched her face with the cool rag her eyes closed.

Leaning forward, I kissed her cheek. "Talk to me, please."

My phone rang showing Derrick's number. I stepped away to answer in case the news was bad. Angel couldn't handle it. "Hello?"

"Hey, man. MJ asked me to call you. The doctor reassured us the baby is fine. The shock to her body caused the cramps but didn't do any damage. She wants Angel to know."

"Let me put you on speakerphone. I'm not sure Angel will believe me."

When Derrick was on speakerphone, he repeated everything he told me. Angel's eyes drifted upward. "Tristan," she said as though noticing me for the first time.

I told Derrick I'd call him later and bent back down to Angel. "Hey, sweetheart, I'm here. MJ and the baby are fine, did you hear?"

"Yes." She paused a moment before breaking into tears again, "I'm sorry."

Slipping my arms beneath her, I lifted her up and carried her to her bed. She grabbed my shirt as I moved from her. "Stay with me, please. I'm scared to be alone. I want a drink right now."

I sat up against her headboard, and Angel curled herself in my lap continuing to sob hysterically. I had no clue what to say or do, so I sat there running my fingers through her hair, letting her release all her emotions. I hated myself for keeping her secret for so long. As things with Melanie progressed, I started to let my focus on Angel slide. I saw her doing better and thought it would last. Something triggered this latest binge and I needed to find out what it was so it wouldn't happen again. My mind kept replaying the scene of Mary Jane falling back. If she'd lost the baby, I'd have blamed myself.

Angel drifted off to sleep leaving me stuck beneath her weight. If I wanted to move her, I could, but I couldn't bring myself to leave her alone. I relaxed my head back and closed my eyes. A light knock on the door caught my attention. "Macy told me I could find you up here." Melanie stood in the doorway to Angel's room frowning at the scene in front of her.

"It's not what it looks like—" I began.

"It appears to be a friend supporting another friend who's in trouble." Melanie wasn't acting jealous, but displayed pity for Angel's situation. She moved next to the bed, leaning down to give me a soft kiss. "She's pretty bad off, isn't she?" Melanie smoothed Angel's hair from her face and felt her forehead. "She's clammy. When she wakes up, she's going to have the shakes pretty badly." Melanie shuffled to the bathroom and came back with a wet washcloth she laid over Angel's forehead. "A cold rag always helps soothe my head when I sleep. Hopefully, this will keep her from having a migraine when she wakes up."

It felt like the right time finally, not the most romantic moment, but the feeling was there, and I needed to express it. "I love you, Lanie."

She froze in place, not moving her eyes up to meet mine at first. When she glanced up, her eyes were clouded over with tears. I feared it might have been too soon and prepared for her to let me down easy until she smiled. "I love you too." Those simple words made me want to jump for joy. And they were spoken as easily as "Good morning." No big romantic production, only an honest declaration of the connection we felt.

My grin was impossible to hide with this kind of elation bouncing around inside me. Melanie leaned forward to kiss me again; this time it lasted a little longer and felt a bit uncomfortable with Angel laying in my lap. "Now we've expressed our feelings, I think we should take a break."

"What? Are you serious?" A break was the last thing I expected or wanted.

"You know my feelings for you now, Tristan. You made a promise to help Angel, and she needs your full attention. I'm giving you the chance to be there for her. It's only temporary."

When I started to argue, she moved to the nightstand beside the bed and pulled open a hidden drawer I hadn't known was there. Inside were more small bottles and a scattering of pills all shapes and colors. "How did you know the drawer was there?"

Melanie sighed. "My mom had a similar nightstand. It's where she kept her drugs and drug money so no one else could find it. One day she passed out before she closed it all the way."

The pills kept my attention. The alcohol I knew about, but drugs? There had to be a hundred pills in the drawer: blue ones, yellow ones, and some were capsules of different colors. "I didn't know about the drugs, but it explains some of the mood swings though." Angel appeared peaceful asleep in my lap, not at all like an alcoholic with a pill addiction. "I'm scared, Lanie. I don't know if I can handle this on my own."

She wrapped her hand around mine. "You're not alone, not really. You told Mary Jane, right?" I nodded. "Then she'll tell the others, and together you all can help Angel. I would stand here and offer my help, but I barely know her. She needs people who she is comfortable with, people who love her. If you need me though, I'll be there. You say the word, and I'll come running. I don't want a breakup, Tristan, just a pause."

"Everything has gotten so complicated," I groaned. The very last thing I wanted was a break from Melanie. We'd worked so hard to be together. Why was nothing ever easy?

"Relationships are always complicated," she placed a

kiss on my lips. She smiled, though it didn't reach her eyes. "I love you, Tristan. A little time apart isn't going to change how I feel."

Before Melanie left, she gathered all the phone numbers for Gracie, Cameron, and Mary Jane. She promised to call them to come to my house tonight so we could all support Angel in some way.

It seemed so simple to promise nothing would change between us with a little distance. In truth, neither of us knew how complicated our lives would get. We couldn't be sure things would stay the way we wanted. I would hold on to hope for Melanie and me to work out, but in the end, only time would tell.

CHAPTER TWENTY

THAT'S WHAT FRIENDS ARE FOR

Before she left, Melanie sent Macy upstairs to see me. Macy helped me roll Angel to the side and offered to stay upstairs and let me know as soon as Angel woke up.

The doorbell rang and Gracie wrapped her arms around my neck the moment I opened the door. "MJ told us everything. I wish you had told us sooner."

Ashton stepped up behind her. "If there is anyone who knows how hard it is to deal with complicated matters on their own, it's Gracie and me."

Gracie stepped back, giving me room to breathe again. "Next time don't try to take on something like this alone, Tristan." She peered out the door for a moment. "Cameron, Gavin, and Derrick weren't far behind us."

"MJ?" I noticed her name had been absent from those

on their way.

Gracie looked around for a moment, glancing up the staircase as well. She lowered her voice to a whisper. "Derrick is worried about her getting too stressed out. He also doesn't want her near Angel. He's afraid she'll get upset with us and go ballistic again."

"I'm here! I'm here, no one fret," Cameron boasted as he came through the door waving his arms as though we were all in a tizzy before he arrived. He stepped forward and hugged me. "We'll get her back, Tri-stud." He gasped as he suddenly remembered something and asked, "Oh, how was the *Risky Business* move?"

"Worked perfectly, Cam. I owe you one."

"One? Psst, I think you owe me a couple." He winked.

"What *Risky Business* move?" Gracie asked with a raised brow.

"I'll explain later," I promised.

Derrick stepped inside next. "Hey, guys." He turned to help someone in the door. As he noticed the surprise on everyone's faces, he said, "You all know how stubborn this woman is, she wouldn't let me come without her."

"I'm fine. Angel is what is important right now. Where is she?" Mary Jane inquired, looking around.

"Upstairs sleeping. I'll go get her."

Macy sat with her feet propped against the bed, leaning back in Angel's vanity chair, reading a book. "Everyone's downstairs if you want to say hi." She took the hint and left me alone with Angel.

I shook Angel until she awoke. She reached up finding

the wet rag on her head and pulled it aside. When she saw me, her face lit up with hope. "Have you been here the whole time?"

"Pretty much. I only left for a few minutes." Pressing the back of my hand against her cheek, I stroked her skin. "Do you feel better?"

"A little. Thanks for the rag, it always helps my head." Angel sat up reaching for the nightstand drawer.

"Lanie did the wet rag. Whoa. You're not taking drugs right now," I said to stop her from opening the drawer. Placing myself between her and the drawer, I knelt in front of her.

"Drugs? Tristan, it's my medication. Alcohol is my drug; I don't need anything else. I can show you the prescription bottles if you want."

My hands rested on her knees, she placed hers on top of mine. "I'll need to see them. Why do you have them spilled out in a drawer?"

She pointed out the different combinations of drugs. "These are set up in the order I have to take them. Some pills I take daily and others I do with flare-ups. It's easier than keeping them in bottles, for me at least."

"What are the pills for, Angel?" Avoiding the question, she reached into the drawer carefully choosing the different selection of pills. With the pills in her hands, I placed mine over hers so she couldn't take them. "What are these pills?"

Overpowered, she sighed. "Earlier this year I saw a doctor because of constant fatigue. I kept having these tingling sensations in my limbs. I became clumsier than normal, and I would get stabbing pains in different parts of my body. I had no clue what it all meant until they began running tests on me. After running several tests and putting all the symptoms together, they told me I have multiple sclerosis."

My chest sank with her confession of this debilitating diagnosis she'd received at such a young age. I'd never known anyone personally who had the disease, but I'd read about it and seen stories of famous people who suffered from it.

"What exactly does this mean for your future, Angel?" How could I have missed so much about her life? Being how important she was to me, I should've seen the signs before now.

"It means a lot of medical treatments, which may or may not work. It means episodes of pain where I may not even be able to get around on my own. It means a lot of issues I'm not ready to say out loud or admit to myself for fear of breaking down. I'm scared, T. The pills sometimes help, but other times the pain is so great I can't handle it. I've been drinking to numb myself and to explain my lack of balance. I guess it was stupid to think I'd rather you believe I'm a drunk than someone with the disease."

"Don't talk like it's the end, Angel. We'll do the research. I'll go to the doctor and ask any questions I can, whatever it takes. This disease will not be the end of your life. You're a young, beautiful woman who has many full years ahead of you." Life got more complicated every minute. Disease had already taken one person I loved from me; I wouldn't let it take another.

"You don't know any more than I do, T. I may not be able to have children. And what man is going to want to take on the responsibility of marrying me knowing he would have to take care of me on the days I am practically an invalid."

"A good man," I responded. "One you deserve. He's out there. And you have to quit keeping all these secrets, Angel. Let your friends help. Speaking of friends, everyone is downstairs waiting for you."

Angel stiffened. "They all know?"

"They all want to help you." I held out my hand until she took hold of it and squeezed for support as we walked down the stairs. Everyone chatted among themselves in the living room as we entered. The room suddenly grew silent. Angel squeezed my hand even tighter, causing me to cringe a bit.

Gracie patted the seat next to her on the couch. Angel moved slowly towards her, and Gracie stood to give her a hug first. "Is this where you guys handcuff me and drag me to rehab?"

Cameron jumped in to answer first. "Oh honey, I know you've always fantasized about being handcuffed by me, but now is not the time for flirting, especially in front of my husband." Angel let out a small laugh and seemed to relax a little. Cameron was the comic relief in our group. His personality was very flamboyant. He was the gay stereotype you saw on screen, such as Hollywood in *Mannequin* or Jack from *Will and Grace*. Believe it or not, *Mannequin* was a movie I'd seen. When Cameron was serious though, everyone took notice.

Cameron knelt in front of Angel, taking her hands in his. "Now, sweetie, we're here to help you. No one wants to force you into anything you don't want to do. The purpose of our visit is to tell you we love you, and we want you to be around for a long time. We aren't here to judge or throw labels around. Gavin and I brought brochures for you to look through and decide which program you'd like to try."

Gavin handed Angel the brochures. "I can't afford these programs, I…"

Cameron patted her hand again. "I'm covering it in exchange for some babysitting time with your niece. Angel, I love you. You're my chica. It breaks my heart to see you in pain." He reached into his pocket pulling out a set of car keys. Holding it up, he pointed out a keychain in the shape of a tree. "Remember when you and MJ gave me this charm. You told me it's a sign of heroism and that I am your hero. Let me continue to be your hero. Please?"

Sniffles filled the room as Mary Jane and Gracie let tears flow at the pleading tone of Cameron's request. Angel felt the pull too as she leaned forward and pressed her lips against his softly. "I love you, Cam. I'm so very scared."

"I understand, baby girl. There's no need for you to be scared. You have all of us."

Angel glanced around the room at all the faces staring back at her, then landed on Mary Jane's face. She covered her mouth, closed her eyes, and began to cry. Mary Jane tried to stand quickly, but her pregnant belly wasn't cooperating. Derrick helped her up, and she wobbled over to Angel. "Don't make me bend over. I'll never get back up."

Angel stood, and Mary Jane wrapped her arms around her in a strong, loving embrace. Angel sobbed as she repeated, "I'm sorry. I'm so very sorry. If anything had happened to the baby...."

Mary Jane pressed her palms against Angel's face forcing her to look her in the eyes. "The baby is fine. I'm fine. Now we want *you* to be fine."

Gracie stood up next. "When Hudson attacked me and I confided in you, you didn't hesitate to step up and go to counseling with me. I never thought I'd be able to repay you, but now is my chance. I'll go to every meeting with you, hold your hand, and support you by standing beside you as much as I can."

"Thank you, Gracie. Thank you all for being the friends I don't deserve."

I stepped up next. "You need to tell them the rest of the story, Angel. Tell them why you began to drink in the first place."

She spilled everything about the depression of being alone to the diagnosis of multiple sclerosis. The girls were huddled together all crying. Gracie and Mary Jane swore to find out everything they could about MS so they could be there for Angel every step of the way.

Cameron and Gavin bunched in an intense conversation across the room. Cameron came forward and pulled Angel out of her group. "Gavin and I spoke about it, and we're going to find you the best specialist money can buy to make sure you have as few episodes as possible."

Angel cried harder as she threw her arms around

Cameron. "You're always my hero, Cam. I don't know what I'd do without you."

Watching the way things played out, I wished I'd told them all about Angel the first time I found her passed out. We should've both had more faith in what our friends could handle.

Chapter Twenty-One

TAKING THE FIRST STEP

Once everyone left, I helped Angel begin packing. Cameron left long enough to take Gavin home to relieve their babysitter, and he was coming back to go with us to get her admitted. She sat on her bed holding up different pieces of clothing. "What do you pack for rehab?" she asked, turning to face me.

"The pamphlet says you have a three-bag limit, and you should bring casual clothes and athletic shoes. It also states not to wear revealing clothes so we may want to go shopping," I teased, hoping to lighten the mood.

It worked because Angel smiled and smacked me playfully. "Nice one." Then she glanced at the stacks of clothes on the bed, placed her finger to her lips, and said, "But you know you might be right. Can we run to the store and buy me some plain T-shirts and such?"

"Sure, we have a couple of hours before Cameron will be back."

"Can I go?" Macy asked, stepping into the room.

Angel wrapped one arm around Macy and the other around me. "I think it would be great to hang out with my two favorite people for a little bit."

Angel drove, and I texted Cameron to let him know we'd be out for a bit in case he beat us back to the house. "Okay, you needed a few toiletries so I'll grab those while you two go look at clothes."

Macy and Angel wandered to the right of the store, and I coasted to the left. There I stood again in front of the feminine hygiene products, and my mind wandered off to Melanie. *How long would she want a break? Would she come back to me once Angel was away at rehab? She told me she loved me, but was my life too complicated for her*? I must have stared for too long because a voice asked, "Can I help you find something, sir?" A young woman in a blue smock stood next to me with an odd look on her face.

"Oh, sorry. Nope, I found them." I held up the hot pink package to prove my statement. Tossing it in the cart, I hurried over to the women's clothing. Macy and Angel were loaded down with plain T-shirts and a couple pairs of jeans. "Is this everything?"

"Yep. I grabbed a few jeans too. Most of my jeans contain fashionable rips or they're incredibly tight, so they leave nothing to the imagination."

"See, Macy, you should always have T-shirts and jeans

that leave much to the imagination."

"In case she has to go to rehab?" Angel asked sarcastically.

Macy laughed. "She got you there."

Macy pushed the cart, Angel and I walked behind her. Angel's leg gave out, and I grabbed her elbow as she began to fall. "Are you all right?" I whispered.

"Don't let Macy see me struggle. I'm all right, just a bit weak today."

Kissing her forehead, I whispered, "I got you." I'd spent a lot of time being angry at Angel lately, but I couldn't imagine my life without her in it. Wrapping my arm around Angel, we kept walking, and Macy never seemed to notice.

Cameron was at the house when we returned. He grabbed a few bags, and I asked Macy to go hang out in her room while we finished getting Angel ready to go.

"You're going to do great, Angel," Cameron encouraged. He lifted up a few of the T-shirts. "Are you going to a nunnery? I've never seen you wear anything this boring."

"The pamphlet suggests boring," I interjected. "She's not going to meet guys, Cam."

Cameron appeared offended. "She should always be prepared to meet guys. You never know where love will find you. At least in rehab, they'd already know they have stuff in common. And they could support each other with their recovery."

"He has a strange yet somewhat valid point," Angel agreed. We rolled her clothes as tightly as possible to fit everything she wanted to take into three medium-sized bags.

Her packed bags sat next to the door. Angel fell back into a seated position on the bed with a stunned look on her face.

Cameron and I sat on either side of her, and each took a hand. "Talk to us, hon." Cameron had been Angel's friend much longer than I had, so I let him try to get through to her first. She didn't speak, so he tried again. "Babe, you're going to be fine."

"Can I have visitors? Will you visit? Both of you?" she asked, panicked.

"It says family can visit. I'm not sure if we'll be allowed to though," I answered.

"You are my family. We'll sign you in as my brothers," Angel suggested.

In the moment, I caught a glimpse of the friend I knew and loved. It renewed my confidence in getting the old Angel back for good.

***

Cameron, Macy, and I took Angel to the facility and helped her fill out all the paperwork. She had to list immediate family members, and she listed the three of us as siblings. She wanted to see the others as well but knew Gracie and Mary Jane were busy being new moms. Both Macy and Angel were in tears when they said goodbye. My sister told her how she admired her for doing this and she would always be a real role model.

Cameron's goodbye included words of encouragement and hope, eliciting more tears. He stepped outside to be with

Macy and gave me a moment to say my goodbyes in private.

"I'm scared, T," Angel professed to me as soon as they left. Wrapping her in my arms, I held her close, laying my head against hers.

"I know. I'm proud of you though. You're going to do great, and when you come home, Macy and I will help you continue your recovery. You'll come through this with flying colors. And I promise, every visitor's day, we'll be here. We'll keep you up to date on the gossip too."

She sniffed back tears. "I love you, Tristan. I owe MJ a lot for bringing you into my life."

"We both do. I love you too, Ang." I pressed my lips against her forehead. "Take care of yourself in here, kid. Call me the first chance you get." I let go of her and trudged away before she could get even more emotional.

Outside, Cameron had his arm around Macy, and though her face still streaked with tears, she was laughing. Mary Jane always praised Cameron for the ability to make you laugh even through the worst pain. I knew this was difficult for Macy. Angel was the second person she'd loved who we admitted to a hospital for longer than a night or two. It would be my job to keep her distracted until Angel came home again. With my focus on Macy, it would help me deal with my own struggles over seeing Angel in this place. When I said goodbye to my mom, she didn't know who I was, which made things a little easier for her. For Angel, we not only saw her pain, but the fear of being alone. Her face, puffy red eyes, and swollen cheeks would haunt me until she returned home to us.

Chapter Twenty-Two

LIKE OLD TIMES

"Macy," I repeated for the third time as I shook her shoulders trying to wake her up. Finally, she grunted and rolled over, facing away from me and toward the wall. I sighed and started again, "Macy, get up."

"Why?"

"You have school today. You're not missing it. You've worked too hard to get to this point. Now get up and get a shower, kiddo."

She groaned and slid out of bed. With her head down and her arms hanging limply at her sides she stumbled into the bathroom, giving a large, loud yawn, before slamming the door behind her.

After her shower, she came downstairs to find a plate of food waiting for her. "Ham, eggs, and toast, it's a breakfast of champions. And, by the way, I'm picking you up from school today because we're going to spend some time together."

Macy paused with a mouthful of food to look up at me, after a moment of thought she nodded. Macy's school let out at three, which gave me a few hours to spend some quality time with an old friend.

Mary Jane opened the door with a smile on her face. "Come on in, handsome." Katelyn was at school, and Derrick was busy making up the schedules for the club. "I'm so glad you wanted to spend the day together. We haven't had a day to ourselves in forever."

"I was hoping maybe we could hang out here and talk a little before we go out to do some shopping?" I wanted to get Mary Jane's opinion on things with Melanie.

"Sit down, and I'll make us a glass of iced tea." Her house was immaculate for having a six-year-old. Katelyn wasn't a normal six-year-old kid though. She'd grown up without a mom, and she was the least spoiled child with the sweetest disposition in the world. It became clear how Mary Jane took on the responsibility of being her mom without a second thought.

Instead of paintings or even family pictures, the walls were adorned with framed drawings Katelyn had done during the years. They progressed from abstract art to a family photo I noticed had a date shortly before Derrick and Mary Jane began dating.

Mary Jane returned, and I pointed at the picture, confused.

"This date..."

"It's wild isn't it? Derrick noticed it a few months back. It's like she predicted we'd be together. The mother is even holding a pink flower resembling a carnation, my favorite."

"I knew the kid was special. Thanks," I said as I took the glass from her and had a quick sip, before setting it on top of the coaster on the coffee table.

"How are things with Lanie?"

"We're on a break... whatever that means."

"Why?"

"Angel. She... um, Lanie, wants me to focus on helping Angel. She believes having a relationship would be too much to handle. Do you think it's an excuse for her? She maintains she loves me, but I mean, maybe she isn't interested in me as much as I thought?" Mary Jane snorted as she took a gulp of tea. "What's so funny?"

"When I dropped Katelyn off this morning I ran into Lanie. She asked about Angel, Macy, even Cameron before she finally asked how you were. She's into you, Tristan. No doubt in my mind. She seemed afraid to ask about you. She kept dancing around it. Trust me. Lanie isn't going anywhere soon. I waited two years hoping I'd be with Derrick. After everything, look at us now."

"Whoa, slow down, MJ. We're nowhere near marriage and kids." I grew nervous at her comparison of this happily ever after life she had and my relationship with Melanie. My bachelor side wasn't sure I was ready for such a strong commitment. The stronger my feelings grew for her, the more nervous I became. I loved how I felt when we're together, but each time we're apart, my mind focused on the fears I had.

"I only meant some things are worth the wait. And since we brought Angel up, I need you to keep me updated on her progress. I hate not being able to see her for a whole month. When it's time for visitor's day, let me know, and I'm going to send a letter with you each time."

"She'd like that. We thought adding too many siblings would be a bit suspicious. Plus," I paused nervously for a moment and then finished, "she's not comfortable around you right now."

Mary Jane nodded sadly. "I know. I understand why, but she shouldn't feel guilty. We're fine," she commented as she placed her palm against her swollen belly. "This little guy is a fighter. He's rooting for Angel too."

"Have you picked out a name yet?"

"Yep, you'll be the first to know. We're telling Ashton and Gracie over dinner tonight. Derrick said it'd be fine if I told you today. Hand me my purse." She pointed at a maroon bag next to the couch. When I handed it to her, she pulled a picture from the front pocket and gave it to me. "Here's our little Craig Jacob Collins."

Noticing the middle name, I laughed. "Hey, it's like a piece of me in there. How'd you come up with the name?"

"Well, Craig was Derrick's father's name and we thought Jacob because of your last name. Plus, we could call him CJ, which is like my nickname."

"Seriously?" I was beyond shocked. "Why me?"

"You mean a lot to both of us. You were there for me

every step of my first pregnancy. I couldn't add your name then because it wasn't mine, but this one is."

Again, I was astonished. She had a knack for surprising me. "I'm truly honored, MJ."

"I'm glad. Can we please go shopping now?" I knew a grin so mischievous had a double meaning. Mary Jane had been aching to go shopping for the baby's room.

"You've been very patient. Come on. Let's go purchase everything blue we can find." She cheered as I helped her up off the couch.

The baby superstore was bigger than I imagined it would be. There were two long aisles for diapers alone. As Mary Jane hustled toward a rack of clothes, I stopped to send a quick text.

Me: Just wanted to say hi.

Lanie: Hi :)

Me: I'm shopping with MJ for baby stuff and I feel my manhood trying to escape through the closest exit.

Lanie: Lol. I think it's very manly to go shopping. How's Angel?

Me: In rehab. It's lonely around the house. She won't be home for a month. You could come by?

Lanie: Spend some time with Macy. I know she misses you.

Me: And you don't?

Lanie: I miss you like crazy. We're not broken up, just taking a breather. Schedule some Macy time, she needs you.

Me: I need you.

Lanie: Soon, I promise.

Me: I'm holding you to that promise.

"You're supposed to be helping me shop!" Mary Jane exclaimed as she dragged me to the cribs where she cooed over a cherry convertible set. Apparently the bed was like Optimus Prime; it transformed into a toddler bed later. We grabbed the barcode for one so they could scan it at the front. Next, she snatched the barcode for the *Terminator* of strollers. It would lead you to safety—"Come with me if you want to live"—and it was a shiny silver. Comparing the items to *Transformers* and *Terminator* made me feel a little manlier.

"I'm getting this one for you," I commented holding a onesie with a bat symbol on the front with a small cape on the back.

"Adorable! Derrick will love it."

"Great. Batman makes me feel a bit more masculine here. Can we go now?"

Chapter Twenty-Three

SIBLING CHIVALRY

Macy ran to the car turning once to wave goodbye to her friend Carter. Hopefully it meant his putz behavior was behind him. She slid into the car, her face aglow with excitement. "Did you have a good day?"

"Carter asked me out again," she squealed.

"Great, see I told you it'd be fine. Guys are idiots when it comes to dating. When's the big date?"

"Two weeks. He wants me to go to the holiday dance with him. I know you have plans for us today. Can it include buying a new dress for the dance?" Cringing at the idea of doing more shopping, I groaned as I prepared to let her down easy. Then I thought about what Melanie suggested and knew I couldn't say no.

"Of course, squirt." There were only a few women in my

life who could convince me to go shopping. Macy could ask me for the moon, and I'd do my best to get it for her. "First, let's stop and pick up an expert."

The expert in question was none other than Cameron McIntosh, our very own "Forget calm, be fabulous" teacher. When I asked him to join us for a day of shopping for dresses, he was elated. Gracie asked to come along as well, so they were waiting for us at her house. "You two are sure you don't mind the three of us joining?" Gracie asked, including Autumn her two-year-old as part of the group.

"We're excited to have you guys. Come here, little one." I scooped Autumn into my arms and stuck my tongue out at her.

"Unca T," she giggled. She had a rough time pronouncing my full name so it seemed the easiest route was to use the letter.

Gracie stepped away for a moment and came back. "Damn. Ash forgot to leave me a stroller."

"I can carry her around." I offered.

"You sure it won't make you feel unmanly?" Gracie teased.

"Carrying this beautiful girl? There's nothing manlier than a dad, right?" I meant it. Since I'd raised Macy for so many years, I couldn't wait to be a dad one day. Well, I could wait because I'd like it to be a few years down the road after marriage, but when it happened, I'd be ready and excited.

It took about five minutes to load the car with all the stuff we had to haul around for Autumn. Then another five minutes to get her car seat moved and locked into a safe position in the back with Gracie and Macy on either side of her.

We took Gracie's minivan so there would be plenty of space. I'd never felt more like a soccer dad in my life. The feeling wasn't as comforting as I thought it would be; it was a little scary. In a way, it made me glad Melanie and I were currently on a break. The utter fright of settling down crept into me, quickly making me doubt I was ready for a committed relationship.

We arrived at the dreaded cluster of stores filled with frilly pastel-colored gowns that starred in my worst nightmares. I paraded around the store with Autumn, who'd fallen asleep on my shoulder. When I bumped into a mannequin, it jolted her awake and the wailing began.

Gracie appeared from the dressing room immediately. "I thought I heard my baby girl." The moment Autumn was in Gracie's arms, she pouted a bit and sniffed back tears as her face shook for only an instant before laying her head down on Gracie's shoulder and falling asleep.

"Any luck finding a dress?" I asked, hoping we'd be moving on soon.

"Several. Cameron's in there with her offering his expertise. If you don't feel comfortable with him being in there, I can go back. She's wearing a slip to try them all on. I know he's gay, but he's still a male so he'll understand if you—"

"Gracie, it's fine if she's comfortable. I'm sorry I panicked. When Autumn started crying, I didn't know how to calm her. Seems like you have the magic touch though." Plus there was a crazy blonde stalking me, and she was still eyeing me from across the room.

"You did great, T. She's a daddy's girl. I'm surprised I could get her to quiet down so fast. Normally Ashton is the one with the magic touch. Come sit with me outside the dressing room. I need to sit down with her."

I followed her to an area sectioned off with a few chairs right outside the dressing area. "I heard you're dating someone now. Tell me about her?" Gracie readjusted Autumn on her lap so the baby could be more comfortable.

"Lanie is amazing. She's sweet, sexy, thoughtful, funny... I'm pretty crazy about her."

Gracie grinned up at me. "I can tell by the way your eyes light up when you talk about her. Seems serious."

"Right now it's on hold. Too many complications."

Rolling her eyes, she shifted Autumn up against her shoulder. "Complications are the worst. If she's worth it, hold on to her."

"She's worth it. There's not a doubt in my mind." No matter what, I knew things between Melanie and me were far from over. I refused to give up on her.

Chapter Twenty-Four

STRONG-WILLED ONE

Angel had been in rehab for two weeks, and the house had been serene. I hadn't realized how much we fought and how much I dreaded going home until she wasn't there anymore. I missed her, but I was glad she would get the help she needed.

"I have to work tonight, kiddo. I need you to go stay with MJ so you can get plenty of rest for school tomorrow. I know you have trouble getting to sleep when you're here alone."

"Cool. I need some help with my art project. Is Ashton working with you? Maybe he could come to MJ's and help? Or perhaps I could go to the bar with you?"

I grinned, knowing what she wanted. "I know you like hanging out at the bar, but you can only be there when it's closed. Otherwise, your uncles could lose their license; no one under eighteen is allowed in during business hours."

She sighed. "Fine. But can Ashton help me? He's the best artist I know."

"I'll call him and see what he says."

Derrick would be running things at the bar, so Ashton agreed to go to Mary Jane's. Gracie and their daughter Autumn would go as well so they could keep Mary Jane and Katelyn company while Ashton and Macy worked on her project.

I helped Macy pack her bags and drove her to Mary Jane's. She jumped out of the car, grabbed her bags, and blew me a kiss before running up the sidewalk. I waited until Mary Jane opened the door before giving a wave and driving off.

My shift began an hour prior to opening, giving me time to set up the bar. As the doors opened, at least one hundred people poured into the building ready for a night of drinking and debauchery. As the holidays approached, business at the bar picked up. I supposed people wanted to get out and meet someone before the holidays arrived.

The first song on the radio was a fast beat hip-hop tune that filled the dance floor with gyrating bodies and even a few show-offs. People surrounded the bar while holding out their arms to display the stamp with proof of age and not the dreaded black X reserved for those under twenty-one.

I swung around to deliver my final beer before going on break when someone grabbed my shirt and pulled me into the backroom. Hands roamed over my body and a soft pair of lips pressed against mine pressing harder and more frantically. The kiss was too rushed and lacking the taste of cherry I associated with Melanie. As hands reached for my pants, I pushed them away and turned on the lights.

"Bailey?"

"Hey, stud. I know you blew me off the last time I saw you, but I was hoping for a second chance. I haven't stopped thinking about our night together."

She moved toward my lips again, and I shoved her back gently. "No. I have a girlfriend now."

Bailey grinned. "I'll be discreet. She'll never know." She lifted her dress above her head and stood there in nothing but a bra and pair of thong underwear. She turned to show me the back. "I know you liked my thong last time. I wore them specifically for you."

She began to remove her bra, and I grabbed her hands. "Stop, Bailey."

She glanced down at my pants. "Doesn't look like you want me to stop."

I'm a guy, and there was a naked woman in front of me, I couldn't help how my body responded to her, but I could help how it connected with her. "I think you know from experience I'm not at full attention." The moment I realized she wasn't Melanie, my erection began to deflate like a balloon.

"Bailey, you're hot. But I have a girlfriend I love, and I do not cheat. Now put this on"—I handed her the dress—"and leave."

When she pushed through the door, it didn't shut all the way, and I glanced up to see Melanie standing there. She looked back at Bailey, who had adjusted her dress after opening the door and then back at me.

"Lanie… I…"

Before I could say anything, she pressed up against me and pushed her tongue into my mouth in a fierce kiss. The sweet taste of cherry lip gloss filled my mouth. And I returned to fully erect almost instantly. We didn't say anything to each other. She unzipped my pants and dropped to her knees in front of me. I laid my head back with a groan as she pulled a condom from her purse and rolled it on. Sucking in a breath as her fingers grazed my cock, I ached to be inside her. Standing up, she pulled her dress up over her hips as she draped her arms around me. With my hands placed under her ass, I lifted her and she wrapped her legs around me. After we had given in to the passion we'd missed for the past few weeks, we collapsed onto the floor gasping for air.

Once I caught my breath, I inquired, "I guess this means you know nothing happened with Bailey?"

"I heard the whole encounter, Tristan. I saw her pull you in here, and I followed to go off in an angry tirade when I heard everything. I've missed you."

"I missed you too, a lot. You came up with a nice way of showing me how much." I groaned as I pulled her into an embrace. "I don't want to leave right now, but I have to get back to work. Things are too busy for Marcus and Xander to take care of on their own."

Melanie kissed me before standing up to straighten her dress. "I know. I came here to talk and check in on you. I didn't plan this, but the moment kind of presented itself to me." She winked. "Do you mind if I hang around a little tonight?"

I jumped up from the floor and pressed her against the wall. Holding her hands above her head, I planted kisses along her neck. Groaning against her neck, I said, "I'd love it. And if you stick around long enough, Macy is staying at MJ's, and we'd have a house to ourselves."

"Guess I'm hanging around for a while then." Shimmying her hips as she sashayed out of the room I thought of the old saying, "I hate to see you go, but love to watch you leave."

Going back to work was difficult, especially when I'd catch a glimpse of Melanie sipping her drink, moving her mouth in a way that made my cock twitch. Tonight would be the longest night of my workweek. A hand appeared in front of my face with a wave, pulling me from my thoughts.

"Hey, Derrick, sorry I was distracted."

"It's cool, Tristan. I understand the distraction of a beautiful woman," he acknowledged with a wink. "How's the night going? Do I need to call in another bartender? Grayson is on call tonight in case we get too swamped."

"I think we have it handled so far."

"Great. Do you have it handled enough to help me with restocking the bar? Marcus told me earlier tonight we were low on beer, so I had to make a run to the distributor. They weren't scheduled to deliver until tomorrow. We need to get some on ice before we run out."

I tossed my bar towel behind me onto the counter and wiped my hands on the half apron I wore around my waist. "I'm all yours, boss."

Derrick had unloaded the cases of beer into his office, and we each grabbed a case putting it up on top of our shoulder to work our way through the crowd. The fact I got it over my shoulder told me my working out, an hour before work each night with Ashton, was improving my muscle tone. Marcus grabbed the case from Derrick and shouted, "Good timing, boss! We're down to the last two six packs in the cooler."

We managed to fill the cooler up and still fill orders without running out of cold beer. Melanie tapped me on the shoulder around midnight. "I think I'm going to head home. I'm working in the morning, but you could call me when you get off work if you want."

I reached into my pocket pulling out a set of keys with my house key attached. "I have a better idea. Go to my house. It's empty, and you can wait for me there." I pulled my hand back toward myself and added, "Only if you want to, of course."

Melanie thought it over briefly before placing her palm out. "I'd love to." With a quick peck on the lips, she waved goodbye, and I sighed knowing the next three hours of work would drag.

A hand slammed down on my shoulder, and I turned to see Marcus grinning at me. "I saw that hot piece of—"

Before he could finish his comment, I interrupted, "Her name is Lanie."

Marcus raised his hands in surrender. "No offense intended, man. All I was going to say is the crowd is thinning, and I saw you hand her your keys. You're always covering for me when I'm sick so give me this chance to repay you. Take off early. We got this."

It didn't take much consideration to take him up on his offer. I untied my apron and threw it onto the bar behind me. Patting Marcus on the arm, I said, "Thanks, man."

Derrick hightailed it out the door at the same time I did and gave me a curious glance. "Leaving early?"

"Yeah, Marcus is covering the bar now. I hope it's cool with you?" It hadn't occurred to me to double-check with Derrick. He's always such a laid-back boss when it comes to our schedules.

"Yeah, it's fine. You know I trust you guys to work the schedules the way it's best for you. You're their boss, and I've seen you cover for all of them too many times. You deserve a night off. Is there someone you're running home to?" Derrick smiled knowingly.

"Why do you ask?"

"Well, Angel is still in rehab, and Macy is at our house, and you're in quite a hurry to get home to an empty house. Unless you want to pick Macy up tonight?"

"No!" I responded quickly. "Sorry, no. I… Lanie's waiting for me."

Derrick grinned and patted me on the back. "Enjoy your evening, T. I won't keep you any longer. See you tomorrow." He waved as he unlocked his vehicle and slipped inside.

As Derrick pulled of the spot, he rolled the window

down and yelled out, "Hey, T, come here."

Sprinting over I noticed he turned and reached for something on the floorboard of the passenger side. "What's up?"

When Derrick turned back to face me, he had a bottle of wine in his hand. "I know you had to get rid of anything alcoholic at the house. I thought you might want this to celebrate with Lanie tonight. You two have had a rough go for a new relationship. Funny enough that seems to be the norm for our group of friends. Take this and enjoy your evening. One of the distributors left it for us to try, so let me know how it is. Macy can come to our house after school too. I know what being a single dad can do to your romantic life."

"Thanks, Derrick. I need a good night away from all the drama of the last few weeks."

"I know. If you need tomorrow night off, just say the word. Now go enjoy yourself." Derrick handed over the wine and rolled his window up before driving off.

The drive home had my mind racing with possibilities. No one would interrupt us tonight, and the idea thrilled me. When I pulled into the driveway, the house was dark but Melanie's car was in front of the house. Stepping inside, I stayed quiet and stopped to pour us each a glass of wine in the kitchen before heading upstairs.

Chapter Twenty-Five

SLEEPING BEAUTY

My bedroom lights were out as I gently pushed the door open. Moonlight shone through the window highlighting Melanie's face; the rest of her was covered up. Seeing her in my bed seemed so normal, as though it should always be that way. For a moment, I thought about how our life together could be. After a long day of work, coming home to find the most beautiful woman in the world lying in my bed, waiting for me. The thought was surreal. A dream within reach, but still so far away. Things were still complicated in my life, and I couldn't ask Melanie to take it all on herself as well. We'd have to go back to taking things slow, but seeing her now, I wasn't sure how possible that was.

I set the glasses of wine down on the bedside table and slipped my shoes off. Pulling my shirt over my head, I threw it into the basket. I sat down on the bed without moving it too much so I could remove my pants and socks. Wearing only a pair of boxer briefs, I slid under the covers and pressed up against Melanie. I groaned when I felt her body and realized she only had on a camisole and panties beneath the covers.

I moved my hand over her stomach and kissed her shoulder blade. She moaned and turned over to face me. "Hi," she whispered groggily.

"Hi. I didn't mean to wake you. You're very cute when you sleep."

She chuckled softly. "Since when is drool and bad breath cute?"

I touched my lips to hers, as our mouths moved together I slipped my tongue between her lips. Her back arched pushing her breasts against me as our tongues danced. After a moment, I said, "No bad breath there. You know I could get used to you in my bed. Especially wearing little to nothing." My eyes raked over her body, as my hands followed their trail.

"It wouldn't be hard for me to get used to this either," Melanie stated as she reached up to push my hair back out of my face. "In case it wasn't clear before, I don't want to be on a break anymore. Do you think we could start seeing each other again?"

"Yes. I can't promise there won't be any drama with Angel when she comes home, but I can promise I'll always be honest with you."

"That's all I need to hear," she said, before pulling me against her body starting the night off with a bang. Luckily

I had a drawer full of condoms.

In the morning, I woke up to an empty bed. The wine glasses sat still full, so I took them to the bathroom sink to empty the liquid. Melanie's clothes were not where she'd left them on the chair, and I checked my phone, but there was no text, and there was no note anywhere. I opened the door to go check for her car when I smelled pancakes.

Relief swept over me, easing my concern she had regretted our reunion. Downstairs I found her in the kitchen dancing around the stove as she piled pancakes on a plate. I stepped up behind her and kissed the spot between her neck and shoulder eliciting a giggle as I hit a tickle spot. "Good morning, sexy."

She spun around to face me and rolled up on her tiptoes to give me a kiss. "Good morning, yourself. I was going to bring you breakfast in bed."

"I woke up alone and thought you'd left. Weren't you working today?"

With a grin filled with mischief, she responded, "I might have called in a favor from a friend who subs for me. I'm using a sick day."

"Good. I was also worried you might have regretted what happened last night."

Melanie shook her head. "Last night was amazing, and no matter what the future holds, I'd never be sorry for what we've shared. I love you, Tristan."

"I love you." I'd spoken the words to her before, but suddenly they scared me a little. Not because I wasn't sure of my feelings, but because of the situation with Angel. *Am*

I setting her up for more heartache? Did we start this back up too soon?

"Good. Now go sit down, and I'll bring you breakfast." She smacked my ass as I walked away to the table. One thing I was sure of, Melanie made me happy.

She brought over a plate of pancakes for each of us and drizzled warm maple syrup over them. Freshly squeezed orange juice was already poured in two wine glasses, so we clinked them together in a toast before digging into our food.

"Tell me about Angel. How is she doing?" Melanie asked with sincere curiosity.

"She's doing good. I talked to her the other day, and she's enjoying the therapeutic part of it. They have different groups you can attend based on why you began drinking. She attends several different ones. I don't want to get into it too much though, I feel like it would be invading her privacy. She should be the one to tell those stories."

"Oh, I agree. I was only curious if she was showing signs of getting better. I didn't mean to pry." Melanie seemed embarrassed, which made me feel as though I should have worded myself better.

"I appreciate you asking, and you weren't prying at all. I only wanted to be as honest as possible with you, as promised." She seemed to feel better, which made me happy. My phone interrupted the moment with a text message.

Derrick: Did things go well last night?

Me: Yep, very well. Eating breakfast now.

Derrick: Macy has a half day. Katelyn wants her to

spend the afternoon with us. We're going to do some Christmas shopping.

Me: Sounds fun. Thanks, D. Call you later.

"Everything all right?" Melanie asked as I set my phone on the table face down.

"Derrick was letting me know he'll pick Macy up from school. We have the house to ourselves for the rest of the day." Wiggling my eyebrows at her, a wide grin spread across my face with the possibilities.

She grinned. "Whatever will we do?"

After spending a few hours keeping ourselves busy in the house with some happy, naked, fun time, we decided to go out for some fresh air. Since I'd been in Nashville, I hadn't done much exploring of the city on my own. Mary Jane had told me I needed to check out the Parthenon sometime. One of my interests was Greek mythology, and she knew I'd appreciate it. Melanie had been when she was younger but was up to explore it with me for the first time.

With only a week before Thanksgiving, the weather stayed in the sixties. The Parthenon sat in the middle of Centennial Park in downtown, and it was the world's only full-scale reproduction of the ancient building. Taking Melanie's hand in mine, I advanced toward the building. I was immediately taken back by the beautiful architecture. When I felt a pull on my arm, I realized I'd stopped, but Melanie had kept going. She giggled and stepped back. "Sorry, I didn't know you stopped."

"I should've warned you I tend to go slowly with this stuff, so I might end up getting on your nerves."

"I doubt it. Once we get inside you'll see I'm the same way," Melanie admitted.

We entered through the bottom of the building and strolled through a small art gallery where we took our time checking out the beautiful paintings. At the end of the gallery, we took the staircase up to the second level, and as we turned the corner, we both gasped.

In the middle of a large, open room filled with columns, stood a statue of the Goddess Athena. Adorned in gold, standing forty-two feet tall, she was quite a spectacular sight to see. We found a small bench off to the side and sat down with our hands linked as we took in every inch.

The security guard tapped me on the shoulder. "Sir, we're ready to close. I need you two to move toward the exit. You can finish your tour in the other room but please do so quickly."

"Thanks. Sorry we lost track of time, I suppose," I said, extending my hand to Melanie to help her up.

"It happens. She's a beauty. I come in here and stare at her many times myself. One of the main reasons why I chose to apply for this job instead of completely retiring. She reminds me of my late wife. We shared fifty years of marriage." The old man stared up at the statue and his eyes grew misty. "She loved Greek mythology. If there was a movie or a book written about it, she had read it or seen it." He shook his head as if to wipe the memory. "Enjoy this beautiful woman, son. They are taken from us way too soon."

He patted my back and walked away from us. I leaned

over and kissed Melanie's forehead, then noticed she had tears in her eyes. "You're so sweet," I said, brushing her hair behind her ear.

"Fifty years. Marriages these days will barely last half the time. It's beautiful." Melanie squeezed my hand.

Fifty years seemed an impossibly long time with someone. The way it moved Melanie to tears made me wonder if we had a chance at a similar story. Perhaps in our seventies we'd be sitting around reminiscing about everything we went through to be together. There wasn't anyone else I could imagine a long future with before her.

"Do you want to see the other room, or would you rather grab some dinner?" I'd heard Melanie's stomach growling earlier, plus I was rather hungry myself.

"Let's go. I don't want to keep them open any later. We'll save it for next time we come."

Melanie and I waved goodbye to the security guard as we passed him on the way out the door. As the evening grew later, the sun began to set, casting a shadow over most of the park. "I hate to end our night together, but I need to go get Macy before she thinks I abandoned her."

Melanie chuckled. "I seriously doubt she'd ever believe you were capable of leaving her. It's fine though. I can grab some dinner after you drop me off."

"Hold that thought," I requested, holding one finger up as I dialed my cell. "Hey, MJ have you guys had dinner yet?"

"No, not yet. We were thinking of going out somewhere. We haven't decided yet though."

"Great. How about meeting Lanie and me for dinner? We're down near Rotier's now. I could get us a table."

"Hell yeah! We love Rotier's. We'll be there in about twenty minutes." I laughed as Mary Jane didn't hesitate to take me up on the offer.

"Where are we going?" Melanie asked after I hung up.

"Rotier's. It's a family-owned restaurant and bar around the corner. They make the best food, especially cheeseburgers. It's quite famous to the locals and a lot of visitors. They have celebrities in there all the time too."

Melanie's stomach growled again, and she placed her palm over it. "My stomach wants to go there."

The place was packed, as usual for a Friday evening. We only had to wait a few minutes before getting a table for six at the back. While waiting, we shared an order of cheese sticks and talked a bit.

"What do you usually do for Thanksgiving? I know you told me you weren't close to your family." I wasn't sure if Melanie and I were at the point where we could share holidays together, but I hated the thought of her being alone.

She shrugged nonchalantly. "It's just a Thursday to me. I normally stay in and watch movies. Put up my Christmas tree if I'm in the mood. What about you?"

"When we were in Florida, Macy and I would make a big dinner for ourselves and eat the leftovers for the next week. Last year we had a similar dinner with Angel and MJ. This year Gracie and Ashton want to have a big traditional Thanksgiving dinner with all their friends. If you're up for it, I'd like you to go with me."

Even though she tried to act as if it wasn't a big deal, her face brightened with the invitation. I loved seeing the glow of happiness on her face. Macy and I spent too many Thanksgiving dinners alone before I realized how sad it made me. The year we shared the holiday with Angel and Mary Jane was one of the best memories for me. We ate a huge dinner, stayed up late watching movies, and then spent the entire next day decorating the house for Christmas.

Before my mom got sick, we would go to an extended family dinner on my dad's side. After her memory lapsed enough for hospitalization, we stopped seeing his family at all. The last time we heard from any of them was just before he abandoned us. Abandonment seems to be genetic. Luckily it wasn't a trait I inherited.

"I'd love to go with you, Tristan. Can you ask Gracie to let me know if there is something I can cook for it?"

"Sure, no problem." I wanted to tell her about my crazy past holidays, but I wasn't ready to bring the conversation to such a depressing level. Hands covered my eyes and a badly disguised voice whispered gruffly, "Guess who."

"Hmm… could it be…" I reached behind my back and tickled her stomach, eliciting a fit of giggles. "Macy," I exclaimed in mock surprise as she sat beside me. "Did you have fun?"

"Yep. MJ helped me pick out the perfect Christmas gift for you today too."

"You guys are shopping early," I remarked to Derrick as he held the chair out for Mary Jane to sit.

"From now until the end of the year the bar is going

to be insanely busy. During the holidays, people drink to forget they're alone, they drink to celebrate, and they drink for no other reason than to feel like they're accomplishing something. I wanted a chance to help my wife do some of the shopping." He bent down and kissed her very extended belly. "Plus our little one will be here any day now."

"I'm glad to help on my days off, MJ. Say the word, and I'll be there," I offered before even considering how Melanie would feel. When I glanced to see if she appeared to be jealous or insecure, I noticed she didn't seem distressed at all.

"I'll have a lot of time off during the holidays too. It's one of the perks of being a teacher. You can consider me available as well," she exclaimed, then something changed, and she grew quiet. Sheepishly she peered up at Mary Jane. "I'm sorry, how insensitive of me."

Mary Jane and I exchanged a look of confusion. It seemed to dawn on Mary Jane first because she reached across the table and patted Melanie's hand. "I would love to spend time with you. You're dating one of my dearest friends, and I'd like to know you better." Melanie's shoulders eased with relief.

"Katelyn, are you excited about your baby brother getting here?" I felt we needed a change of subject before the two girls started questioning the odd moment between Melanie and Mary Jane.

"Oh yeah, I plan to teach him everything I know," she stated proudly.

All of us guffawed over her comment until the waitress

came up to take our orders. Mary Jane ordered one of every appetizer and a grilled cheeseburger with fries for her main course. She had been such a healthy eater before this pregnancy it was still strange to see her eat so much. Mary Jane raved to Melanie about the quality of food at the restaurant. Together they bonded over the deep-fried deliciousness of zucchini.

Witnessing her interactions with Melanie, they seemed like lifelong friends without a weird history of any kind. Occasionally I marveled at her forgiving nature and wished I could be the same with people who had done me wrong. My dad being one in particular.

Around the holidays, I grew sentimental and wished my parents were here. Once my memory caught up to my sentiment, I knew Macy and I were better off without our father.

Mary Jane leaned over and whispered in my ear, "Are you all right?"

I draped my arm over her shoulder and whispered back, "I'm great. Thanks for what you expressed to Melanie before." Without saying a word, she smiled, then kissed my cheek and nodded in understanding.

Mary Jane's phone rang, and she beamed with excitement as she asked, "How are you?" She paused a moment and glanced at me, "Yeah, he's right here. Hang on." She handed me the phone. "It's Angel."

Melanie's face fell when I grabbed the phone and gave my normal greeting. "Hey, beautiful, how are you?" Mary Jane kicked me under the table, and as I rubbed my sore shin, I tried to maintain my conversation with Angel. "We're all good. Can Macy and I come see you next week?"

"Please do, Tristan, I miss you two so much," Angel spoke sadly.

"We miss you too. It's very quiet around the house without you," I teased.

"I'd smack you right now if I were close," Angel teased back. "I can't talk long. I wanted to thank you for helping me get here. It's been eye-opening."

"Glad to help. I want you back good as new. And as for the next visitor's day, we'll be there." The house had been quiet without her, and at times, I missed the bickering because it always seemed to end in laughter.

"Thanks, T. I love you guys."

"Love you too, Angel." When I glanced up, I noticed Melanie squirm uncomfortably. Once again, Mary Jane kicked me under the table. After hanging up, I turned to Mary Jane and through gritted teeth I asked, "Do you have a twitch?"

Mary Jane pursed her lips in anger. "Why don't you take Lanie outside to get Macy's stuff out of our car?"

Melanie took the hint immediately, though I remained confused. "Now?"

Melanie grabbed my arm and commanded, "Come on."

Once outside, she crossed her arms due to the chill in the air. I removed my jacket and wrapped it around her shoulders. "What did I miss in there?"

"We're still new, Tristan, and we don't know if we're forever yet." She sighed and added, "And it's okay if you're confused about your feelings for Angel. I saw the smile on your face when you heard her voice."

My lips answered with actions instead of words. "You don't need to be jealous of Angel. We're friends only. I care about you, Lanie. My feelings for you are new, and they're exciting and scary at the same time. We need to trust each other if this will work. I have a lot of women friends, but there's only one woman I want to be with… you."

"All I need to know." She smiled and gave me another kiss before insisting we go back inside.

CHAPTER TWENTY-SIX

A LOT TO BE THANKFUL FOR

I knew Thanksgiving Day would be hectic, but I couldn't have prepared for everything. The morning started fine; I woke up as usual and had breakfast with Macy. We cleaned the dishes and began to make our contribution to the potluck dinner at Ashton and Gracie's. Sweet potato casserole was the dish Macy volunteered for us. We'd never made it before, so we started early in the morning so we could taste test and possibly make another one if the first turned out gross.

"Do we want to put pecans, marshmallows, or cornflakes on top?" I asked as I searched for the multiple recipes online.

"Marshmallows, of course. Eww, cornflakes, really? Sounds too weird," Macy acknowledged with a sour look.

"I agree," I commented while tossing her a bag of

mini-marshmallows out of the cabinet. "What's the next ingredient?"

"Brown sugar," Macy called out. I grabbed a bag from the pantry and set it next to the marshmallows. "Lastly, sweet potatoes."

A resounding smack filled the kitchen as my palm hit my forehead. "I forgot the sweet potatoes."

Macy belly laughed. "How do you forget sweet potatoes when making sweet potato casserole?"

A knock at the door saved me from further embarrassment. "Great, Lanie's here to see what a doof I am."

Macy rolled her eyes. "A big doof."

Melanie greeted me with a smile and handed me a casserole dish.

"What is this?"

She glanced over my shoulder, and as I turned, I caught Macy waving her hands in the air. When she saw my head turn, she dropped her hands, but it was too late. "Sweet potato casserole," Melanie stated timidly.

Macy sighed. "I forgot to tell you not to tell him."

"Tell me what?" I asked curiously, still confused about the situation going on.

"Neither of us are great cooks, T. This is our first Thanksgiving with a big group of people. I asked Lanie if she had ever made it before, and she boasted about making it for school and that everyone loved her recipe. So, I asked her to make a casserole for us in case ours was a disaster."

"Thanks for the vote of confidence, squirt." Defeated by my sister's lack of faith in my cooking skills, I lowered my head.

The three of us loaded up the car. I surrendered radio control to Melanie, who sang along to pop music with Macy for the entire drive. As much as I hated the boy band concert happening, it made me smile to see Melanie and Macy getting along without effort.

Gracie's house was filled with excited voices when I arrived with Macy and Melanie next to me. At the table, Mary Jane sat stuffing egg whites with deviled egg filling. "Happy Thanksgiving!"

I kissed her cheek. "Happy Thanksgiving, gorgeous. What are you doing in here alone?"

"I was ordered to stay off my feet and this is the only way I can help." Feet propped up on the chair next to her I could see how swollen her legs and feet had gotten.

"Mind if I keep you company?" I asked just as my arm was tugged in the opposite direction.

Gracie interrupted us. "Nope, sorry, T, I need you in the kitchen. Lanie is our guest today. She can keep MJ company."

Melanie grinned. "It would be my pleasure." She handed me the sweet potato casserole as Gracie dragged me away.

"You're making the men slave away in the kitchen?" I teased as I saw Derrick, Ashton, and Gavin all working on a separate dish.

Hands on her hips, Gracie gave me a seriously scary look of distaste at my choice of words. "You think the women belong in the kitchen instead?"

"It was just a joke, Gracie."

She chuckled. "I know, mine was too. I suck at cooking under pressure though, and I think the more time Lanie and MJ spend together the better. You two are getting serious, and they have a weird history. It seems to be the best solution to everything."

"I agree. Thanks. Now do I have a bird to stuff or potatoes to peel?" There was so much food everywhere I wasn't sure where I'd be needed.

"Step over here to my station, T. I can use some help with this veggie tray," Gavin requested. He handed me a knife and led me to the counter full of carrots, celery, broccoli, and tomatoes.

"It's been a while since we've seen each other. How are things with you and Macy?" I saw Cameron all the time at the club, but Gavin traveled for work so I rarely saw him. Their marriage didn't seem to suffer from the distance.

"Things are going well. She's doing well in school, and I think she has her first boyfriend. They had a few dates. I don't know if they've decided to go steady or whatever kids call it these days."

Gavin snickered. "I don't think people 'go steady' anymore. I'm glad you're both happy though."

"Where's Cam?"

"He's on toddler watch. He's in Gracie's bedroom keeping Autumn and Addison entertained. Things must be pretty serious for you and Lanie if you invited her for the holidays." Gavin pressed for information.

"Yeah, they are, I think."

Gracie moved over next to us, sliding a large dish with separate bowls for each vegetable. "Here guys, fill it up, and we'll set it out for dinner. Mrs. Collins will be here soon, as will Marcus.

"Marcus? My bartender?" I inquired.

Gracie nodded. "Ash found out he'd be spending Thanksgiving alone, so he invited him to join us. I think he might be bringing a date too, a girl who frequents the club who'd also be spending it alone."

The doorbell rang, and a few minutes later Marcus came into the kitchen. "Happy Thanksgiving, T." He gave me a one-armed hug, and then grabbed a carrot and tossed it in his mouth.

"Good to see you outside the club, Marcus. What girl did you bring?"

"The one you introduced me too, the gymnast, Bailey," he gloated, grabbing another handful of veggies.

I dropped the last bit of vegetables into the bowl and cleaned my hands off. "Gracie, I need to get in the living room. I'll be back in a few minutes."

Bailey throwing herself at me, even with the knowledge I had a girlfriend, didn't sit well with Melanie, and I completely understood why. I didn't want our first holiday to end with a catfight. The moment I entered the room, the temperature dropped. Bailey sat on the couch and when she saw me, she jumped up.

"Tristan, hi," Bailey exclaimed, coming up and kissing my cheek. I pushed her away, politely greeting her.

"Bailey, did you meet Mary Jane, Derrick's wife?" They shook hands, and Mary Jane glanced over at Melanie nervously. "And Lanie, my *girlfriend*."

It seemed to dawn on Bailey suddenly why Melanie and Mary Jane had barely spoken a word to her. "Oh, um, hi."

Melanie glanced at Mary Jane, took a deep breath, and replied, "Nice to meet you, Bailey."

Sighing with relief, I asked Melanie to join me outside for a minute. Once we were outside without an audience, I said, "I had no clue she'd be here. She's dating Marcus, I guess."

"It's fine, Tristan." I'd learned a long time ago that anytime a woman uttered those words she really wasn't.

"You're being extremely nice to her."

"When I was interested in Derrick, I implied things to Mary Jane I'm not proud of, thinking it would get me a second chance with Derrick." Distaste filled her tone. "Granted, I didn't get naked and throw myself at him, but Mary Jane granted me a second chance. I feel this is my way to pay it forward." Pointing her finger toward the door her voice rose an octave. "If she happens to rip her clothes off again and try to have sex with you though, I swear I will—"

I yanked her forward into a kiss, interrupting her threat against Bailey. As I pushed my fingers through her hair, she ran her hands over my back. Her fingernails grazed down my shirt sending shivers along my spine. I pressed my forehead to hers. "I love you, in case I haven't told you today."

When we stepped back inside Bailey was explaining to

Mary Jane about our one-night stand and how she threw herself at me the other night. Melanie sucked in a breath and whispered, "I cannot believe you'd spill that story over Thanksgiving dinner."

Bailey scoffed. "I don't see anyone eating dinner yet. I thought MJ would want to know why you two scurried outside."

Keeping her voice as calm as possible, Lanie responded, "Look, Bailey. I'm trying to be as gracious as I can by asking you to please keep our business private. What happened between you and Tristan before we met is nobody's business but yours and Tristan's. To speak about it with strangers shows very little tact on your part."

Bailey rolled her eyes. "Don't be a prude, Lanie."

Melanie gritted her teeth. "I'm not a prude. And I'd like you to leave."

Bailey smirked. "You have no right to ask me to leave, this is Gracie's house, and Marcus invited me as his date."

Gracie stepped into the room with her hands full of napkins and silverware, glanced at Melanie and me and asked, "Is everything all right?"

Fists clenched at her sides, eyes misting over with tears, Melanie attempted to stay composed. "Everything is fine, Gracie." As the words left my mouth, I noticed the hurt on Melanie's face deepened. "If you don't mind though, Bailey isn't feeling well and decided she needs to go home."

It seemed I was on a roll for the day because Bailey's expression turned to hurt. "Thank Ash for the invitation, Gracie. Tell Marcus I'll see him at the club sometime."

As she was leaving, Melanie sighed and followed her out. At first I wanted to follow after them, but Mary Jane stopped me. "They're adults, let them work it out."

After ten minutes, the two girls came back inside laughing at something. "Feeling better, Bailey?" Gracie asked as she looked up while setting the table.

"I am. And I'm starving."

Melanie followed Gracie into the kitchen to help while Bailey stepped over to me and offered a sincere request for forgiveness. "I'm sorry for how I acted earlier, Tristan. Lanie's a sweet person."

"Tristan, come help me with the rolls?" Melanie beckoned, peering back into the living room. When I entered the kitchen, she whispered, "Bailey has no family. She was crying when I stepped outside. We talked, and she had a similar upbringing to mine. We worked things out, and she even apologized when I explained to her my luck with men and trouble in trusting people."

"Thanks for fixing things. I don't want to ruin the day for Gracie and Ashton. I appreciate how calm you stayed during the entire thing. I'd have been a bit louder if the situations were reversed." Melanie's forgiving nature was as endearing as Mary Jane's. I supposed it made sense I'd fallen for them both. Bailey wasn't a bad person. I had no hard feelings toward her, but I didn't want anything else coming in the middle of my relationship with Melanie. I was glad they worked through things, because I also hated to see anyone spend the holidays alone.

"I didn't want it ruined for us, either. It is our first

Thanksgiving together," she reminded me with a sly grin. After a quick kiss, we grabbed the last of the food and carried it into the living room.

Dinner was perfect. Ashton carved the turkey, and the rest of the food was passed around the table until our plates overflowed. I stood up and tapped a fork against my glass. "Ashton, Gracie, I wanted to thank you for including Macy, Lanie, and me to your family dinner today. Since Macy and I moved here, you guys have been the family we never really had. I think I speak for Macy too when I say we love you. I'm very thankful for everyone at this table, in fact. Though we are missing one of our members, this feels like a perfect day. Happy Thanksgiving," I ended the toast by holding up a glass.

Cameron stood up next and announced, "I have a surprise. Gracie, may I use your laptop?" Gracie grabbed her laptop from her bedroom and brought it to the table. Cameron checked his watch and then urged, "Oh, sign in, please. We only have about a minute." Gracie logged in, and Cameron grinned when a ringtone sounded. He pushed some buttons and greeted the face on the screen. "Hello, beautiful."

Lifting the laptop, he turned it to face everyone, and Angel smiled back at us. "Happy Thanksgiving!" she exclaimed with a wave. Everyone cheered and returned the sentiment. "For the holiday, they allowed us to Skype our families. I only have ten minutes, but it's so good to see you all." She choked back tears.

As Gracie and Mary Jane dominated Angel's attention for a moment, Marcus leaned over to me. "Who is that gorgeous creature?"

"Angel, my roommate. And don't forget you're here with Bailey."

Bailey waved nonchalantly. "Marcus and I are just friends who didn't want to spend the holidays alone."

Hearing my name mentioned pulled me from this awkward conversation. I moved closer to the screen. "You are very much missed today, Angel. In your honor though, I'm eating a plate for you."

Angel chuckled softly. "Thanks so much, T." She rolled her eyes playfully. "Only one week to go and I'll be home with all of you. I only have about two minutes left today though. Is Macy there?" I was confused why she didn't see her if she could see me until I noticed Macy wasn't in her seat.

"I'll go get her real quick." I found Macy in the guestroom, pretending to be engrossed in a magazine article.

"Hey, come say hello to Angel. She's on the computer asking for you." The magazine in her hand was a bar manual so I knew she wasn't interested in whatever was on the page.

Without looking up, she responded, "Say hi for me."

"She has one minute left now, come tell her yourself." Without her looking at me, I couldn't read the expression on her face.

"No." Macy had never acted like a stubborn teenager before this moment. Before I dealt with her, I had to say goodbye to Angel. Keeping her spirits up to help her recovery was important. I hurried back to the dinner table and poked my head in as everyone said goodbye. "Sorry Angel, Macy's in the restroom. She asked me to tell you she loves you and can't wait for you to come home."

Angel gave a teary wave goodbye and blew a few kisses our way before the screen faded to black.

Macy's behavior had me concerned. She knew how important our support was for Angel's recovery to be successful. I had to act as normal as possible for Angel while the call was active, but afterward, I had to find out what had Macy acting so strangely.

Chapter Twenty-Seven

FEELING DESERTED

Once Angel's call was over, everyone helped clean off the table in preparation for dessert. Leaning into Melanie, I whispered, "I don't want you to feel deserted, but I need to go deal with Macy for a moment. Are you okay in here?"

She pressed her hand against my chest and leaned up to kiss my cheek. "I'm fine, go take care of her." She loaded her arms down with dirty dishes and followed Gracie into the kitchen.

Macy had given up the charade of thumbing through a magazine. She had curled up against the mountain of pillows on the bed. The bed sunk under my weight as I sat next to her. I ran my fingers through her hair, waiting for her to speak or get annoyed with me. Instead, she stared straight ahead at the lava lamp on the bedside table.

After a few minutes of rather awkward silence she exhaled deeply. "I always thought lava lamps were soothing. Watching the bubbles transform into different shapes, forming as one giant bubble and then stretching out and breaking apart into two."

"Now that you're talking, do you want to tell me why you wouldn't speak to Angel?"

Macy sat up, pulling a pillow from the opposite side of the bed, and curled her arms around it in a hug. "What's the point? She's another person I'll have to say goodbye to, and I'm tired of saying goodbye. Mom left me, Dad left me, and now Angel. You're the only one still here."

"Angel is coming home in a week, Macy. She didn't abandon you. She's getting the help she needs for her alcoholism." Even with her level of intelligence, matters of the heart still took a toll on her.

"What else?" Macy asked.

"What do you mean?"

"She's not only drinking, but also doing drugs, isn't she?"

"No. Angel didn't want you to know this, but she's been diagnosed with multiple sclerosis. It's a disease, which affects your brain and spinal cord. It's why you see her stumble so much. It causes you to be off balance. It can cause numbness; problems with her eyes are possible too. There is a lot I don't know about it. Together we can do research and learn how it will affect her and what we can do to help. She loves you, Macy. We need to make sure she knows we all support her or she won't make it through recovery."

Macy began to panic. "Now she thinks I hate her because I didn't come to talk to her. Can we call her back?"

I steadied her with my hands on her shoulders. "Not today. Don't worry. I told her you were in the bathroom, and you love her."

Macy's mouth dropped open in shock, and she spouted, "The bathroom? That's not embarrassing at all!"

I threw my head back in laughter and mussed her hair. "It's Angel, Macy. It's not like I told Carter."

"Never tell Carter I'm in the bathroom… even if I am."

"Deal," I promised, pulling her in for a hug. "I'm going to pick up Angel next week. Will you come with me, please?"

"Absolutely. I'm sorry, T. I shouldn't have acted like a brat earlier."

"Hey, you rarely act like a bratty teenager, so I'll let one slide." I kissed her forehead and got up off the bed. "Let's go back in and get some of the fantastic-looking dessert. I think there was a chocolate pie, and I know it's your favorite."

Macy bounced back to her old self and sprinted into the dining room. We came back to find a table covered with pies and cakes ready to be cut. Melanie stepped over to wrap her arm around my waist. "Better?" she asked, without making a scene. I nodded and bent to give her a kiss. The touch of her lips on mine made me want so much more. She uttered a soft laugh on my lips when I pushed for a deeper kiss. Gently her hand pressed against my chest as she pushed me away.

My phone vibrated in my pocket, and I had to step away to answer it. The number wasn't familiar but it was a Florida area code. I stepped outside on the front porch before answering. "Hello?"

An older woman's voice answered. "May I speak with Tristan Jacobs, please?"

"This is Tristan."

"My name is Trudy, and I'm calling from Oceanside Nursing Home." My body tensed hearing the name of the facility where my mother resided.

"Did something happen to my mother?"

"Your mother has reached the final stages, and she doesn't have much time left. She hasn't been eating on her own, and her organs are beginning to fail. We thought you and your family might want to come and say goodbye. You are the only ones listed as next of kin in her chart. Can you contact the rest of her loved ones?"

No words justified the level of despair I felt. I'd given up hope on seeing my mother again, but hearing the end was so close made it more permanent.

"Mr. Jacobs?" she asked worriedly.

"I'm here. I'll get the first flight out. Call me if anything changes." I hung up the phone before she could even acknowledge what I'd said. Dizziness and nausea washed over me. I lowered myself to the cold concrete porch. My long legs bent, my knees pulled up to my chest, and I rested my elbows on my knees with my head against my hands. Memories flooded my mind as I pushed my fingers through my hair, trying to decide what to do. *I told the nurse I'd get a flight out, but how would I tell Macy? How could I subject her to saying goodbye again? Was it even worth saying goodbye to someone who didn't remember us?*

"Tristan?" Melanie's voice pulled me from my turmoil. I turned to face her, and she could tell from the look on my face something was wrong. "What was your phone call about?" I shook my head without uttering a word. She lowered herself down on the porch next to me. "Do you want to talk about it?"

"It was the nursing home where my mother is living, if you can call it living. She has no clue who anyone is from one day to the next. She doesn't use the bathroom on her own, someone has to wipe her ass, and now she's not even eating and her organs are failing." It all spilled out of me, each word getting angrier until I was screaming. It hadn't occurred to me how loud I was until Ashton and Derrick both stepped on the porch.

"You okay, T?" Derrick stepped down in front of Melanie, putting himself between us. "Calm down, man."

Melanie patted his shoulder. "He's not angry, Derrick. He's grieving." She wrapped her arms around me and all the emotions I felt spilled out of me as I shook in her embrace. I let the tears flow, closing my eyes tightly.

"Grieving who? What happened?" Forehead creased with worry, Ashton stepped toward me.

"Can you guys give us a few minutes? I promise I'll fill you in once I know." Melanie kept her arms tightly around me as she explained this to them. The next noise I heard was the sound of the screen door shutting behind them as they marched back inside. "I'm here when you're ready to talk, Tristan. Take your time."

She held me for a few more minutes before I felt calm enough to talk. I filled her in on everything the nurse had explained to me. "What should I do?" I wanted her opinion, but mostly I wanted someone to make the decision for me.

"You have to go. She's your mother."

"She doesn't remember me though. What's the point?" I never intended to come off as a heartless ass, but no one understood the difficulty of the situation.

"The point is you will never see her again. I know you had made peace before, but there is a reason you received the call to say goodbye. You can get closure for yourself, for Macy. Tell her you love her. Everyone wants to feel loved." Normally Melanie's close proximity and soft touch would set my body on fire, but I was so numb she barely affected me.

"How do I put Macy through that heartache again?"

"She is one of the most intelligent fifteen-year-olds I've met. Ever," Melanie began.

"She's still a kid, Lanie. She didn't want to talk to Angel earlier because she told me she felt Angel will be one more person to desert her in life. How do I ask her to go say goodbye to the woman who has unconsciously caused her the most pain in her life? As smart as she is, no one can comprehend why their mother can't remember them."

Melanie pressed her hands against my face. "I'll help you."

Hearing those words from Melanie lifted a small weight off my shoulders. I'd always been alone when it came to helping Macy deal with our parents. Knowing she'd be by my side gave me greater hope for getting through the next few days.

Chapter Twenty-Eight

WE ARE A FAMILY

Before we left the Collins' house, I took Mary Jane to the side and explained everything in private so she could fill in the others once we were gone. After I had dropped Melanie off at her house, I sat Macy down to talk to her.

"It's time to go say our goodbyes to Mom, Macy." She didn't need a big explanation; like me, she knew this day would come sooner rather than later. She took the news with strength and silence. No tears shed, no words spoken. She gave a simple nod of understanding before she coasted to her room for the night. Before bed, I called Melanie to let her know everything went as well as expected.

"How's Macy?" Melanie asked the moment she picked up.

"She's fine. She took it better than I did."

"It doesn't make you weak to show emotions, honey. You're human."

"I like when you call me honey." I encouraged a subject change, and it was nice to hear the term of endearment from such an amazing woman.

She chortled tenderly. "I like how it sounds myself. Are you sure you want me going with you and Macy on this trip?"

"Absolutely. I'll admit it's probably not the ideal way to meet your boyfriend's mother, but I'd like you to be there. Even if she isn't aware of me, I want to let her know I'm happy." I'd never introduced a girlfriend to my family. In fact, I'd never considered it before.

"You are?" Melanie asked, not sounding surprised as much as questioning whether it was because of her.

"I love you, Lanie. Besides all the craziness going on with my friends and family, I've never been happier than when I'm with you." The words were true, even if they scared the hell out of me.

I heard the sound of her fingers tapping away at a keyboard and then she said, "Tickets purchased. We leave in the morning." I was both excited and nervous about Melanie going with us on this trip. Things were already so complicated in my life; I wondered when they would be too much for her to handle.

My mind raced all through the night with how things would go once we arrived at the nursing home the next day. Tossing and turning, I couldn't get a moment's rest. Daylight shone through the curtains the moment I finally got to sleep. The alarm on my phone began to blare out "Bring Me to Life." I rubbed my eyes and smacked the phone to make it stop. I hit snooze and rolled over to take advantage of the next eight minutes of silence.

After two more snoozed versions from Evanescence, I reluctantly rolled from the bed and straight to the shower. The hot spray from the massaging showerhead gave me the ability to feel more human and less zombie-like.

When the water ran cold and started to make me less of a man, I dried off and slid on my jeans. The doorbell rang, and I heard Macy shout, "Tristan! Get the door, I'm in the shower!" My lack of hot water made sense, since teenage girls seemed to live in the shower. I sacrificed a hot shower many times for her. In fact, it must have been a woman thing because Angel took forever as well.

Shirtless with my hair sopping wet, I opened the door to Melanie. Eyes raking over my half-naked form, mouth hanging open in midspeech, she stood in the doorway. She stumbled over her words. "I… um, hi. I… here." She handed me a paper bag and a cardboard carrier with three drinks in it.

"You brought breakfast? Thanks! Come inside, sweetheart." I moved aside to let her in. Setting the food and drinks down on the kitchen table, I turned to give her the proper greeting. Her hands gripped my waist as I kissed her.

"Go put on a shirt please. We don't have enough time for me to get worked up." Melanie pushed me toward the stairs. I chuckled at her adorable shyness and sprinted upstairs to grab a T-shirt. While in my room, I decided to pack my bag so we could eat breakfast and leave for the airport in time.

Tapping Macy's bathroom door with my knuckles, I called out, "Lanie's here. Get your bag packed and meet us downstairs for breakfast. We only have about an hour before we leave."

"Be right out!" Macy yelled back.

Staring at my closet wasn't getting my bag packed, but I couldn't seem to move. A light touch on my shoulder caused me to turn around swiftly, almost knocking Melanie down. "Did I scare you?" she asked. "I called your name twice, but you didn't answer."

"You did? I never heard a thing." Somehow I completely blocked the world out for a few minutes.

Melanie took my hand and led me over to the bed to sit. "You were staring at your closet pretty intensely. Are you nervous about today?"

"This is going to sound stupid but I was looking for something nice to wear. She hasn't seen me in over a year."

"Doesn't sound stupid to me."

"She isn't going to remember me being her son, let alone remember it's been a year since she saw me. I doubt she'll judge me on my choice of T-shirt and jeans as attire instead of a dress shirt and slacks." My anger had subsided, and I'd moved toward sadness over the situation.

Without a sound, Melanie moved toward my closet. She pulled out a few plain colored T-shirts and nice jeans. Lastly, she pulled out a dark maroon button-down dress shirt and black slacks. "It's not stupid, Tristan. She may not remember you, but you remember her. Saying goodbye is for you, in this case. If you put this stuff in your bag, I'll go check on Macy and see if she has the same dilemma."

My bags were finally packed so I checked on the girls. Through a cracked door, I heard Melanie speaking to Macy. "Tristan would never make you speak to her if you didn't want to. Tell him how you feel."

Macy sniffed back tears. "I don't want to disappoint him."

"You could never disappoint him. He loves you more than anything in this world, Macy. He'd never make you do something you didn't want to do. I'm going to tell you a secret though. If you go with him, it will give him the strength he needs to say goodbye too. He's more scared than you are." I'd been a teenager when my mother's health began deteriorating so it had hit me harder than Macy because I had more time with her.

"He is?" Macy asked, looking up at Melanie with confusion. Though I didn't want to admit it to myself how afraid I was, Melanie had it right. She apparently saw through my tough façade on the entire thing.

Macy asked Melanie to help her choose a dress to wear, so I eased away from the door and let them have a few private moments. Time ticked away as I sat on the couch with my bag next to me.

"Hello?" Mary Jane called out as she opened the front door. She saw me on the couch and sat beside me. "You ready to go?"

"I thought Derrick was driving us to the airport? You're supposed to have your feet up."

"I'm driving, which involves sitting. You know I'm

stubborn. Derrick wanted to come, but I asked him to let me. I wish I could go with you. I don't want you and Macy doing this on your own." She placed her hand over mine and squeezed.

"They won't be alone," Melanie commented as she came down the stairs.

Mary Jane appeared surprised to see her and then replied, "Oh good. I'm thankful you're going with them. I had no idea."

Melanie gave Mary Jane a quick hug as she sat down next to her. "Like you, I couldn't bear to see them go through it alone. Macy is upstairs finishing her packing, but I gave her a two-minute warning."

When Macy came downstairs with her bags, I took them outside to fill the minivan up. Only planning to stay for three days, we each had one bag for carry on.

Mary Jane let us out at the drop-off spot in the airport. Melanie and Macy started inside with their bags, and I stopped to give Mary Jane a hug. "If you need to talk or anything, don't hesitate to call me. I wish I could be there with you. I love you both."

"We love you too, MJ. I'll call you after I see her. Don't have the baby before we get back." I gave her a quick kiss on the cheek and made sure she got back in the car and drove off without any issues before I ran to catch up with Melanie and Macy.

Once through the security gate, we still had an hour before our flight. The holiday weekend brought quite a crowd to the terminal. Every restaurant had lines with at least ten to twelve people, and they didn't seem to be moving quickly. We had been so distracted at the house getting ready we'd left the breakfast on the table without eating. Melanie had thought ahead and pulled out a box of Pop-Tarts handing us each one. "I packed these in case we needed a quick breakfast over the next couple of days."

The seats at the gate didn't allow for much cuddling, but Melanie still managed to wrap her arm around me and lean her head in, staying as close as possible. It was what I needed to keep from falling apart. Mostly I was terrified of how Mom would react and whether bringing Macy would be worse than not saying goodbye at all.

Chapter Twenty-Nine

A MOTHER'S LOVE

In Florida, we rented a car at the airport. We checked into our hotel, and Macy put on a dress while I put on my dress shirt and slacks. My hands trembled with nerves as I tried to button everything up. Melanie noticed and placed her hands over mine to stop me. She finished fastening my shirt and then smiled and whispered, "You look very handsome. You're going to be fine, and Macy will too."

One thing I loved about her, she always seemed to know exactly what I needed to hear. She grasped my hand, and as we were leaving, I noticed she took Macy's too. She also offered to drive while I sat next to Macy in the back seat.

"You okay, squirt?" Wrapping one arm around her shoulder, I placed my free hand over hers.

"I guess. I'm not sure what to say when we see her."

"It'll come to you. I'm not sure what to say myself either." Macy grasped my hand and held it tightly for the remainder of the ride. When the hospital came into view, her breathing sped up, and I noticed she started to panic a bit. "Kiddo, you can stay with Lanie if you don't want to do this."

"No. I need to be there with you."

"I love you, squirt," I whispered and then kissed the top of her head.

The nurse at registration recognized me from when I visited before. "Tristan? I didn't expect to see you again."

"We came to say goodbye. Has she gotten worse?"

The nurse placed her hand over mine and offered a sad smile. "I'm sorry, Tristan. She passed away an hour ago."

Melanie embraced Macy, who began to cry the moment she heard the news. The sounds intensified around me; machines beeped louder, Macy's sobs grew heavier, and I could hear my heart beating. The nurse's voice was the only thing I couldn't hear anymore. My head spun with images of my mother before her diagnosis. Macy barely had much memory of her, but for the first fourteen years of my life, I had an amazing mother.

"Tristan!" my mother called out. I was supposed to be on the playground with my friends, but I'd wandered off into the woods behind it. Her voice grew more frantic as she yelled my name. Finally, I came running out and saw her cheeks covered with tears as she looked around anxiously. She spotted me and ran over to snatch me up in her arms. She spun around, holding me against her tightly, pressing

my head against her chest. "Don't ever scare me so much again!"

That night when she put me to bed she asked me why I'd run away. "You were talking to your friends, and Tommy dared me to go into the woods with him. Since you were talking, I didn't think you'd miss me."

"I'll always miss you when you aren't around. You're my little Tristan-bull."

"I'm sorry I ran away today, Mommy. Do you still love me?"

"Always and forever, Tristan."

"Tristan?" Melanie's voice brought me back to the present. Her face crinkled with concern as she waited for me to answer. "Tristan, let's take them up on the offer of the private room where we can talk."

The nurse had mentioned a private room for families to congregate. I followed behind them silently, still lost in memories.

My mother always picked me up after school. Normally she was the first one in the pickup line, standing there smiling with her arms open as I ran to the car. One Thursday afternoon in third grade, she didn't show up. The teacher took me inside to the principal's office when I was the last one waiting for a ride. I sat outside in the hallway while they called my parents. She ran into the building. "Tristan! I'm sorry sweetheart. My car had a flat tire."

"I thought you forgot me."

"Nothing could ever make me forget you. You're my favorite special little man and all I think about is you."

"Drink this," Melanie commanded, offering me a steamy cup of coffee.

"Thanks." That was the first word I'd spoken since hearing the news. It shocked Melanie as much as it stunned me. Her face relaxed into a compassionate smile as I came back into the world with them.

"Macy," I spoke her name realizing I hadn't checked for her reaction.

"I'm fine, Tristan. I miss her, but she left a long time ago." The fifteen-year-old was taking it better than the twenty-four-year-old.

"The nurse informed me your mother is still in the room, waiting for transport. You can go in and say your goodbyes if you'd like. Or you can wait for the funeral. We'll have to make arrangements soon, Tristan. I know this is hard, but I'll help however I can."

"Thanks."

"I'm going to leave you two alone and go check with the nurses about how to make arrangements." Melanie used the excuse as a chance to give me time to see how Macy was holding up. She loved Melanie, but she hadn't known her very long, and she may have felt embarrassed to talk too much about her feelings.

Before I could ask again how she was doing, Macy began to tell a story. "I have a couple of memories before Mom got sick. I was five and I wanted one of those fancy dollhouses. She told me we couldn't afford one because they cost half her week's pay. Instead, she gathered up shoe boxes from all her friends and glued them together to make rooms. The lids were perfect for forming a roof and patio. She covered the outside with construction paper and left the inside blank. When she presented it to me, she told me we'd decorate the rooms together. We made furniture from Popsicle sticks and pipe cleaners. It ended up being the best dollhouse in the world."

"Wow, Macy. I don't remember your dollhouse."

"We worked on it the summer you'd gone camping. You probably never paid attention to it in my room."

"What happened to it?"

"I tried to bring it when we moved. It fell apart when I tried to move it. I got angry and threw it away." Macy's eyes stared at the floor as she relived the sad memory.

The door creaked open, and Melanie popped her head inside. "Hey, there's someone here who claims he knew your mother. He'd like to speak to you?"

I nodded approval as I tried to imagine who was about to come through the door. When his face came into view, I stood up knocking the chair back. Melanie caught it before it fell over. "What are you doing here?"

My father stood there with a smile on his face as if we should be happy to see him. It began to fade as he realized we weren't. "I left my number with one of the nurses and asked her to call me personally when your mother passed."

"What? So you wanted to be divorced from her and never see her again but wanted to make sure you knew the minute she was dead?"

"Don't act like I'm the only one who left. You and Macy moved hundreds of miles away." His indignant behavior angered me.

"We left to spare ourselves the heartache of a mother who didn't know us on top of a father who abandoned us! Don't pretend as though we are anything like you." Stepping forward, I was nose to nose with the man I despised. I clenched my fists trying to convince myself not to punch him, though I desperately wanted to.

Melanie moved to Macy's side. I hadn't noticed she was crying. "I'm going to take Macy to the cafeteria. She doesn't need to be around this. You two need to sit down and talk this over. You're in a hospital environment. People do not need to hear such anger." She gave me a quick kiss on the cheek. "Text me if you need me back here."

"Beautiful woman you have there. How long have you been together?"

"None of your business. You lost the privilege to know anything about me when you skipped out on us six years ago. You can't even imagine the hell Macy has been through because of you." Assuming he could show up and reenter our lives as though he'd done nothing wrong angered me the most.

The last time I spoke with him was the day he'd come to me with the paperwork. He handed me a manila envelope with documents to look over and informed me he'd answer any questions I had. He explained how taking care of my mother had taken a toll on him. *Poor baby, a grown adult dumping his problems on his children.* He couldn't handle seeing her losing her mind, couldn't handle not having a wife waiting at home for him each evening. *Who cares if his children would be abandoned by two parents?* Taking care of Macy was too much for him alone. He loved her but felt I could raise her better. A businessman with a steady job and tenure felt a kid just graduating high school with no job would be a better father. If it hadn't been incredibly pathetic, I might have laughed.

"You never even told Macy goodbye. Once I signed the paperwork, you whisked away leaving her a note. 'Be good for your brother' with a check for ten thousand dollars to get us started. I stretched the money to supplement my income while I worked as many odds-and-ends jobs as possible. I'd graduated from high school at the top of my class expecting to go to college. Instead, I spent my life flipping burgers, waiting tables, picking up garbage, cutting lawns, and finally I landed a job at Disney where our lives changed completely, no thanks to you."

"Why did you leave Disney? I could find you in Florida and then you disappeared." Something still made the man believe he deserved an explanation of anything I'd done to survive.

"The job at Disney gave me the opportunity to take Macy there since she'd never been. It gave me a chance to offer her some semblance of a normal childhood. We visited Mom up until we moved. We were going three times a week, and then it trickled down to once a week and finally to about once a month. Each visit I asked the nurse if you'd been by, and every time it was the same answer. After signing away your children and divorcing your wife, you never looked back. And now you want to question my choices, my lifestyle, or living arrangements?" He was a coward, and I wanted nothing to do with him; even being in the same room with him made me sick.

"I care about my children and what happens to them."

I laughed. "Really? Well, you saw Macy. She's gorgeous and the most intelligent fifteen-year-old I've ever known." I stood up and walked toward the door. "We're arranging the funeral. If you come, don't speak to us unless we speak to you. Stay away from Macy."

"You can't keep my daughter from me, Tristan."

Holding back my laughter took all the strength I had left. "I'm not like you. I won't take the choice from her. As I was saying, stay away from Macy unless she comes to you. I'll ask her if she wants to speak to you. It's her choice, no one will force her to speak to you." He handed me a business card with his number on it. I still had it programmed in my phone, thinking one day I might need to speak to him again. I wouldn't admit this to him though.

"Don't pretend to think you know why I left. You think you've been through hell? I have missed every moment of the last six years of my children's lives. The woman I've loved for thirty years died not knowing who I was, what we shared, or the two lives we created out of love. I've been through hell too."

"You didn't have to leave," I stated through gritted teeth.

"I did. Perhaps one day you'll understand why." Gesturing out into the hall he asked, "The woman you love out there, do you want to marry her?"

"I told you it's none of your business." No part of my life

was his business, not since the day he left.

"Let's say you do love her. Imagine for a moment you go to see her one day, and you mention a memory of your first date. She doesn't remember it. You may shrug it off as no big deal and move on without a second thought. One day she leaves your five-year-old daughter on the playground by herself for hours because she forgot she had brought her there. You get a call at work from the police officer who found her crying on the swings late at night. You have to fight child services to prove you aren't a neglectful parent." No matter what sob story he provided, I refused to let him get to me.

"Then you have to make the decision to put the woman you love in a hospital so she has constant monitoring. You go to see her every day. You take her a bouquet of her favorite flowers and play your song of twenty years hoping to see her smile. Instead, she smacks the flowers out of your hand and screams for the nurses saying a stranger is in her room. I hope you never experience such pain, Tristan. I hope you get to live to a ripe old age with the love of your life. I pray she remembers every second of your time together. You can call me a coward, and I agree. You're stronger than me, and Macy needed someone strong. Don't think for one second I don't know what kind of pain you've gone through."

His words stabbed at me. I knew the pain because I'd experienced it from a different angle. It didn't justify the fact he abandoned his two children in my eyes. I couldn't feel sorry for him and forgive him so easily. "I have to go. I need to get back to Macy." I exited the room without responding to his guilt-trip story.

In the cafeteria, Melanie and Macy had their heads together in a serious-looking conversation. "You ready to go back to the hotel, squirt?"

"Is he coming?" she asked with fear in her eyes.

"No. I told him not to speak to you unless you came to him first. I won't keep you from talking to him if it's what you want, but I won't force you to talk to him either."

"You've been a better dad to me than he would have ever been, Tristan."

My voice caught in my throat as I choked back tears. I struggled to take care of her and had always been scared she'd resent me, thinking I hadn't done enough.

"Why don't we go to the hotel and take advantage of their indoor pool. We need a little relaxation," Melanie suggested.

"Sounds great to me," I replied.

Relaxation was exactly what I needed. Not that I expected to find any. With Macy and Melanie though, I'd do my best to put on a good front. Knowing my father was in town made it hard to find any kind of peace.

CHAPTER THIRTY

SO MANY EMOTIONS

Macy changed into her swimsuit and grabbed a towel the moment we stepped into the hotel room. "Can I go on down while you guys get ready?"

"Sure, kiddo. I need to talk to Lanie a moment. We'll be down shortly."

The door shut, and I turned to Melanie, who appeared concerned. "We need to talk?"

"Talking isn't what I need. I need you." My fingers dug into her waist as I pulled her against me. Our mouths moved together as our hands pulled at the clothes hindering our connection. As my hands fumbled with the clasp of her bra, I dipped my head to taste her skin. She moaned as my tongue grazed the nape of her neck. Her hands moved to my boxers, pushing them down before she moved towards the bed. Grabbing a condom from my bag, I slipped it on as I gazed at her naked body in front of me.

Propped above her, I left the world of emotional despair and entered her world of ecstasy and love. She rolled over on top of me, and I lay back to enjoy the ride, my escape from reality. When we both reached our peaks, she fell forward, pressing her face next to mine. Melanie whispered in my ear, "I'm here. Let everything out." I enveloped her in my arms and held her tightly as I released the emotions I'd bottled up.

Her skin against mine was smooth as silk. As I let the emotions out, I ran my hands over her porcelain skin, relishing the feel of her body on top of me. I wanted to get lost in passion with her again instead of feeling this pain. I rolled over and began to make love to her once more. She cried out in surprise as I entered her, and the next noise from her mouth was a sigh of pure bliss as we disappeared together again. I grabbed the headboard and held on as I pushed deeper, flew higher.

After the second round, we were both spent. We lay on our backs gasping for air as we stared at the ceiling. I rolled over and pressed my lips to her shoulder. "I love you so much, Lanie. I couldn't have gotten through this trip without you here."

"I love you, Tristan."

"Shit. We didn't grab a new condom." It occurred to me in my need to forget reality I didn't stop to put on a new rubber for our second time. Unwanted pregnancies resulted from such stupid mistakes.

"Don't worry. I'm on the pill so we should be fine. And I have regular checkups each year so I know I'm clean." Her eyes drifted up to mine curiously.

"I'm clean too. I've never been without a condom with anyone else. And I've been checked." After my one-night stand with Angel, considering the amount of our promiscuity combined, I made sure to get tested just in case. The used condom wrapper implied we were safe, but as drunk as we were, I wanted to be sure.

"Okay, now that's settled, we need to get downstairs to be there for Macy."

I jumped up. "You're right. I didn't mean for us to be up here so long."

"You won't hear me complain," she replied with a wink.

The pool area was loud with a few young kids screaming and splashing. Macy sat in the corner of the deep end talking to another girl who appeared to be her age. She waved us over as we stepped out of our shoes and slipped into the water. As we approached, the other girl swam back to her family. "We didn't mean to chase off your friend."

"It's no big deal. She saw me by myself and wanted to chat. She's from Wisconsin, and they're here for the beach and to visit Disney. I told her we were here to see family."

"Have you thought about talking to Dad?"

"I don't want to," Macy answered without pause.

"Then you don't have to." No one would cause her any more pain if I had anything to say about it.

Melanie interjected, "While you two were in there talking, I called the funeral home. We are to meet with the director first thing in the morning to start the arrangements. For tonight, why don't we swim for a bit and then order room service and relax."

The crowd at the pool died down after about an hour, and we took advantage of the empty room to swim for a little while longer. Once our skin started to prune, we decided it was time to head upstairs again.

Room service delivered an hour after we ordered. We had burgers, chicken tenders, and fries for dinner with ice cream for dessert. My phone rang in the middle of our meal, another number I didn't recognize with a Florida area code. I stepped away in case somehow our father had found my number. "Tristan Jacobs," I answered, to avoid the question later.

"Mr. Jacobs, my name is Harvey Windsor. I'm your mother's attorney and the executor of her Last Will and Testament. I'd like to offer my condolences for your mother's passing."

"Thank you. How did you get my number?"

"I called your father who had a Florida number for you, but he told me you'd moved out of state. I ran a background check which gave me your new number and address. I need to speak with you regarding the details of her will. How long will you be in town?"

"Only for two more days, long enough for the funeral," I responded. The idea my mother had a will never occurred to me. It never dawned on me she had any assets to leave.

"I'm booked pretty solid for the next few days, but I'll have my secretary reschedule a few appointments if you could meet with me tomorrow?"

"Sure." He gave me the address of his office with a time that worked out perfectly. We could go straight there after making arrangements.

Macy's phone rang while I finished up with the attorney. When she finished talking to whoever was on the line, she handed it to me. "It's MJ."

"Hey, Mary Jane."

"Macy told me about today. I'm sorry, T. Is there anything I can do?" Her voice alone gave me comfort.

"No, but thanks. I was on the phone with my mother's attorney when you called. I heard you beep in but couldn't change over."

"It's fine, sweetie. How's Lanie holding up?"

I stepped out of the room to answer her question. "She's been a lifesaver for both Macy and me. She's one of a kind, MJ. We haven't been together long, and this family drama doesn't spook her. I've been thinking a lot the last couple of days, about the future. I think I'm going to ring shop when I get home. What do you think?"

A loud squeal resonated from the line, causing the connection to cut out. "In case I was unclear, I think it's a fantastic idea."

I laughed for the first time in two days. "I love you, MJ."

The door shut behind me, and I turned to see Melanie standing there. "I wanted to make sure you were okay." She must have only heard the last part of the conversation, and I could see the hurt in her eyes.

"I'm good, give me one second." Back on the phone, I said, "I'll call you tomorrow if I get the chance, to let you know how things go with the attorney and the funeral home. We'll come see you when we get home too. Take care of yourself."

"You too. Love you, T."

Placing the cell phone in my pocket, I prepared to explain myself to Melanie. Before I could speak, she explained, "It's weird to hear you say you love her because I know the history you have. It throws me for a loop, but I'm not jealous, and I do understand it. Let's move on now."

Again, I felt myself laughing for a change, and it felt good. "Moving on. Mind if we call it a night? I'm exhausted."

"Sounds perfect. Macy's tired too. Her eyelids were heavy during dinner. You both need a good night's sleep."

The day's emotional roller coaster had left me exhausted. A good night's sleep would be the first step to starting fresh in the morning. I was positive the next day would be another heart-rending experience.

Macy asked to stay at the hotel the next day while we made the arrangements and spoke with the attorney. I didn't argue with her on the matter. She had been through enough emotional turmoil this weekend already. The director scheduled the funeral for the following day. It would be a very small occasion, immediate family only. After details had been finalized, I texted my father with the particulars and told him Macy didn't want to speak with him. He responded, stating he would respect our wishes on the matter.

When I arrived at the attorney's office, I expected to find my father sitting there too, but he wasn't. Mr. Windsor welcomed us inside and motioned to the seats in front of his desk. "Are you Mrs. Jacobs?"

"Not yet. This is Lanie, my girlfriend." I didn't mean to say not yet; it came out before I could stop myself. Melanie seemed pleasantly surprised at the answer. "When did my mother make this will?"

"After your little sister's birth, she decided to get the genetic testing to determine if she had the markers for Alzheimer's. She'd found it had occurred to several relatives in her genealogy. When her test came back showing a high risk for the disease, she wanted to protect the two of you if something happened to her."

"What about my father?"

"She had strict instructions if they were divorced, then he was to be excluded from any details of these proceedings."

"I don't understand. They seemed happy, why would she assume they'd be divorced?"

Mr. Windsor opened a file and pulled a manila envelope from it. "Your mother put all the paperwork in here and wanted to leave this with the will including a few other things in case he tried to contest the contents."

"Can I see what is inside?"

Melanie placed her hand on top of mine. "Are you sure you want to know? He abandoned her in the worse part of her life, do you need more reason to detest the man?"

Mr. Windsor cleared his throat and leaned forward with his hands folded in front of him. "In all honesty, I have no clue what the envelope holds. But son, she was fighting a disease that messes with your brain. Whatever's there may not be anything more than a fear she brought into reality."

"I'll hang onto the envelope in case we need it later. Maybe we'll get lucky, and he'll leave us alone. What's in the will?" I didn't need material things; I simply wanted this day over with already.

"Your mother set up a trust for you and Macy. You each have a fund with twenty thousand dollars in it. Any bank accounts were to be transferred to you in the event of her death as a divorced woman. The total of her bank accounts adds up to seventy thousand dollars." If I hadn't been sitting down, I'd have fallen over in shock.

"How did she have all of this money? We grew up cutting coupons, making toys from trash, and wearing hand-me-downs from cousins. I don't understand where this came from?"

"Besides being her attorney, I was your mother's friend. She believed saving for your college and future was more sensible than giving you expensive toys and clothes as a child. As for Macy, I understand you have custody of her?"

"Yes, sir."

"Then you will be in charge of her inheritance until she turns eighteen." Inheritance sounded like a foreign word to me.

"Wait, she's in her senior year of high school. She'll be

in college two years before she turns eighteen. Can we use the money for school?"

"My recommendation would be to use the main account and when she turns eighteen, give her control over her money through a bank account. The stipulation shows no access to her account until her eighteenth birthday. Fighting would probably take more time than it's worth."

"Fair enough. I'm sorry. I don't know what to say. I'm in shock about this whole thing."

"I understand completely. All I need from you is a few signatures, and I can turn everything over to you once the paperwork is complete. Because your father was named in the will, I have to inform him why. He'll be meeting me later today. He asked for a separate meeting for your sake, which seems like a good sign. But, if he decides to contest the will, things could get ugly."

"I understand. Will you call me after your meeting?" I didn't need more surprises where my father was concerned.

"I will." He stood and extended his hand to me. As I grasped his hand in a firm shake, he stated with sincerity, "Your mother was a good woman. I'm sorry you and Macy didn't have more time with her."

"Thank you, sir." I pressed my hand against Melanie's back leading her out the door. We walked in silence. I was left speechless by the entire meeting, and Melanie seemed to be waiting for me to speak. She would glance up at me with a smile and look away when I said nothing. I held the envelope out to Melanie. "Can you hold onto this for me? Only give it back to me if I ask?"

"And you're sure you don't want to look?" She must have noticed my confusion because she continued by saying, "I know I suggested you don't, but this is your family. It's your decision whether you want to read it or put it in the past."

"I'm going to wait and see how the next few days go. If Macy wants a chance with him, I don't want to know what's in that envelope."

"What if it's something proving Macy shouldn't be near him?"

The thought had crossed my mind as well. "If it was something terrible, my mother would have told me, not left it in a letter."

She nodded and tucked it away in her purse.

In the car, Melanie reached over to take my hand before I turned the key in the ignition. "Not yet?" she asked with a small hopeful smile.

"You caught that, huh?"

"A little bit. Do you think we're marriage material?"

Bringing her hand to my mouth, I gave it a soft kiss. "I hope so."

"Me too," she replied softly.

If I could sweep Melanie off her feet and have the happily ever after moment she dreamed of, I'd do it in a second. Life wasn't as simple as just wishing for something and making it happen. My father's reappearance had ignited new fears inside me. With Macy, I'd been a better father than he'd ever been. Would I be a better husband than he was too? Or would I abandon Melanie the way he'd left my mother.

Chapter Thirty-One

IT'S SO HARD TO SAY GOODBYE

The funeral went as well as any funeral could. Other than the few nurses who came to pay their respects, the room held only Melanie, Macy, and me. During the service, I noticed my father sitting at the back of the chapel. When it was over, he turned to leave, respecting my wishes of not speaking to Macy. My mother requested she be cremated, so there would be no burial to attend.

"I'll be back in a minute," I leaned over and whispered to Melanie. I needed to get closure. "Mr. Jacobs," I called out.

He turned, shocked to see it was me. "I don't deserve to be called Dad now?"

"Dad's don't walk away."

"Fine. What do you want, Tristan? I did as you asked and

came quietly and was trying to leave quietly." He fiddled with his key ring, looking anywhere but straight at me. When I didn't speak, he peered up with red, swollen eyes. He'd been crying over a woman he deserted at the worst point in her life.

I refused to let him affect me. "Did Mom's lawyer contact you?"

"Yes. I won't contest the will. It's the least I can do for you two. I signed off on his paperwork. It's all yours."

He began to walk away, and I called out to him again. "Dad." One word stopped him in his tracks.

"If Macy changes her mind one day and wants to talk to you, I have your number, so she has the chance. You have mine, and you can call and check in with me anytime. I won't make her talk to you, ever. It will be her decision alone. She may not be an adult officially, but she acts more like one than most of the people I know. She's been hurt a lot too, and I won't be the one to allow her to be hurt by you."

"Thank you, son, this gesture means more than you know."

Macy's happiness came before any grudge I had toward our father. Each gesture I made was with her in mind. "One more thing. Macy graduates this coming May. I'll text you the info. Again, you can come and sit in the back. When it gets closer, I'll ask her if she wants you there. I'll text you so you know it's safe to show your face to her. Do we have an understanding?"

You'd think I'd given him a million dollars the way his

face lit up. "You don't owe me anything, Tristan. The fact you want to do this for me means the world."

"None of this is for you. It's for Macy."

"I agree. And no matter what you think about my decision to leave, I know I did the right thing by having you raise her. She's a beautiful young woman, and you've been a wonderful influence on her." I didn't fucking need him to tell me anything about how Macy turned out.

Anger boiled inside of me. I regretted opening up to him. If he knew how many times we had been close to eviction or how often I had begged a neighbor for food for Macy. I learned the schedule at the grocery store for the days they offered the most samples, and it saved me from eating food at home those days. Ramen noodles were a staple in our house. The first couple of years, I was so scared I couldn't take care of Macy I almost put her in foster care. It would've killed me to do, but getting the job at Disney saved my life.

After a few deep inhalations, I simply responded with "Thank you. Macy makes it easy. She's about the best teenager ever."

"And the young woman with you, she's quite beautiful. How long have you been together?"

"About six months."

"I can tell you love her." His statement made me sick to my stomach. As though I wanted to hear him tell me he recognized love? He was the last person I wanted to compliment me on a relationship. Again, I bit my tongue.

"I do. Macy's very fond of her as well. I need to get back to them now, thank you for coming today." Reluctantly I shoved my hand toward him to shake. He surprised me by taking it and then pulled me into a hug. At first my body stiffened in shock. After a moment, I reciprocated the hug.

"If she asks, tell Macy I was here and I love her, please?"

"If she asks, I won't lie to her about you being here." Part of me hoped she asked. As much as I hated him, I wanted Macy to know she was loved. But I gave her the choice, and I wouldn't push.

Inside the funeral home, Melanie had her arms around Macy as she stroked her hair and spoke softly to her. I couldn't hear the words, but I knew Melanie enough to guess they were what Macy needed to hear. My phone rang grabbing their attention. I mouthed "sorry" before stepping back outside to answer the call.

"Derrick?"

"Hey, T. I'm sorry about your mom. MJ filled me in. I wish we could have been there for you."

"It's okay. Macy and I are fine. How are things there?" Talking about work was better than thinking about the last several years of my life.

"That's why I called. MJ's in labor. We wanted to make sure you knew your namesake was on his way into the world." A huge grin filled my face. My family was welcoming a new member. No matter how hard the move had been, being in Nashville had given us back the family we lacked in Florida. It made me homesick for Tennessee.

I laughed at his announcement. "You called at exactly the right time like MJ always does. I needed good news. As soon as we get home tomorrow, I'll call to see if we can come to the hospital. How is she?"

"Good. Everyone is here with us, except you guys. We all miss you, and we're all thinking about you."

"Thanks, man. It means a lot. Tell her I'll see her soon," I said.

"I'll tell her you love her too, T. See you guys soon. Have a safe trip home." Derrick and Ashton Collins had to be two of the nicest guys ever born on this planet. The person who decided nice guys finished last hadn't met those two.

As my two favorite girls stepped outside, I shouted, "Mary Jane's in labor!"

Macy squealed with excitement and ran to hug me. Her face was still red and puffy from crying; her hair matted to her face from sweat and tears combined. Through all the grief and despair, she felt joy over this news, and it let me know she'd get through this just fine.

"Can we go see her as soon as we get home?" Macy asked.

"Absolutely. I already told Derrick we'd be there. You'll come with us, right?" I posed the question to Melanie, so she didn't feel left out.

"Of course. Is everything with the estate settled?"

"Yeah, it is. I wish we could leave tonight."

"I need to make a phone call," Melanie excused herself.

Macy asked the question I feared coming. "Did I see Dad?"

"He was here. He wanted you to know he loves you."

For a brief moment, her eyes lit up. It broke my heart a little. "Oh" was all she said.

"He respected your wishes about not talking to him. However, I did get his number and told him if you want to talk to him someday, I'd give it to you. It's completely up to you, Mace. I'd never keep you from him if you wanted to get to know him again."

She flung her arms around me tightly. "Thanks, T. One day I might want to. I'm not ready yet."

"We can fly out tonight if you two are ready," Melanie called out as she held her phone to her ear. "I paid to have our flights rescheduled."

"Thank you!" Macy and I replied in unison.

We wasted no time getting back to the hotel and packing up. All three of us were anxious to get back home. And three hours later, we were on an airplane on our way back to Nashville.

After saying goodbye to my mother, I was ready to close the Florida chapter of my life.

Chapter Thirty-Two

NEW BEGINNINGS

The frigid air in Nashville was a shock to our system after the warmth of Florida. Before we boarded the airplane, Melanie contacted a friend of hers to give us a ride to the hospital. Familiar faces filled the waiting room when we arrived. We were swallowed up in hugs repeatedly by Ashton, Gracie, Cameron, Gavin, Katelyn, and Maria, who was Derrick and Ashton's mom. Each offered condolences with a comment about how much they missed us. Moments like these were the reason I moved Macy to Nashville without too much thought. She needed a family, and they'd become ours.

"Is he here yet?"

"Not yet," Ashton answered. "Derrick is back there with her. I know she'll be happy to see you. She has been worried about you."

"I can't wait to see them all."

Derrick burst into the room. "It's a boy!" The statement came as no surprise; we all knew it was a boy. I suppose it's better than saying, "It's a baby!" The room erupted in cheers all around. Derrick was the next one bombarded in hugs. When he spotted me, his smile widened. "You made it!" He grabbed me in a hug and tugged me toward the door. "I want you to be the first to meet him."

Mary Jane's hair was pulled back into a ponytail, and she was sweaty and looked as though she hadn't slept in a week. Witnessing her staring at her baby boy with such love made her look like the most beautiful woman in the world. Derrick gave me a light push into the room and then shut the door leaving us alone.

She glanced up and gasped. "Tristan," she whispered happily. I leaned over and kissed her cheek. "Do you want to hold him?"

She placed him in my arms, and I watched his tiny face scrunch in different positions. His wrinkled brow, his tiny nose, his bright pink lips, ten tiny fingers, and moving the blanket, I checked and found ten tiny toes. "He's beautiful, MJ."

"Thank you. I'd like to think I had something to do with that," she teased.

"He looks like you. He has Derrick's dark hair though." I kissed his forehead and handed him back to her.

"I thought you weren't coming in until tomorrow?" Bouncing the baby gently in her arms, she made faces at him as she spoke.

"Lanie arranged for us to come home early when she found out you were in labor. I have so much to tell you about my trip. Maybe when you get home, I can come by and visit."

"Not maybe. You better."

"All right, quit hogging the baby now," Cameron demanded as he barged into the room. "Hand him over."

Cameron confiscated the baby from Mary Jane, freeing her arms. She held them out to me, and I leaned in to hug her. "I'm so glad you're home. We missed you and Macy. Katelyn has been asking about her nonstop."

I hadn't had a chance to explain the will information to Macy, so I had to be quiet as I relayed the message to Mary Jane. I moved my mouth to her ear and whispered, "I have the money to pay you and Derrick back for camp. And I have more than enough to send Macy to college next year."

Mary Jane beamed with excitement but kept things quiet. We researched for hours on ways I could afford Macy's college education. There was a high chance she would get an academic scholarship, but in the event she didn't, I needed a backup plan. Derrick and Ashton had offered to give us a loan I could pay back over the years. With the inheritance, I could make sure Macy achieved everything she wanted.

Taking a moment, I glanced around the room noticing everyone cooing over the baby or checking on Mary Jane. Gracie handed Craig to Melanie, and it looked like the most natural thing in the world for her to hold the baby. She didn't seem nervous at all. Though she was smiling, her eyelids were heavy. It hadn't occurred to me how much she had been through the last few days; she had to be as exhausted as I felt.

Once she handed the baby back to Derrick, I announced, "Congratulations you two. He's a handsome kid. I don't want to run, but we've had a long day, and I need to get my girls home."

Hugs were handed out again with promises of getting together for a celebration once Mary Jane and Craig were home. The three of us had stepped out of the door before I remembered we'd been dropped off. "Shoot," I mumbled.

Melanie chuckled. "Did you have the same realization I did just now? We have no car?"

We both broke out in a fit of delirious laughter with Macy staring at us in confusion. We must have been loud because Cameron opened the door and asked, "What's so funny, Tri-Stud?"

"We have no car," I emphasized each word through bursts of laughter, my stomach aching at the hilarity. It wouldn't have been as funny if we hadn't both been sleep-deprived.

Cameron gave a small laugh, nothing close to the ridiculous guffawing coming from Melanie and me. "Give me a second." A moment later, he returned keys in hand. "I'll give you a ride home. Where's your luggage?"

"My friend Sara dropped us off. She's leaving the luggage in my garage, so we didn't have to bring it in the hospital." Melanie offered an explanation since she calmed down from her fit of laughter. "Tristan thought we could bum a ride with one of you guys, but in all the excitement, we completely forgot to ask."

"Have no fear, SuperCam is here. You two need some sleep."

Melanie and Macy took the backseat together. Halfway home they grew quiet, and I turned to see Melanie's head resting against the window with Macy's head against Melanie's shoulder. Both were sound asleep and looked adorable.

"Have you heard from Angel since Thanksgiving?"

"I saw her yesterday. I told her about your mom because I knew she'd want to know. She sent her love and—" He reached into the console between us and pulled out an envelope. "—she sent you this letter." I folded the letter and placed it in my pocket to read when I was more alert.

"How's she holding up?"

"Angel is one tough chica. She looked fabulous. She was a bit weak, so they had her using a wheelchair. She told me it has been good for her being in there because she never misses a dose of medicine. They are on top of it."

"Good. I've been thinking about her a lot. I hate she spent Thanksgiving in there alone. At least she'll be out in time for Christmas with everyone."

"Angel's been through a lot, and she bounces back like a champ every time. Not to be nosy, but did your dad show up for the funeral?" I laughed out loud, startling Cam a little at first. "What's so funny?" he asked, confused.

"Not to be nosy? Isn't it painful for you… not being nosy, I mean?"

Cameron nodded and replied, "Touché."

"To answer your question though, yes, he did show up.

It was awkward, but it's over now. All I want is to go home and get some sleep. None of us slept well in the hotel room. We're all emotionally drained."

"I get it. In all seriousness, I'm glad you're home. And on that note, you are *officially* home."

Once in the driveway, I woke the girls, who grumbled out moans and groans at being disturbed. Cameron let Macy lean on him while I lifted Melanie out of the back and carried her inside. I accompanied Cameron to the door and thanked him for the ride.

Macy yawned, mouth agape, arms stretched above her head, and then gave me a hug. "I'm going to bed. You two could use some alone time I'm sure. Love you, T."

"Love you too, squirt."

I left Melanie on the couch for a moment and went to use the restroom after the long drive. With a moment alone, I reached into my pocket and pulled out the letter from Angel.

Tristan,

Cameron told me about your mom. I wish I could have been there for you. I'm sorry for all the complications I've added to your life lately. You have so many responsibilities already, and I made things worse. I hope one day you will forgive me for all the trouble I caused. One of the steps to recovery is making amends. The person I need to make amends with most is you. I love

you and Macy more than I can say.
You're my family and I never wanted
to hurt either of you. When I come
home, I promise to make things right,
even if it takes a lifetime.

I love you, T. Give Macy a hug and
kiss for me and tell her I said, "Siempre
estoy aquí para ti, no importa lo lejos
que parezca." Because you aren't in
honors Spanish, I'll translate for you.
"I'll always be there for you no matter
how far away I seem." And the same
goes for you, T.
Your friend,
Angel

I carried the letter to my room and placed it in a drawer. Taking a moment to gather my thoughts over the past few days, everything with Angel, and my life in general, I sat down on the bed. I missed my mom. She'd been gone for years, but now it was real. In a way, I was relieved. Not only was she not in physical pain anymore, but she didn't have to wake up in terror every morning wondering what was happening around her.

Something the attorney said had me thinking about a future I'd never considered before. He said my mother was tested for genetic markers, which meant one day I could end up just like her, or even worse, I'd relive her struggles through Macy.

CHAPTER THIRTY-THREE

SAVE THE LAST DANCE FOR ME

After taking a moment to myself, I walked downstairs and found Melanie sound asleep, snoring softly, curled against the arm of the couch. Slipping my arm behind her back, she stirred enough to wrap her arms around my neck and shoulders as I lifted her. I tried to carry her up the stairs, but I was too tired to keep from falling backward each time I tried to take a step. I kissed her forehead softly and implored, "Baby, can you wake up long enough to walk to bed?"

She grumbled as I lowered her feet to the ground. She had on heels, so I removed them before she trudged up the stairs with her head bowed, arms hanging beside her. At the top of the stairs, I scooped her back up in my arms, and she squealed in surprise. When I laid her on the bed, she was asleep in no time. I unzipped her jeans and placed them on the chair. She woke up at the movement and sat up to remove her shirt and bra. My lips pressed against her collarbone, and she moaned my name.

"Baby," I whispered as I kissed my way up her neck and then flicked my tongue against her earlobe. When I nibbled on her ear, I felt her hands move to my pants. She wrapped her hand around my length and stroked. Now wide awake, her mouth was eager for mine. I dipped to taste her luscious rosy lips and ran my tongue across her bottom one before sucking it into my mouth.

Pulling her hand away, I reached for her hips and slipped her panties off. Each thrust was slow and methodical; each moan captured the bliss we both felt. Once we reached our peaks, Melanie rolled to her side, and I pressed up against her back, kissing her neck.

"I love you."

Her skin had goose bumps from the chill in the room. I pulled the sheet up, covering her sexy body, and wrapped my arms around her for warmth. She fell asleep before saying the words herself, but I knew she felt the same.

As tired as I was, I couldn't sleep. Instead, I watched Melanie sleep, enjoying the soft purr of her snores. At times she'd smile in her sleep, and I thought she might have awakened, but instead it seemed like a good dream instead. The curls in her hair were limp from our rolling around. I twirled the silky auburn strands around my finger, pulling them away from her face. Her skin smelled like coconut and felt like warm silk. I pressed my mouth against her ear and whispered, "Marry me." Melanie gave a small chuckle in her sleep. "I'm serious Melanie Harris, marry me."

Her eyes popped open, and she flipped over to face me. "Do you have a ring?" she asked in a panic of excitement.

"Not yet," I admitted sheepishly, "but if you say yes, we'll pick one out together."

"Yes."

The proposal came out of nowhere. I hadn't planned it any more than Melanie had expected it. As soon as she said yes, I closed my eyes and smiled. My life had taken a turn upward.

Chapter Thirty-Four

WHAT HAPPENS IN VEGAS

Melanie was my fiancée. Melanie was going to be my wife. Melanie and I were getting married. No matter how I phrased it, it scared the hell out of me. In the moment of proposing, it seemed like the most natural thing to do. We'd hit every relationship step in such a short span of time this seemed the next logical one. At the time, I hadn't considered all the obstacles involved. *How would Macy feel about me getting married? How would this affect Angel who already felt like the last single person on Earth? Am I sure Melanie's the one? Last year I was in love with Mary Jane. How could I know this time was for life?*

These thoughts zoomed through my mind as I kept my eyes closed lying in bed. I sensed the emptiness of the bed. The groan of the bedroom door opening caused me to finally face the day. Melanie had on one of my T-shirts, which rode up her thighs as she sat next to me on the bed. "I took Macy to school this morning. I'm off work today, so I made you breakfast. I can bring it to you in bed if you want to stay up here?"

Looking at her, I wanted to wake up every day for the rest of my life next to Melanie. I trailed my fingers along her smooth calf and moved them up to her inner thigh. "You drove her to school like this?" I teased.

She gasped as my fingers grazed over her panty line. "Tristan, your eggs will get cold," she advised with unconvincing concern. My hands moved up under her shirt, softly caressing her skin until I could cup her breast. The moment my hand found her taut nipple, she gave in. "We'll microwave them."

She removed her shirt and panties before she straddled my waist. "Since I'm on the pill, is there any reason I should worry if we don't use a condom?" Shaking my head no, since I'd never gone without a condom with anyone else, she replied, "Good, I always want to feel everything with you."

Afterward, we sat with our hands pressed together, fingers entwining. With a resounding sigh, I said, "I suppose we need to get up. Breakfast is waiting, and we have shopping to do."

"Shopping?" Melanie asked.

I lifted her left hand and pointed to her ring finger. "This finger needs some bling, don't you think."

She bit her lip as she held back her smile. "We're engaged?

I thought maybe it was a moment you'd regret. I wasn't going to mention it in case you wanted to take it back."

I never regretted asking her, only questioned whether it was the right time. "Do you regret your answer?"

"No. Tristan, I've never felt this way about anyone in my entire life. You're sweet, funny, charming, and incredibly sexy. Most of all, you have the biggest heart of anyone I know. I couldn't imagine a better husband and father for my children." I tensed up at the mention of children. "Don't worry, no kids for a few years. I simply meant I see us having children one day. And with the way you've raised Macy, I know you'll be wonderful."

"And you'll be an amazing mother. So let's get dressed and go find you a ring. I want to tell Macy when we pick her up from school. She needs to be the first to know, before anyone else."

"I agree. There's one more thing I need to tell you. She's scared to tell you herself but talked to me about it this morning."

My mind immediately shot to a worst-case scenario, and I sat up in a panic. "Is she okay? What's wrong?"

Melanie stroked my back. "Calm down, she's fine. She wants to call your dad. She's scared it will hurt your feelings. She wants to hear him out though. She'd like to see if he can be a part of both your lives now."

"Oh. Um… no it's fine. I got his number for her." The truth was it did hurt a little. It shouldn't, but it did. I needed a few minutes to deal with it, so I got out of bed quickly. "I'm going to get a shower."

"Want me to join you," she asked with a wink.

"Not this time. I need a moment."

"Okay, no problem. I'll go finish breakfast for when you get out." She gave me a quick kiss and left the room.

The hot water beating down on my skin felt like heaven. As I soaped up, I regretted one decision I had made in the last twenty-four hours, telling Melanie not to join me in here. I don't know what made me think I needed time to myself. Macy deserved to know her father. He was an ass for leaving her behind, but we made it. We both survived, and if he hadn't left, we wouldn't be here in Nashville. I'd never have met Melanie. For once I felt the saying was true: everything happens for a reason.

Once out of the shower, I stood in front of the mirror, and grinned at myself. Everything in my life was falling into place for a change. I closed my eyes and breathed out a sigh of relief. "Mom, if you're listening, because of you, Macy and I are fine, and she's going to her dream school next year. And you'll be the first to know I'm getting married. You'd have loved Lanie. She's… well, there are hardly words worthy of describing her. None of them match how extraordinary a woman she is. I wish you could be here. I miss you, so much."

Forgiving my father for abandoning his family would be difficult, but for Macy, I was willing to try. I owed my father nothing. He'd made his choice to walk away without looking back for several years. Macy had lost too many people in her life. After seeing how she reacted to Angel on Thanksgiving, I hoped our father would make her see people do come back. There'd be no third chance. If he hurt her again, I'd never forgive him.

Gathering my composure, I dressed in jeans and a tee. Melanie had the table set for breakfast. She ate while I got my shower so I could eat while she took one herself. "Do you think Angel would mind if I borrow some clean clothes? I'll get them back to her too."

"No, she wouldn't mind at all."

Melanie flitted upstairs, and I grabbed my phone and dialed Mary Jane. "Hello, new momma. How are you feeling?"

"Tired, but happy. I'll be going home in the morning. I fed him last night. It was the coolest thing, T."

"When you get home, Lanie and I would like to come over and make dinner for you. It would give us a chance to tell you about the trip too."

"Anything else you want to tell me?" she hinted. He knew what she was asking but couldn't give it away. Macy had to be the first to know for certain.

"Nothing else right now."

It would be hard to keep our secret for long. Macy would be hurt if she wasn't the first one to know. I knew she'd be excited, especially since she and Melanie had grown so close.

It only took one stop for Melanie to find the ring she wanted. She picked out a very simple gold band with a petite diamond. "Are you sure you don't want something fancier?"

"We don't need to go broke for an engagement ring, this

is beautiful and says 'I'm taken,' so it seems perfect to me."

"Aren't I supposed to spend three month's salary on it though? This amount is barely a month's."

She rolled her eyes. "I never understood where someone came up with such a number. I chose the ring because of its beauty, not its price. I'd rather you spend three month's salary on a down payment for a house or something we can both enjoy."

"Damn. If I hadn't already proposed, I'd do it again right now."

Melanie giggled, and we waved the jeweler back over. "We'll take this one," she decided, handing him the simple gold band with a quarter-karat diamond in the middle and three smaller diamonds on each side. When she slipped it on her finger, it was the perfect fit.

With a smile on her face, she held her hand out straight ahead and stared at the ring the entire ride to Macy's school. As we pulled into the parking lot, she put her hand down to hide it until we could break the news.

Macy slipped into the backseat a few moments later. "You two have fun today?"

"We did a little shopping." I winked at Melanie. "How was your day, squirt?"

"Carter and I are officially dating."

I groaned, but Melanie expressed enough excitement for both of us. "Awesome, Macy! Do you have a picture? I must see this guy you've told me so much about."

Macy quickly handed Melanie her phone, who in turn showed me before I drove off. The picture was a selfie of the two teens with their faces pressed together smiling happily. "Oh, he's cute," Melanie gushed. "I may have to fight you for him."

"Hey now." I teased back. My girl and Macy both laughed at my attempt at jealousy. "We have something to tell you, Macy."

Melanie handed the phone back, and Macy screamed. I swerved the car out of surprise. "What the hell?" I shouted.

Macy grabbed Melanie's hand. "You guys are getting married!"

"I guess you're happy?" Melanie noted with a laugh.

"Ecstatic! You two are perfect together. Can I be a bridesmaid?"

"I was hoping you'd be my maid of honor," Melanie replied, taking both of us by surprise. "I don't have any sisters. There's no one I'd rather have stand beside me."

"Am I old enough to be a maid of honor?"

Melanie shrugged. "I don't see why not. You're too young to sign as a witness on the certificate, but we'll have plenty of people there. Tristan and I both want you standing up there with us."

Macy unbuckled and thrust forward to hug Melanie. I pulled the car over. "Buckle back up, squirmy. We need you in one piece for the ceremony one day. I spoke to MJ earlier. When she gets out of the hospital, the three of us are going to go make them dinner and break the news. For now, you're the only one who knows."

Macy squealed again. "I want to help with all the planning."

"I hoped you would," Melanie exclaimed.

"I thought maybe we'd go to Vegas and elope," I half-joked. The idea of planning a large wedding seemed scarier than just running away to get married in a more intimate setting. The disappointment on Melanie's face implied my joke was not funny. "I'm kidding." Once I added those two little words, she seemed relieved.

"I don't want to spend thousands of dollars on a wedding, Tristan. I'd rather be surrounded by our closest friends in a small chapel here than in Vegas getting married in a tacky chapel with an Elvis impersonator performing the service as he gyrates his hips in character." Her tone wasn't full of anger, only a plea for understanding.

"What if we got married at A Shot in the Dark?" The idea to get married in the bar came to me as a cheap venue but after saying it, I thought it might be offensive to her.

Instead, it received the opposite result. Her eyes misted over with tears, and she asked, "The place we met? How amazingly romantic."

Hmm, who knew being cheap would be construed as romantic for a change? "Great. I'll check with Derrick and Ashton as soon as we tell them."

"Carter's uncle is a preacher. I could see if he would perform the ceremony for you guys."

"This is coming together quite nicely," Melanie replied.

For the rest of the afternoon, I could not get the girls to drift away from marriage talk. Macy's animated emotions over the entire thing made it so I didn't even mind being ignored. She needed a good dose of happy and this seemed like the perfect distraction.

Chapter Thirty-Five

GOING BACK IN TIME

The house looked like a bachelor pad since Angel left. I hadn't stayed on Macy about chores with everything going on. Angel would be home in just a few days, and I wanted things to be nice for her. Since it was my day off, I told Melanie I'd have to see her later because I needed to get the house in order. She offered to help, but it felt wrong to let her clean my mess.

The living room took me an hour to finish. I ran the vacuum, and the loud noise must have made me miss the doorbell. As I rounded the coffee table, I glanced out the window and in time to spot someone walking away. Turning the vacuum off, I ran to the door and called out, "Did you have something for me?"

The deliveryman turned back with a package in his hand.

"Yes, sir, I need you to sign for this."

I gave my electronic signature and apologized. "Sorry, I almost missed you because of the vacuum. I knew cleaning was bad for me." The delivery guy laughed and waved as he rushed back to his truck. The package was only an inch thick, and the return address label showed the name of my mother's attorney. Inside the thick envelope was a letter with a disc.

Mr. Jacobs,

I've been going through your mother's belongings from the safe-deposit box per your request. Most of the contents inside were the papers regarding the accounts you inherited. You will have access to those accounts in the next few weeks. I will contact you by phone to give you all the details. The other item was a DVD addressed to you and your sister. I have enclosed this disc without viewing it. I hope it brings you some peace.

Sincerely,
Harvey Windsor

Macy wouldn't be home for a few hours, and I needed to watch this before she did to make sure it wouldn't be too hard for her. "Can you come over?" I asked as soon as Melanie answered her phone.

"Is everything okay?"

My voice cracked. "Not really."

"I'll be right over," she promised without any further questions.

The DVD felt very fragile in my hands as I wondered what it contained. Treating it as though it were made of glass, I carried it to the player to be watched as soon as Melanie arrived. She knocked on the door twenty minutes later.

Silently she wrapped her arms around my neck and pressed against me. "What happened?" After showing her the note and package, we sat down to see what was on it. Melanie offered to take control when she saw my hand shaking. She pressed play on the remote, and my mother's face appeared on the screen.

She was seated at my father's desk, the painting behind her always hung there in his office. Looking beautiful, so full of life, she smiled. "This is my memoir to the two most important people in my life, my children, Macy and Tristan. If you're watching this, it means I have passed away. Today I was diagnosed with early-onset Alzheimer's." Her voice choked as she held back tears.

"I'd have welcomed any other diagnosis but this one. The idea of losing my beautiful memories of the two of you is worse than anything else they could have told me.

I wanted to preserve a few of my favorites so you know how much you mean to me. The doctor explained to me I might get violent or spout cruel words out of fear in the final stages. If I ever express anything to hurt either of you, I want you to know from the deepest part of my soul how sorry I am. You two are the lights of my life. Before you, there was a dark time I feared I'd never have children. Soon, there will be a dark time again when I forget you exist. The concept tears at my heart more than you can know."

Melanie grasped my hand, never taking her eyes from the video.

"I probably shouldn't tell you all of this and make things worse in your grief, but I'd rather you know how I feel while I was still lucid. Macy, my little girl, you're only four right now, and it pains me to know I will not be at your wedding or remember it if I am. I may never see your first date or recall the excitement you felt over a boy asking you out. I pray that even though my mind doesn't know you, my heart will."

The screen skipped and the next scene she was sitting outside in the garden. She continued as though she'd never stopped. "My favorite memory of you is the day you first spoke Tristan's name. From day one, he was a king in your eyes. Your first word was 'dizzan'. We thought it was gibberish until we noticed you only repeated it when he was close, and after listening to it many times, we knew it was your way of pronouncing his name. You worshiped him from the beginning, and because of this, I know he will make sure you become the woman you're meant to be."

She held up a photo of Macy in Tristan's arms. "You two are my perfect angels. Tristan." The moment she mentioned my name, tears fell from her eyes. "My sweet boy, you're thirteen now. Your voice is beginning to change, and you had a growth spurt practically overnight. I pray I will see you graduate high school. I feel more confident I'll see your first date with a girl. You're so handsome I know you'll be a heartbreaker. And the one you choose for a wife someday will be the luckiest woman on earth. I hope she knows how lucky she is."

I glanced at Melanie wondering if my mom had any idea I'd be watching this with my future wife. The mere thought seemed silly since she couldn't have known. With tears filling her eyes, she peered up at me and admitted, "I do know."

"I've left a request with your father and after much arguing, he agreed to it. When my mind goes and it becomes too difficult to visit or I lose my memories of you all, I want him to move on. Your father has always put work first above everything else. When I'm not around, Macy will need guidance and love. Tristan, you've helped me raise her from day one. She looks up to you more than anyone else. For this reason, I've asked him to give custody of Macy to you, Tristan, on your twenty-first birthday."

Melanie paused the video. "Didn't he sign her over at eighteen?" The fact my mother was even the one who suggested I raise Macy had me dumbfounded. The age matter was not my biggest concern; it was why he didn't tell us. Melanie placed her palm on my knee and gave it a gentle shove. I shook my head to clear my thoughts. "Sorry. Yeah, I was eighteen. He never told me she had anything to do with his decision. Why wouldn't he tell me?"

Melanie wrapped her fingers around mine. "Because he loves you? Because he loved her? Who knows? There's one way to find out though, call him."

"Let me finish watching this first."

"By twenty-one you'll have almost finished college and he's promised to help you financially, but I want stability for Macy and you can provide that for her."

The scene changed again. She still sat in the garden, but she wore a different dress. A child's laughter rang out, and a four-year-old Macy jumped up in her lap. My mother tossed her head back in amusement before smothering Macy in kisses. "Who are you talking to?" Macy asked innocently.

"Myself, I remembered all my favorite things about you."

"Like what?" Macy asked, laying her head against Mom's chest.

"Like your beautiful curly hair. Your favorite color is the shade of Ariel's hair. Your favorite stuffed animal is Harley, the black teddy bear. Tell me who your favorite person is, I forget."

"Tristan, my brother. He's my best friend." Macy's words inflated my chest with joy. I couldn't remember her as much back then. "You and Daddy are my favorites too though."

"I know. Why don't you say your ABCs for me?"

While Macy sang her ABCs, Mom closed her eyes and

smiled as if she didn't have a care in the world. When Macy got hung up at the letter Q, she asked for help, and my mother joined in.

As hard at it would be to show Macy the video, I knew she had to watch it. Even with my years of memories, I'd forgotten so much about my mother. Hearing her speak of us with such love in her voice was the closure I needed. No matter how many times I reminded myself she loved me, that the disease was making her forget, I had trouble believing it. Watching the words come from her own mouth lifted a weight of confusion off my shoulders.

A car pulled into the driveway, and I quickly shut off the disc. Carter helped Macy from the passenger's seat of his truck and leaned in for a quick kiss. At least he was smart enough not to press her against the vehicle in full make-out mode in front of our house.

As soon as she came in the front door, Macy called out, "Hey T, can Carter stay for dinner?"

"Not tonight, we have a family matter to discuss."

"Lanie's here and she isn't family yet. Please."

"Don't be rude. Lanie *is* family." After a little reconsideration, I relented, "We'll talk later. Carter can stay."

"Thanks, Mr. Jacobs," Carter replied in a typical ass-kisser tone.

"Look, kid. If we're going to be cool, then call me Tristan. I'm not old enough to be Mr. Jacobs yet. Carter, this is my girlfriend, Lanie." Carter wouldn't know any of our friends, but I didn't want to take a chance of calling her my fiancée until everyone else knew.

"Carter, will you help me set the table while Tristan talks to Macy?" Melanie stated.

"Yes, ma'am."

Melanie cringed. "I'd rather you call me babe, than ma'am."

Carter looked thrilled at the prospect so I interjected, "I think calling her Lanie will suffice."

Carter cleared his throat and followed Melanie silently to the kitchen. I'd sufficiently frightened him, which meant I did my big brother duty. Macy rolled her eyes and requested, "Can you be nice to him? He's sweet, and I know you'll like him."

"I'll give him a chance, but you need to know something first. Come sit down."

"This sounds serious, what's wrong?" Macy bit her bottom lip nervously.

"We received a package in the mail today. It was from Mr. Windsor, Mom's attorney. It's a DVD she made for us. I'd like you to watch it if you feel like you can handle it."

Her hands trembled with anxiety. Her gaze drifted to the television set across the room. "Have you watched it?"

"Yes. I wanted to make sure you could handle seeing it before we watched it together. I didn't finish it yet though. I don't know how it ends."

"After dinner, I want to watch it with you. Can we watch it alone though?"

"Sure, kiddo. I needed Lanie here for moral support, but it'll just be the two of us tonight."

"Thanks. I love Lanie, but I think we need to do this together."

After dinner, Melanie and Carter left us alone. Macy continually apologized to Melanie for not wanting her to stay, but she never seemed offended by it in the least. She even told me Macy needed my full attention for the moment. With a quick kiss goodnight and a promise to call her before bed, I watched her get in her car before shutting the door.

I started the disc from the beginning again and watched as Macy went through many of the same emotions I had gone through. The moment she saw her younger self on screen seemed surreal. Her mouth was agape as she cherished seeing her mother laughing with her.

Once we reached where I left off, I turned my focus on the screen and took her hand in mine to add support for both of us. The disc skipped, and my mother's chest was in front of the camera as she backed away from it after obviously hitting record. She looked despondent as she said, "I'm back. I haven't recorded anything for two years now. Memories are becoming fuzzy for me. I was at the grocery store and ran into my best friend from college. I didn't recognize her or remember her name at first. She hasn't changed a bit, and I have photos of her on the wall at the house. It's scary. *I'm scared.*" She began to cry. Unable to control her tears she reached forward and turned the camera off.

In the next clip, she was in a sundress. "This is my final taping. I'm going to be quick because my mind is leaving me so often now I'm afraid I won't say what I need to. All I need to say is I love my family. Tristan, Macy, my husband Blake.

You three mean the world to me and even if I forget you, I'll never truly forget you. Please don't ever feel I didn't love you completely and deeply."

She sat there a moment not saying a word. Gazing at the screen, something in them changed. Her head turned toward a noise in the room. She jumped up out of the chair and yelled out, "Who are you?"

Our father approached her with his hands out in surrender. "Loretta, it's Blake, your husband." Her eyes grew with fear and then recognition. Her shoulders slumped, and she leaned into his embrace and broke down crying. He comforted her for a few minutes before he said, "The kids are waiting for dinner." The couple stood up and left the room. We watched for a few more minutes, and nothing happened. We hit the fast-forward button until the disc finally cut off.

"He must not have known she was recording." I guessed at the only logical explanation.

"So she forgot she was recording. As hard as it was to watch, Tristan, it made me feel better. I began to doubt if she ever loved me. Seeing the two of us together made the grief easier and harder at the same time."

"I feel the same way." I wrapped my arm around her shoulders. "I've got something else to talk to you about now."

She backed away from me. "Lanie talked to you? You're okay calling Dad?"

"I am. Are you ready to see him?"

Her shoulders rose and fell before she exhaled a breath. "Might as well."

Chapter Thirty-Six

MAKING AMENDS

To say our father was more than happy to meet with us would be an understatement. Blake Jacobs had always been an eloquent speaker, yet when I called him, he fumbled over his words repeatedly. We agreed to meet at a restaurant, just the three of us. Macy sat quietly for the first part of the meal. I discussed the details of the disc and asked him to explain about the divorce and the custody of Macy.

"Your mother was the love of my life. Her diagnosis devastated both of us. I tried to prepare myself for the moment she'd forget everything. I convinced myself I could make her remember, I could save her. When I couldn't, it shattered me." He loosened his tie as though it was choking him up instead of the emotions themselves. "The envelope the attorney had contained paperwork with the disc. It was an agreement signed by me and notarized, which stated I would give you custody and I would divorce her. When it came time to follow through, it devastated me. I watched you on visits with your mother, the way you cared for her and knew the right things to say. You were eighteen, and I felt you were in a better state of mind than I was so I signed Macy over early."

"And then you just went on with your life like nothing happened?"

He wiped his mouth and placed the napkin on his plate. Sitting back, he reflected for a moment before speaking. "For two years I walked around in an emotional fog. I threw myself into work even more. Longer hours meant shorter times alone in the house. I had lost everything. Though it was my own choice to leave you two, it felt more like you'd died. My grief was overwhelming, and I couldn't think rationally. Work literally came naturally to me because I barely remember anything of those two years except work stats."

"At any time did you wonder about us?" I asked.

"One day the fog cleared and I broke down. My first moment of true grieving since I'd lost you. I sought out therapy and decided after I was better, I'd find you and beg forgiveness." Clearing the emotion from his throat, he turned to face me. "I saw you one day. The two of you were with a blonde woman on your way into the park. I'd found your address and showed up as you were leaving so I followed you. The three of you looked so happy I assumed you were a family. I convinced myself entering back into your life would only complicate things for you."

"The blonde woman you saw is my best friend, Mary Jane. She's the one who convinced us to move here to start over. I hated leaving Mom behind, but being here has been a better life for us." I looked toward Macy for reassurance and she smiled and nodded. "After seeing us that day, which had to be over a year ago, did you ever consider trying again?"

"Yes. But by the time I got up the nerve to see you, I found out you had moved from the apartment. I wasn't sure where to find you until the day I got the call from the nursing home."

"Why didn't you try harder?" Even with his explanation I couldn't understand his reasoning.

"Shame. Facing you again terrified me. I neglected my children and my wife. Like a coward I abandoned my family. I regret the decision, not because you didn't do a good job, but because I was a terrible father."

Macy spoke for the first time since we sat down. "You weren't a terrible father. Tristan just happens to be a better one."

Ouch. You could see the pain flash in his eyes over her hurtful statement. I tried to ease the brewing tension. "I appreciate the sentiment, Macy."

Macy scoffed at my wording. "It's not sentiment, Tristan, it's the truth. If I'm going to sit here and listen to him defend his actions, then he is going to listen to me tell him the consequences of those actions."

To a passerby, it would seem my father was a mute. He sat there staring straight at her without a word or any movement.

There were no emotions in his expression, no anger, no tears, nothing.

"Macy, be respectful, please. You're better than this. He made mistakes, and we're here to give him a chance to make up for them."

Macy crossed her arms and slumped in her seat. "He'll screw it up again," she ranted. I had never seen her act this way before.

"If he screws up this time, then it's on him. We are going to make the best effort we can though."

Pushing up to a stiffer position, she took a drink from her water glass and cleared her throat. "I apologize for acting childish."

"Neither of you owe me an apology or anything."

"Stop," I interrupted before he could go over the same drivel again about mistakes. "The past is the past. Will you join us for Christmas this year? Our friends will have a celebration at their home, and they've extended the invitation to you. I'd like you to get to know Lanie under better circumstances. And, while we're here, you should know Lanie and I are engaged."

My father's face brightened with sincere happiness. "Congratulations!" He stood up and embraced me in a firm hug. "She's a beautiful young woman, son."

As if she sensed we were speaking of her, my phone sounded with her ringtone. "We were just talking about you," I answered.

The voice on the other end of the line resembled Melanie, but it was deeper and scratchier. "I'm sorry to interrupt your dinner. I wanted to let you know I'm sick. I'm not sure if it's a stomach bug or food poisoning, but I don't want you to be sick. Until I'm feeling better, I think we should stay at our own houses."

It would be futile to argue with the woman in her current state, so I wished her well and hung up the phone. "I need to get Macy home. I'll call you with the details of Christmas dinner."

"Sounds good. Thank you both for this. I'll do my best not to let you down again."

His words were exactly what we both needed to hear, which was why I had reservations. I'd keep my guard up with him until he proved those words were true.

***

Angel had been home for a week, and she had been in a better mood than I could ever remember her being in. She bounced around the house singing as we walked in the door. There were days her disease made it difficult to walk and other days she seemed like the healthiest person on earth.

"How was dinner with your dad?"

"Fine. Can you do me a favor and stay home with Macy tonight? Lanie is sick, and I need to go over and check on her."

"Sure, T. We can have a girl's night," she exclaimed, wrapping her arm around Macy's shoulders.

On my way to Melanie's house, I stopped to buy chicken

soup, sports drinks, saltine crackers, and a few fashion magazines. We exchanged keys once I proposed, so I let myself into her house. I could hear her coughing upstairs. To calm her stomach, I poured the orange sports drink in a cup of ice and grabbed a sleeve of saltine crackers.

Her bed sheets were tousled, and her clothes were strewn all over the floor. Another gagging sound came from the bathroom where I found her slumped over the toilet with her head against the seat in exhaustion. "Lanie," I spoke softly, trying not to startle her.

She could barely lift her head enough to scold me. "Tristan, I told you not to come over."

"I wasn't about to leave you here alone and sick." I grabbed a washcloth from her cabinet and ran cold water over it. In the drawer of her vanity was a basket of hair scrunchies. I grabbed the first one I saw, reached down pulling her hair away from her face, and braided her hair to keep it out of the way and make it easy to lie down. I used to braid Macy's hair when she was younger, who knew the talent would come in handy in a relationship as well? She sighed with relief when I pressed the cold rag against her forehead.

I slumped to the floor behind her, and she laid back on me. To cool her off, I moved the rag over her face. "I look disgusting." She began to cry. "You shouldn't see me this way."

"You're beautiful. And I have to see you this way eventually, you know in sickness or in health and all." The heat of her skin came through the washcloth. "You're burning up, baby. Do you have a thermometer?"

She pointed up towards the medicine cabinet above the sink. I felt bad moving her, but it worked out at the right time because she sat forward to get sick some more. After a moment, I pulled her into my arms again and placed the thermometer under her tongue. It beeped a moment later showing a temperature of one hundred one.

Her teeth chattered as she pressed up against me struggling for warmth. To keep her from getting dehydrated, I grabbed the cup of orange drink and held it to her lips. "Take these two Tylenol to help with the fever, and this Gatorade is full of electrolytes. Drink and it will help keep you hydrated. I bought you a few different kinds, plus I brought some soup and crackers for when you want to try to eat again."

"You're too good for me. Right now, I am freezing. Can you get me back to the bed, please?" She put her arms around my neck as I lifted her up and moved her from the bathroom floor to the comfort of her bed. Seeing her so sick filled me with worry and made me glad I ignored her suggestion to stay away. Taking care of her was important to me.

I tucked her into bed with three layers of covers before she finally stopped shaking. The cold rag had gotten warm, so I drenched it once more in cold water. Under the sink, she had a bucket for mopping, which I placed by the bed for an emergency.

I removed my belt and shoes and slid into the bed next to her, wrapping my arms around her. "Honey, you're going to be sick," Melanie whined.

"Shh. Don't worry about me. I'm here to make sure you

feel better. I'm not leaving until your fever drops. Go to sleep, and I'll be here when you wake up."

While she slept, I slipped out of bed and cleaned her room. Melanie's house was always spotless, so I knew when she got better the mess would annoy her. I fixed myself a large glass of orange juice from her fridge to get a dose of Vitamin C to boost my immune system and popped a few Tylenol.

I called Angel and arranged for her to get Macy back and forth to school the next couple of days just in case. Next, I called Derrick and asked for the next two nights off. He had scheduled everyone due to the crowds getting larger lately. He assured me it wouldn't be a problem; that he and Ashton could take turns covering if needed.

Angel dropped off a bag of clothes for me too. I had her leave them on the front porch and ring the doorbell instead of coming inside. I didn't need to make her sick when she had so much going on already.

I'd been there for three hours, and Melanie still slept soundly. I refreshed her rag and checked her temperature; it seemed to have fallen from the feel of her skin. I didn't want to wake her by using the thermometer. I crept back downstairs to watch TV and grabbed Season one of *Doogie Howser MD* to give it a shot since she made such a big deal about it. I laughed when the credits open with him typing on a blue screen with white block letters. This show wasn't hiding its age. Even though bits of it were cheesy, I was getting into it. His pal Vinnie had me laughing hysterically at his awkwardness.

"I love this episode." Melanie stumbled across the room all bundled in her comforter. I sat up on the couch and held my arms out to her. She curled up next to me and laid her head against my chest. "Mind if I watch with you?"

"As long as you don't puke on me," I teased.

"No promises," she replied glumly.

She should've been in bed resting, but I couldn't argue with having her next to me. Plus, I'd run myself ragged getting things fixed up, I was too exhausted to carry her upstairs again.

***

Melanie's stomach bug lasted for two days. The morning she finally felt better, she let me sleep in and made me breakfast in bed. I awoke to the smell of bacon, and when I opened my eyes she stood over me holding a strip of bacon in front of my nose. "Good morning, fiancé."

I pushed myself into a seated position, and she placed the tray of food on my lap. "Good morning to you. I hope you're hungry."

"Aren't you going to eat?" It had been two full days since she had anything other than Gatorade and saltines.

"Not yet. I'm going to stick with a cup of soup and some crackers just in case." Before I took the first bite, she took my hand in hers. "Thank you for taking care of me. I can't remember the last time… I can't remember anyone ever taking such good care of me."

"It was my pleasure. You can get used to this kind of

treatment from me, baby." The couple of days spent taking care of Melanie gave me a glimpse of our future, and I loved it. Waking up to her every day, eating breakfast, reading the newspaper, growing old together, everything about it gave me a feeling of peace. Normalcy was what I craved, and I could have it with Melanie.

Chapter Thirty-Seven

LOOKING AHEAD

Ashton and Gracie had a Christmas Eve party for everyone at their house. They were the unofficial head of our little family. They had extended an invitation to my father for this event, and he accepted. Of course, they asked my permission before contacting him with the details.

Macy reveled at the prospect of sharing the first holiday with him in several years. The decorations in their house put mall displays to shame. The couple was very much into the Christmas season.

With the extra holiday money coming in at the club, Ashton, Derrick, and Gavin created a fund to purchase presents for children. This year they bought toys, and each took turns dressing as Santa to deliver them to the homeless shelter and the local children's hospital.

We all pitched in to help as much as we could as well. Melanie and I did all our shopping together for gifts for everyone. We were engaged, so buying joint gifts for our first Christmas together seemed right. The temperature outside was a brisk thirty, but my feet were cold for a different reason.

Melanie and Gracie had been in the kitchen preparing appetizers when Melanie ran into the living room. "Tristan, it's snowing!" she exclaimed. We dashed to the window, and fluffy white flakes of snow were falling. Some were even beginning to stick. Although in Nashville, they usually got ice or barely an inch of snow. Being a native Floridian, I was ecstatic to experience my first snow.

I pressed up behind her, arms around her waist, placed my head on her shoulder, and watched the snow fall. She sighed with contentment. "Isn't it beautiful? I love when the snow blankets the ground, and it's the only time the dead trees of winter are picturesque instead of dreary. I've thought about getting married in the snow." I tensed at the mention of wedding plans again. She pulled away from me. "I'm going to finish helping Gracie."

Derrick watched as Melanie marched back into the kitchen. As soon as the door shut, he walked toward me. "Are you two having issues?"

"Not that I know of, why?"

"She looked a bit... perturbed... when she turned away from you."

I shrugged, completely unaware of what could have upset her. "We've been very happy together, Derrick.

Nothing's changed."

He patted my shoulder. "Okay, good."

"Where's MJ?" I needed a subject change before I dwelled too much on my reactions and became paranoid.

"She's in the back. As soon as we got here a few minutes ago she had to change Craig's diaper."

Outside the snow picked up, the back porch was blanketed in white. "Do me a favor and give me two minutes, then go get Lanie and send her outside to see me." Derrick agreed, and I did something hoping to put a smile on my fiancée's face.

The snow had covered the deck enough to give me a message board on their picnic table. I used my gloved hand to write it out. Melanie stepped outside and crossed her arms over her chest when the cold air hit her. "Derrick indicated you needed me?"

"You ran off abruptly before. Derrick said you looked unhappy." Unhappy seemed a better way to describe it than pissed off.

She stared down at the ground and said, "You tensed up when I mentioned the wedding. Do you still want to get married?"

I stepped forward and rubbed her arms for warmth, then led her over to view my note. "What is this?" she asked.

"I wanted to see how it would look, and I gotta say it looks pretty great to me." I had written out 'Melanie Jacobs' on the table.

The stern, unyielding look on her face had me worried. "What if I want to keep my maiden name?"

"Well, I guess it would be fine," I answered with uncertainty. In this day and age, a lot of women kept their maiden name for professional reasons, but it still was a blow to a man's ego.

She must have noticed my disappointment because her nonchalant look broke into a grin. "Aw, sweetie. I'm teasing. Of course, I'm taking your name. And this"—she gestured to the name—"is the sweetest thing in the world."

Wrapping her arms around me, she gave me a loving kiss. "You taste like chocolate."

"Gracie pulled out the chocolate fountain they used at Derrick and MJ's wedding. We might have tested it out for flavor once or twice."

"Tastes pretty good to me." I grinned and bent forward once more for a kiss. We were interrupted by my father coming to tell us dinner was ready.

After dinner, we exchanged gifts and around midnight, we began our ride home. Melanie came home with us, and our first Christmas together turned out to be a happy memory.

New Year's didn't go as well as Christmas, however. Early in the evening, things were going well. I worked since it's a huge night for the bar business. Melanie wanted to be with me so she spent the evening at the bar. She hung out with Gracie, Mary Jane, and Angel most of the night. Maria and Macy were babysitting the children together and watching the ball drop on TV.

Just before midnight people hustled to find someone to kiss as the music note, Nashville's version of the ball, dropped downtown.

The bartenders found single women in the crowd to kiss, and I made it to Melanie's side just as we got to the five-second point. At the stroke of midnight, I took her in my arms and pressed my lips against hers, dipping her in the process.

"Happy New Year, baby."

"Happy New Year," she exclaimed, before using the blower in her hand and making it shriek in celebration. "Come to my house tonight so we can ring in the New Year appropriately?" Melanie requested.

"I already arranged for Macy to spend the night with Maria. I get off in two hours."

"And then an hour later," she teased with a seductive smile.

"Mmm… I can't wait."

Melanie waited for me in her bed wearing a black nightie with lace over her breasts and nothing else underneath. We made love and fell asleep in each other's arms. Up until then, the night had been perfect. The next morning, things got a bit complicated.

"I've been thinking about something and wanted to get your opinion. I have an extra bedroom here, and since you're renting your place, I'd like you and Macy to move in here with me. What do you think?"

"Right now isn't a good time. Angel just came home from rehab, and I can't leave her alone."

Melanie stopped me from explaining further. "Of course. I meant after the wedding. She'll have time either to find a new place or possibly a new roommate to share the expense. You do want to move in with me, right?"

"Absolutely. But Angel began drinking because she felt alone and like the last single person on the planet. Now I'm getting married, what if she slips back into the rut and falls off the wagon?" Even I had to admit it sounded like a poor excuse for not moving in with my soon-to-be wife, especially using another woman as the reason.

"Tristan, you can't put your life on hold for Angel. She's an adult. She's strong, and she has faced her problems head on and come out the other side unscathed. Give her some credit."

"It's not so simple, Lanie. I trust her, but alcoholism and depression are diseases, not to mention the MS diagnosis she is coping with." I cared about Angel too much to leave her alone at the time she needed her friends the most.

"MS is a lifetime disease," she stated the fact as though I didn't already know.

"I know. It's just I don't want to move Macy around so much, and she loves Angel like a sister. It will be difficult to leave her there."

"And how do you love, Angel?" she asked in an accusatory tone.

"She's a friend, Lanie. I've told you several times before now. I don't understand the big deal. We probably won't even get married for at least a year."

Melanie stood up and marched toward the door. "Forget

I mentioned anything, Tristan. I have errands to run. Thanks for last night. You can let yourself out."

It hurt deeply knowing she still couldn't trust the depth of my feelings for her. I had to find a way for her to see she was the only one I wanted.

Chapter Thirty-Eight

TOO COMPLICATED

Instead of running after Melanie, I gave her a few hours to calm down and think more rationally. I couldn't blame her for being upset with me. We were planning a wedding, and I was arguing how I should be living with another woman, putting her needs before my fiancée. Her anger was justified, but I hoped she would understand where I came from and that it would only be temporary.

Melanie was supposed to be home around four, and I went to work at six, so while getting ready I kept my phone next to me waiting for her to call. As it grew closer to time for me to leave, I sent her a quick text.

Me: I'm on my way to work for the night. If you feel like talking, shoot me a text and I'll call you on break. I love you.

No response came through, but I knew Melanie loved me, and she'd talk when she was ready.

We had three other bartenders on duty that night: Marcus, Xander, and Grayson. Being the first day of the year, lonely people filled the bar looking to drown their sorrows with someone. Ashton and Gracie had been by earlier and removed all the holiday decorations left over from the New Year's Eve party.

"Hey, man, did you ring in the new year with a bang?" Marcus asked as we each stood filling up a pint of beer for a customer.

"Nice one," I complimented his sexual pun.

Bobby cruised up to the bar and held out an envelope. "Your girl left this at the door for you." I opened the manila envelope and found a letter inside.

Tristan,

Your life is full of complicated relationships, and I can't be one of those complications. You're not ready for us to get married. I understand, and I'm not angry. We've been together a little over six months, and we probably rushed into things. I love you and probably always will, but I can't marry you until you're ready to commit to us. I'm sorry.

Love always,

Lanie

Remaining in the envelope was her engagement ring. "Marcus, cover me," I yelled out, throwing my towel down on the bar and running towards Bobby. "Bobby! Is she gone?" Bobby pointed toward Melanie standing at her car. Even from across the parking lot I could see her shoulders shaking as she cried. She got in her car, and I ran out calling after her. "Lanie! Don't do this, Lanie!" She turned to look at me before driving out of the lot.

It felt like being punched in the gut. I had no idea how intensely hurt she had been this morning. I wanted to call her, hear her voice, and explain things. I knew her well enough to know she wouldn't answer. I sent her a quick text.

Me: Please, Lanie. Don't give up on us. I love you, and I do want to marry you. We need to talk. Can I come by after work?

Lanie: No. I have to work tomorrow.

Me: Please talk to me!

Lanie: In time. When I'm ready, I'll let you know.

Derrick was talking to Bobby when I stepped back in the club. "Hey, T, you have a minute to talk?" I followed him to his office, and he closed the door drowning out the music from the club.

"Is something wrong?" I asked, not needing more heartache.

"I wanted to ask you. I saw you run out of here like a bat out of hell, and I figured you might need a friend right now." I handed him the note to read. Once he finished, he closed his eyes and folded it again. "I'm sorry, T. You two are great together. What does she mean by you don't want to commit? You proposed. Did you give her some reason to think you aren't ready?"

I sighed and leaned my head back. "I'm an idiot, Derrick. She asked me to move in with her. My response was I would move in after Angel gets better."

Derrick nodded. "Angel came home from rehab, Tristan. If she weren't better, then they'd have recommended a longer stay."

"She could relapse or the MS could get worse."

Derrick interrupted. "You're right, but she isn't your fiancée. She's your friend, and you can still be there for her even after you marry Lanie. Maybe the real problem is Lanie is right, and you aren't ready for marriage."

"No, it's not true," I stated, not completely sure of the validity. I'd had my doubts, but doesn't everyone? Marriage was the biggest commitment you could make, tying your life to one person. But every time I wondered if I was ready, I thought of what it would be like to lose Melanie, and that hurt more than any fear I felt.

"Then maybe Lanie isn't the one you want to marry. Have you developed feelings for Angel now?"

"I love Angel as a friend, nothing more. But…" I hesitated in my admission, not wanting to say it out loud.

"But…?" Derrick urged.

"But Lanie may have been right about the marriage thing. I proposed while grieving my mother. I want to be with Lanie, but I think I might have rushed into it." The words felt wrong. I loved Melanie. Why was I being so stupid about all of this?

"So, tell her," Derrick advised.

"How do I tell her I'm not ready to marry her without breaking her heart? Can we go back to only dating after being engaged?"

Derrick picked up his phone and dialed someone. "You up for a visitor? Our friend Tristan needs a little advice. I'll send him your way."

After hanging up, he handed me back the letter. "MJ is going to make some coffee for you. She asked you bring a chocolate milkshake with whipped cream for her."

"I can't bother her, she has a newborn."

Derrick chuckled. "Exactly why she jumped at the idea. She doesn't sleep most nights until I get home. She needs the company. I've got things covered here. Go talk to your best friend. She'll give you the woman's perspective you need."

On the way to Mary Jane's house, I thought about how lucky I'd been to meet her at Disney. My life had changed so much since she came into it. I had friends I could count on to help me with any obstacle I faced. Friends who were my family now. When it was just Macy and me, I had to bear the load myself.

They brought Melanie into my life, maybe not directly, but they definitely had a hand in it. With their help and my determination, she would come back to me.

With a large chocolate shake in hand, I stepped up to the Collins's door. I sent Mary Jane a text to alert her to my presence

Me: On the porch. Didn't want to knock in case the baby is sleeping.

Mary Jane opened the door and waved me in. She whispered, "Thanks for the text, he just fell asleep. Katelyn's in bed too so we can go to the den and talk. I have the baby monitor."

I repeated my conversation with Derrick to Mary Jane to get her up to speed on what was going on. I showed her the note, and she handed it back to me with tears in her eyes. "Those dang baby hormones, right?" I teased, trying to make her smile.

She frowned instead. "It's heartbreaking, Tristan. She's in a lot of pain."

"I'm aware. I saw it first hand after I chased after her. What do I do, MJ?"

"If Derrick had proposed and then told me he wasn't sure he could marry me yet, I'd have been devastated. But it wouldn't have been a deal breaker for me. She's going to hurt. She's going to feel insecure about your feelings, and she's going to be even more jealous of your relationship with Angel. What she is saying in this letter is she wants to be your priority. And she doesn't mean in front of Macy, but it does mean in front of other women. You made her feel as though Angel is more important than moving forward with your relationship. Deep down, she understands you're a concerned friend, but she also knows it's an excuse."

A shrill cry sounded through the monitor. "Duty calls… which may even be a terrible pun if his diaper needs changing. I'll be back."

To pass the time waiting for her return, I flipped through the pictures on my phone and stopped to stare at one of Melanie and me from the day we traveled to Fall Creek Falls. She'd taken a selfie of us standing on the cliff in front of the falls. We both looked blissful. Pre-engagement, pre-rehab for Angel, pre-parent issues, pre-complications in general. A simpler time in our relationship. Part of me wanted to go back. Why couldn't we? Although we technically already started over once, the day she was mugged. It shouldn't count when it happened before our first official date.

I thought back to the endless one-night stands I had before I met her. They didn't make me happy; they made me feel a little emptier like Angel felt. I couldn't put my life on hold because my friend might take it too hard.

Mary Jane returned holding Craig in her arms. "Would you like to hold him?"

I held my arms out, and she gently placed him in my grasp. "He's a tiny little man."

She laughed. "I know. I wish he had felt so tiny inside me."

Glancing up at Mary Jane, I admitted, "I'm going to tell Lanie I can't marry her yet. I'm going to tell her the truth. I'm not ready. If she loves me, she'll give us a chance. If she doesn't, well, then I guess I'll have to accept it." Sadly, I didn't know if I would be able to accept it if she walked away for good.

"I think it's the best idea for you both, T. And for the record, I hope she sticks around. You're good for each other, and she's very good for Macy."

A groan escaped me as reality hit me hard. "Macy is going to be almost as wrecked as Lanie."

Mary Jane placed her hand on my shoulder. "You can't worry about Macy's feelings either, T. You have to do this for yourself. You worry about everyone else too much. It's one of your best traits as a friend, but one of the worst for finding your own happiness."

I handed the baby back to her and gave her a kiss on the cheek. "Thanks, MJ. I'm going to go. It's still early, I think I'll swing by her house and see if she's still awake." I only hoped she would listen to me and not slam the door in my face.

The light was on in Melanie's bedroom, so I took a chance and knocked on the door. No noise came from inside, and I looked at my watch and noticed it was midnight and I probably scared her. "Lanie, it's me, Tristan. I won't stay long. I didn't want to use my key unless you wanted me inside."

The door creaked open, and Melanie stood there holding her robe closed, her hair tousled, her eyes half-closed. "Were you asleep?"

She shook her head and moved aside to let me in. "I've got a headache and couldn't sleep. I was watching something in the den. Did you leave something here?"

I ran my thumb across her cheek, over her bottom lip, and down her jaw, her skin trembled beneath my touch. "I wanted to talk."

I pulled her close and was about to press my lips to hers when she pushed me away. "Talk," she instructed and then took a seat on the couch. She bent her legs beneath her to sit.

"You were right in saying we rushed things. I don't think I'm ready to get married yet." She bit her lip and turned away from me so I wouldn't see her tears. "But you were wrong thinking it has anything to do with Angel. I love you, Lanie. I want to marry you, but it terrifies me. I'm so scared I'm not going to be the husband you deserve. I'm afraid of being like my father."

"You'd never be like your father, Tristan. You're so much stronger than he is."

"Lanie, don't give up on me, please," I begged, my voice breaking as everything I felt overwhelmed me.

"I'm not giving up on you," she promised, reaching to take my hand in hers.

"Don't give up on us either," I added. She shied away from me again, and I reached out to grasp her hand. "Please, I'm begging you to give us a chance. I want to marry you… one day."

"There's still…"

"Angel, I know. I got some great advice on that dilemma, and I'm going to take it. Angel is a grown woman who can take care of herself. I can't fix everyone. I want to be with you, Lanie. You've done so much for me."

She stood up to pace out of reach. "Okay, so show me gratitude, don't force yourself into a commitment you aren't ready to face."

I moved closer to her. Bending to kiss her, relieved

when she didn't push me away, so I pressed further. I tugged her robe tie to pull her close, and it slipped open revealing her negligee underneath it. Pushing the bathrobe off her shoulders, it fell in a puddle on the floor. She moaned against my mouth, and I slipped my tongue between her lips and my hands around her waist. Trailing my lips down her jaw, I nibbled on her neck and collarbone and slid the straps of the negligee off her shoulders. She grabbed it before it could fall and backed away from me. "I can't."

"Let me stay here tonight?"

"Why?" The word came out strangled with emotions.

"Because I want to talk some more, I don't want this to be over."

"We need to chalk this up to what it is, Tristan, a failed relationship. We had fun, we shared good times and bad, but it's over. You can't get engaged and then unengaged and still have everything be fine. I can't move backward," Melanie stated earnestly.

"I'm not accepting this is over. I don't want to be unengaged. I just want to postpone getting married for a while. I want you to wear this one day." I held up the ring. "I'll give you some time. We're still in a relationship as far as I'm concerned. You call me when you're ready to see me, and I'll be here. And Lanie, when you want this ring back, I'll give it to you. All you have to do is ask."

She walked to her door and held it open for me. "Good night, Tristan."

I decided not to dwell on her nonresponse, but instead on the good night and not goodbye.

CHAPTER THIRTY-NINE

BECOMING LESS COMPLICATED

Angel adjusted my tie, and it felt as though it were choking me to death. "Who created these torture devices?" I asked as I pulled at the knot.

She smacked my hand. "Stop fidgeting already. It's your big day. You've been waiting years for this moment. Macy is graduating high school! Dads wear ties for these occasions."

"Since our father is back in the picture now full time, I've sort of been demoted to brother again. I think I should be able to get away with no tie."

"You'll always be more than just her brother, T." Kissing my cheek, she smiled. For five months Angel helped me get

Macy prepared for this, and we'd become as close as any family could be.

Macy entered the room frantically tossing sheets and towels. "Where is my other shoe?"

Angel chuckled. "Chillax, girlfriend. It's right there." She pointed at the shoe sticking out from the open closet door. "You guys need a drink or something to calm your nerves."

We both stared at her for the terrible joke coming from a recovering alcoholic. "Not funny, Angel."

"Sorry. MJ asked me to video the entire ceremony. They're so sad you couldn't get more tickets. And, by the way, I appreciate you giving me one."

"Well, you're practically family since we all live together," I replied. Macy ordered four tickets back around Christmas. The four tickets were for me, our dad, Angel, and Melanie. After the night at Melanie's house, I didn't hear from her again for a while.

After the first month of no response, I sent her a text message to see how she was. From then on, we texted each other about once or twice a week for small talk. We talked about how work was going, the weather, and other awkward, boring subjects to avoid the big picture, our relationship status.

I regretted not marrying her when I had the chance. I kept the engagement ring in my wallet behind the business card she left me with her number almost a year ago. Macy missed her all the time. She constantly asked me about her.

"Why don't you see if MJ wants the fourth ticket, Macy?"

It seemed silly to not let anyone use it.

"It wouldn't be fair to invite her and no one else. Plus, Dad is bringing someone."

"He is? Since when?" I asked confused. I didn't know he had been seeing anyone, much less someone serious enough to bring to his daughter's graduation.

"I don't know, some chick. We're going to be late. Let's go!"

Graduation was in the auditorium of a local college. We had tickets but not assigned seating so Angel and I grabbed the closest set of chairs we could, and I texted my dad to let him know where we were. We could meet up afterward.

Macy graduated at the top of her class as valedictorian. Unabashedly, I cried when they called her name and during her entire speech. She spoke of what the future held, second chances, and grabbing what you want and not letting go. I needed her speech five months back.

The eloquence of her speech earned her a standing ovation from the senior class. It made my chest swell with pride. When the closing music played, I checked my phone and saw a text from Dad stating he'd meet us at Gracie's.

Macy wanted to ride with Carter, so Angel rode with me. Everyone was inside waiting when we got there. They all screamed their "Congrats" when Macy walked in the door. Mary Jane pulled me aside. "Look at you in the suit and tie! You look like such a proud dad."

"I am, MJ. She's made me incredibly proud. She's blossomed so much since we moved here. I owe you. I'm not sure I'm thrilled she's dating, although the kid is good to her. But look at her. Can you remember seeing her smiling so much back then?"

We stared at Macy like proud parents. Mary Jane helped me raise her for two years. I couldn't believe how far she'd come from the scared little girl who was afraid to go to school and deal with bullies. "Excuse me a minute, MJ." Macy was talking to Carter, and I tapped her shoulder. "Come with me for a minute?"

Macy and I stepped out on the back porch. "Is something wrong?"

"Not at all. I wanted a moment alone with you to say a few things. First of all, I love you more than life itself. You're not only my baby sister, but my very best friend."

"I feel the same way. I owe you my life, T. You have been the best role model any girl could ask for." Macy began to cry, and she wrapped her arms around me. "I love you, Dad."

I laughed through the choked back tears. "I always thought it would sound sweet, but it makes me feel so old."

Macy giggled. "We'll stick with big bro."

"Much better."

Mary Jane poked her head outside. "Sorry to interrupt, but your dad's here and he wants to see the valedictorian. And Tristan, can you go down to the basement and get the two gallons of ice cream out of the freezer?"

The basement lights were set on dim, but I saw enough to get to the freezer. I pulled out the containers of chocolate and vanilla ice cream. When I turned around, I almost dropped everything on the floor. A set of feminine hands grabbed the carton threatening to spill forth to the floor. "Hi," Melanie greeted me with a smile of uncertainty.

"Hi."

"What are you doing here?"

"Macy invited me months ago. She gave me the ticket, and I couldn't pass up seeing her graduate. Her speech was amazing."

"I didn't see you there?" My hands were freezing as the ice cream cartons stung my skin. I set them on the table and Melanie followed suit with the one she'd been holding.

"I sat with your father. He and I came together."

"Oh… please tell me you aren't dating my father?" I cringed, not sure whether I wanted to puke or go punch my father in the face.

"What? No! He called me and implied you haven't dated anyone else since we broke up and asked if I'd attend with him and speak to you."

"In my mind, we never broke up." I'd confided in my father the other day about my regrets about not marrying Melanie.

"Can we sit down?" Melanie asked. We moved to the couch and sat next to each other. "I haven't dated anyone since we… parted ways," she said, seemingly to appease my comment on there being no breakup. "I've done is a lot of thinking about my life, my future, what I wanted. And as I was questioning whether I should give up on you for good or come begging for you to take me back, your father called."

"I didn't ask him to call you." He'd have been the last

person I would've asked for a favor so huge. We were closer than before, but things were still uneasy at times.

"He told me you didn't. I took his call as a sign. We needed to address what went wrong and find closure or fix it." She reached for my hand and I closed my eyes and smiled. We hadn't touched in so long I wanted to relish in the feel of her skin against mine.

"Since we've been apart, all I've done is think of you, Lanie. I was wrong to put Angel in front of our relationship. It was a cop-out I used instead of admitting my fears. I was scared of turning out to be a disloyal husband like my father. But, more than that, I was terrified of ending up like my mother. The way I felt… the way I *still* feel about you, made it even scarier. I never want you to go through the pain of watching someone you love forget all about you."

Her hand tightened around mine and she pulled it against her chest. "I love you, Tristan. If you do end up there, I will do everything I can to take care of you. I'd rather have decades of time together, than to never be with you again."

"What if it's not decades? What if we only get a few more years and then my memory fades?" These fears were ones I'd never voiced out loud. I convinced myself to stay strong and positive for Macy's sake.

"Who cares about what-ifs? We were supposed to be married or at least planning a marriage right now. Life doesn't always go the way we think it will. I'm tired of what-ifs, I'm tired of giving in to fear, and I'm tired of being apart from you." Scooting closer to me on the couch, she pressed her hand against my cheek. "The pain was so fresh before I couldn't think rationally about what to do. In our time apart, the thoughts became clearer. I told you before how strong you are. Look at Macy and the woman she's become. You did that. When things were tough, you never abandoned her. You could've put her in foster care and gone on with your life, but you didn't. That's how I know you will never abandon me."

Tears threatened to spill forth, but I suppressed them. Melanie was right. I'd never stopped to think about how ridiculous my fears were. I'd already been challenged with things my father could never handle and I'd succeeded. Genetics and blood didn't make us who we were, we chose that path ourselves.

"Our relationship hasn't been traditional. We haven't followed a timetable or rules of dating, we made our own way. I know we've been apart for several months, but in my mind and heart nothing has changed." She peered up at me through her eyelashes, possibly searching for my reaction, I wasn't sure. "Are you—"

"Yes. I'm still in love with you. Nothing has changed for me either. I've spent the last several months wondering what grand gesture I could do to get you back. Instead, you show up here today surprising me. After the last time we spoke in person, I wasn't sure I'd see you again."

"The last time we spoke in person, you meant everything you said?" She seemed to be testing my memory, but I knew exactly what she was asking.

"Every single thing."

"Can I have it back?" She asked for the ring, which

currently resided in my wallet. Her hands and voice trembled with the request.

I reached into my back pocket, pulled out my wallet, took the ring from the sleeve it was in, and stepped forward. "I thought you'd never ask."

"You've been carrying it with you this whole time?"

"Yep, in this sleeve where I keep the most important things to me: Macy's picture, my mother's picture, the business card you gave me with your phone number, and for the past five months your engagement ring."

She slipped the ring on her finger and pulled me into a passionate, long-awaited kiss.

Epilogue

A PROMISING FUTURE

After Macy's graduation, we'd had plans for a road trip to the mountains for some time together. When she found out Melanie and I reunited, she invited her along. Melanie hadn't started a summer job yet so she was able to come.

The three of us bonded again, and Melanie and I started back where we left off as though we hadn't spent five months apart. The day we came home, Melanie walked into the house and Angel was there. She turned to me and said, "Can we talk a moment?"

My gut churned assuming the fight over Angel would recommence. Instead, she said, "I was wondering how you'd feel if I moved in here… with the three of you?"

"What about your house?"

"I'll sell it. We can put the money into a savings account

for another house when we're ready."

I pulled her into my arms and kissed her. "You're possibly the most amazing woman in the world. You've sacrificed so much for us. I don't even know what to say."

"Is that a yes?" she asked breathlessly. I nodded. Her idea gave me confidence in things working out better between us.

A few months later, we were packing up Macy to move her to college. Melanie helped her load up the luggage as I ran upstairs to grab a present for her. Searching the drawers for what I'd put away for this day, I came across an envelope.

"What do you have there?" Melanie asked as she stepped into the room.

"This is what the lawyer gave me. The information my mother had to convince my father to walk away." When we came home after my mother's funeral, I asked Lanie for it, but couldn't bring myself to read it. I placed it in the drawer to look at it one day if needed.

"Did you look at it?"

With my hand on the tab, I ripped it open and pulled out a set of documents. They were all notarized and signed by my mother and father. They appeared to be exactly what my father had told me. I considered reading them word for word, curious if there were other promises he made and broke. My mind went back over the past several months. Thursday night dinners with my dad had become a regular event. He and Macy were closer than I ever imagined they'd be. And of course, he brought Melanie back to me. Things had changed so much between us, for the better, that I didn't want anything to ruin it.

With one hand on the top and one on the bottom, I tore the letter in half, placed the pieces on top of each other and tore them again, and then threw it in the trash. "He's proven himself to Macy and me in the last few months. Whatever happened was a long time ago and doesn't matter anymore."

When I first received the letter, I tried to throw it away several times but couldn't bring myself to do it. After ripping it up, it was a relief to no longer have it looming.

Melanie and I drove Macy to college together, said our teary goodbyes, and drove home in silence but holding hands. "Do you think she'll be homesick?" I asked when we pulled into the driveway.

Melanie smiled up at me. "She's going to miss you terribly, Tristan, but she's going to do great things. You should be very proud of the young woman you raised."

Proud seemed too simple a word to describe the way I felt about Macy's accomplishments. I had no doubt she'd have an impact on society one day.

While Macy was away at her first year of college, we made plans for the wedding to be the following summer at A Shot in the Dark. We wanted to give ourselves plenty of time to be certain marriage was right for both of us, and we wanted Macy to focus on her studies. The girls—Gracie, Mary Jane, and Angel—grew closer to Melanie as they worked together to make the arrangements and shopped for dresses.

My fear of commitment, or repeating the history of my father's failure as a husband, had diminished. On the calendar, I kept a running countdown of the days until Melanie would become my wife.

The complications in my life had lessened. My mother was gone, my father had immersed himself in our lives, Angel was in recovery, and Melanie and I were better than ever. We may not live happily ever after like in the fairy tales, but I'd make sure we gave it one hell of a try.

THE END

Acknowledgements

First and foremost, Hot Tree Publishing, thank you for believing in my series and helping to make these stories the best they can be. Your team of editors and beta readers dig in and put a lot of thought into the details of the story, and they certainly keep me on my toes!

To my Hot Tree family of authors, thank you for the support you offer every day and for the confidence boosts—something we all need at times! I'm incredibly thankful to be a part of such a great group.

Some of my biggest supporters have been right here at home. My mom "pimps" me out to everyone she knows. She has sold more books for me than I have sold for myself! Both of my parents have been fantastic in supporting me in this endeavor in my life.

Some local authors have inspired me lately: Stacie O'Brien who helped talk me through my first public speaking panel at a convention, Susan Burdorf who has given me many tips for making more connections in the writing community and has included me in local signings. She's always offering up her time and help, and I appreciate it more than I could ever say.

Last, but in no way least, my amazing husband, Daniel. He has been my muse on each story, allowing me to bounce ideas off him, even acting as an illustrator on some of them. He has been my biggest supporter, and I am more grateful than he will ever know.

About the Author

Amy McClung was born in Nashville, TN. She is the second oldest of four girls and occasionally suffers from middle-child syndrome. She met the love of her life online in August of 2004, on his birthday of all days, and married him in September 2005.

Currently they have no human children, only the room full of colorful robots that transform into vehicles and the large headed Pop Funko's who represent their favorite characters. Collecting movies, shot glasses, Pop Funkos, and dust bunnies are some of her favorite pastimes.

Amy began writing in September of 2011 and independently published her first YA novel, *Cascades of Moonlight*, book one of the Parker Harris series the following May. Her first book was a means of therapy for her, enabling her to escape reality for a while during a difficult transition in her life.

Amy loves to connect with readers. You can reach her:

FACEBOOK: facebook.com/AmyKMcclung
WEBSITE: amykmcclung.blogspot.com
TWITTER: twitter.com/AmythaMcclung
GOODREADS: www.goodreads.com/author/
  show/6421342.Amy_K_McClung
NEWSLETTER: facebook.com/AmyKMcclung/
  app/100265896690345/

About the Publisher

Hot Tree Publishing opened its doors in 2015 with an aspiration to bring quality fiction to the world of readers. With the initial focus on romance and a wide spread of romance sub-genres, we envision opening up to alternative genres in the future.

Firmly seated in the industry as a leading editing provider to independent authors and small publishing houses, Hot Tree Publishing is the sister company to Hot Tree Editing, founded in 2012. Having established in-house editing and promotions, plus having a well-respected market presence, Hot Tree Publishing endeavors to be a leader in bringing quality stories to the world of readers.

Interested in discovering more amazing reads brought to you by Hot Tree Publishing or perhaps you're interested in submitting a manuscript and joining the HTPubs family? Either way, head over to the website for information:

WWW.HOTTREEPUBLISHING.COM